THE
DO
OVER

SHARON M. PETERSON

THE
DO
OVER

bookouture

Published by Bookouture in 2022

An imprint of Storyfire Ltd.
Carmelite House
50 Victoria Embankment
London EC4Y 0DZ

www.bookouture.com

ISBN: 978-1-80314-638-6
eBook ISBN: 978-1-80314-637-9

To Mom,
Thank you for always letting me read when I should have been cleaning my room.
Love you bunches.

ONE

"Know your worth.
Then add tax."

—*MIMI*

There was a rumor my grandmother, Mona Raye Perkins, bashed my grandfather in the head with a frying pan. A cast iron one that still sat on her stove where it had lived for as long as I could remember.

"Mimi," I asked one day as a child, when curiosity got the best of me, "did you really put him in the hospital?"

She smirked and took a long pull on the cigarette that might as well have been surgically grafted to her fingers. The smoke clung to her clothes, mingled with the flowery undertones of White Shoulders and the faint, yet permanent smell of canned green beans from her years working as a school lunch lady.

"I sure did. That lying, no-good rat bastard deserved it too," she said before eyeing me through the cigarette smoke. "How old are you?"

"Nine."

"Well, that's a story for when you're older." She winked and pointed at the chipped coffee table taking up prime real estate in the cramped living area of her single wide. "Now, hand me the remote. *Days of Our Lives* is on."

I knew she wasn't lying or putting me off in the hope I'd forget. Mimi differed from every other adult I knew. She always told me the truth, and she never softened it. "Shit by any other name is still shit," she'd say. "Why call it anything else?"

Mimi had a million of these sayings—Mimi-isms, I called them. My mother forbade me to repeat them, but that didn't stop me from memorizing each one and writing them in the Lisa Frank journal I kept in my nightstand.

Then again, my mother disapproved of everything about Mimi—from the tiny green trailer she lived in at the Forest Lake Mobile Park in the small border town of Eagle Pass, Texas, to the garden gnomes she let the neighbor boys arrange in compromising positions in her yard. Mother hated that Mimi laughed too loud, never watched what she ate, and didn't care one bit what anyone thought.

On the list of People I Wanted to Be Like When I Grew Up, Mimi was number one.

I wanted to wear loud clothes, heavy on the animal prints, and tight pants and prance around in sky-high heels. I wanted to brush off my mother's impatient disapproval. I wanted to be unafraid to just be me.

Even now, at twenty-seven, I spent most of my life being a square peg my mother tried to cram in a round hole. The look of utter exasperation—lips pursed, fists stuck on her hips, all accompanied by a heavy sigh—it was always for me, never my sister.

When I was very young, I'd crawl into Mimi's lap and inspect the dangly earrings she favored. She'd whisper tongue-twisters in my ear until I giggled and wrapped my arms around her neck, melting into the softness of her. That was another thing I loved about Mimi. She embraced her curves; the way her cheeks rounded when she smiled, how her entire body shook when she laughed. Confidence oozed out of her, and I prayed some would transfer to me.

Although three years younger, my sister Phee was on her way to being skyscraper tall, like our daddy, with curly blonde hair and huge blue "take-care-of-me" eyes. Nothing like me. The Perkins side of the family gave me my dark hair and eyes, and short, curvy stature.

My mother disapproved, of course.

When I complained about my shape, compared myself to my sister or the women in Mimi's soap operas, a knowing little smile settled on my grandmother's face. She tugged her cigarette from her mouth and leaned toward me, dropping her voice so only I could hear her say, "Perci, darling, a man wants a spoon, not a ladle. Remember that."

I did. I wrote it down even though I had no idea what it meant.

When I was thirteen, she finally told me the story of my grandfather's run-in with the frying pan. The evening before, Mom dumped me off at Mimi's on her way to Laredo. Phee was competing in the Little Miss Outrageously Adorable Cowgirl Beauty Pageant, or some contest with an equally lame name, and the very last thing I'd wanted to do was watch.

Now, I huddled around the tiny built-in kitchen table while Mimi whipped up sausage hash in the very same pan in question.

"Me and your grandfather, we got married real young because we were stupid and fixin' to have a baby." She paused and stabbed a finger in my direction. "Listen up, do not get yourself in the family way before he puts a ring on it. A minute of pleasure is not worth the hassle."

Seeing as how boys didn't realize I was alive, I figured that wouldn't be hard advice to follow. "Yes, ma'am."

"Good. I was nineteen when your mama came along. Her daddy never could keep a job for longer than a flea's hair, so I worked two just to keep us in food and diapers." She dumped a bowl of chopped peppers and onions in the pan where the sausage was browning. My stomach rumbled in response. Sausage hash was my favorite.

"I'd work at the school cafeteria and then head off to the grocery store for a shift. Sometimes I'd run home in between and freshen up and such." The potatoes followed, a little salt and pepper, a few stirs with a spatula, then she lowered the heat and plopped down at the table across from me.

I waited impatiently while she dug out a Virginia Slim, lit it, and took a long drag.

"Well, I saw a car I didn't recognize in front of the trailer, and I had a suspicion. Marched right up to the door and burst in. Do you know what I found?" She waved her cigarette in the air, dark eyes blazing in remembered anger. "There he was with some blonde floozy in my bed while our baby napped in the next room."

Gnawing on a fingernail, a nasty habit per my mother, I leaned closer. "What happened?"

"I got mad is what happened. There was some screaming, and the baby woke up and started wailing. That woman jumped up, grabbed her clothes and ran out of the trailer buck naked. But I only had eyes for that ass I called a husband." She tapped the end of her cigarette on the little misshapen clay ashtray I'd made for her in the third grade.

"He started whinin' about how lonely he was because I worked so much. I went a little crazy, I guess you could say." Her head tipped toward the pan our breakfast sizzled in. "I picked up that pan and swung." A corner of her mouth tipped in a smirk. "Guess his head got in the way."

"He fell like a tree right there in the kitchen. I picked up the baby, went next door and called for an ambulance. He told everyone it was an accident 'cause he didn't want to admit his wife flat knocked him out."

"Wow," I breathed, more than a little in awe of her.

"I changed the locks while he was in the hospital and saved enough money to divorce his good-for-nothing ass." She pressed her cigarette out and stood, strutting to the stove. Mimi strutted everywhere—the grocery store, the doctor's office, funerals—like life was one long catwalk.

The hash finished, she pulled it from the burner and flipped off the heat. She turned to face me and leaned a hip against the counter. "That was one of my moments, honey."

"One of your moments?"

She nodded, her helmet of dark hair wobbling. "See, there are moments in life—sometimes they're big, sometimes small. Some are happy, like meeting the man you'll marry or having a baby. But sometimes they're ugly. It's the moments that make us who we are. The day I opened the door to the trailer? That was one of them moments. It changed me."

I mulled this over as Mimi pulled out two of her blue and white dishes and set them on the counter before piling them with hash.

"How'd it change you?" I asked when she brought the food to the table.

"I finally took charge of my life, peeled that man off me, and never looked back. You'll see. No one escapes those moments. One day, when you least expect it, it will hit you. You might not realize it at first, but it'll change you. Now, eat up. *The Price is Right* is almost on."

In the fourteen years since that conversation, I've waited for The Moment That Would Change Me—I held my breath on each birthday, the first time I met a handsome man who made my heart skip, when I graduated from college—but it never arrived. I made it all the way to twenty-seven years old, disappointed my life seemed to be following the same predictable path it had been set on.

Then, one day, in the least likely place, it happened.

And it was not pretty.

TWO

"When life gives you lemons,
   give them back and ask for grapes.
   You can make wine with grapes."

—MIMI

On my list of Places I Hated, the dentist's office was firmly at number two. Slightly worse than shopping with my mother, but not as bad as a visit to my gynecologist, who was also a family friend. My parents had him over for barbecues and I couldn't quite look Dr. Sullivan in the eye without remembering where his eyes had been. I was, of course, a fully-grown woman who could easily change doctors, but then my mother would find out, I'd have to explain, and the battle would be lost before it began.

All that to say, it was late morning on New Year's Eve, and I was perched in a pink reclining dental chair waiting to get the filling I'd procrastinated over until the last possible hour.

"How's your mouth feeling? Numb?" Dr. Kelly peered down at me, a blue mask covering half her face. I couldn't remember ever seeing more of her than two fiercely tamed dark eyebrows balanced over blue eyes.

I nodded and slid my phone under my thigh.

The corners of her eyes crinkled. "We'll wait five more minutes and get started. How's your mom?"

Yes, Dr. Kelly was Mom's dentist too.

"You know Mom, she keeps busy." She also kept herself firmly planted in the lives of her daughters. Not quite like a tree with widespread roots that nourished; more like vines that were suffocating and impossible to kill.

"And that sister of yours? I saw her on the morning show last week." Her eyes took on a dreamy, wistful look. "Such beautiful teeth. I bet she flosses every day. Her dentist must be so proud."

"They're very nice teeth."

Her eyes narrowed. "Flossing prevents cavities. You wouldn't be here today if you did it a little more."

My cheeks flamed. "You're right. Sometimes I fall asleep or forget. One time I dropped the whole package of floss in the toilet and—"

"How are you today, Ms. Mayfield?" Callie, the hygienist, sank into the stool opposite the dentist and smiled. "Getting one last thing taken care of before the new insurance year, hmm?"

"Yes, actually I—"

Dr. Kelly interrupted me. "Turn up the radio. This is my favorite segment."

Callie leaned and fiddled with the radio on the counter. A second later, a voice filled the room.

"Folks, listen up! Today for Friday Cry Day, we're giving away two sets of tickets to Houston's most popular local band, AB/CD, an AC/DC cover band."

"Bro, they're awesome," another voice said, sounding like the Texas version of a surfer dude. "Here's how this works. You call up and if we choose you, you break up with your significant other right here on the radio. That's all you gotta do and the tickets are yours. Phone lines are open now." The radio cut to a power ballad by an 80s hair band.

Dr. Kelly rubbed her hands together. "These are always hilarious."

I smiled with the part of my mouth that wasn't numb. It seemed a horrible way to break up with someone. If I was going to break up with my boyfriend, Brent, I'd write him a gently worded letter, or we'd meet over coffee and discuss our issues like rational adults. Perhaps an email with clear, logical reasons for the proposed split.

Not that I'd thought about it much.

Brent was a great guy—smart, driven, handsome in the slightly-balding-dad-bod sort of way, and exactly who my mother wanted me to marry. As she liked to remind me. Daily. By text. In person. An occasional email. If she could get her hands on a billboard...

"Let's get this party started." Dr. Kelly gloved up, slipped on giant plastic protective glasses, and picked through her instrument tray. All of this with a bit more glee than seemed necessary.

Sweat beaded on my forehead as the chair reclined. Dr. Kelly adjusted the light with its police-interrogation-level brightness until it shone in my eyes. Blinking to clear my vision, I could just make out the posters plastered on the ceiling of the room, meant to keep us captives entertained. Each featured an animal—an eagle soaring, a lion roaring, a giraffe... giraffe-ing—along with an inspirational, if slightly lame, quote.

I paused on one with a bird, a scruff of feathers sticking up on its head, and bulging, wild eyes like he'd walked in on his bird-parents in a compromising position and could not unsee it. The quote below it read, ALWAYS BE YOURSELF. YOU'RE THE ONLY ONE WHO CAN.

Like I said, lame.

"Open wide," Dr. Kelly said. She placed a contraption in my mouth to prop it open. A moment later, a cloud of tooth dust accompanied the whir of the drill, the sound scraping my nerves. I reminded myself this would be over soon. If I could survive monthly mother/daughter brunches, I could survive anything.

The song on the radio ended and the announcer, his voice deep and dramatic, returned. "Ladies and gentlemen, boys and girls, we have our first contestant. Tell us your name, where you're from, and who you're breaking up with today."

"I'm Sheila from Houston and I wanna break up with my boyfriend, Todd."

"What's Todd done to deserve this?"

Sheila harrumphed. "What hasn't he done? He's lazy, doesn't pay me any attention. For Christmas, he got me a vacuum cleaner. Who does that?"

Callie rolled her eyes. "I would totally kill my boyfriend if he did that."

The whirring stopped. Dr. Kelly balanced the drill on my bottom lip. "One year, I got a toaster for Christmas. Isn't that terrible?"

"Aaat ih errble." My eyes crossed as I focused on the drill. What would happen if that thing slipped?

"Don't talk, dear."

Nodding, I twisted my hands in my lap until my fingers went as numb as my mouth.

"There's a reason I divorced that man." The whirring resumed. "He forgot our first anniversary. Completely forgot it. Not one single word." She met my eyes. "Should have been my first clue, don't you think?"

"Aaa cooos."

Dr. Kelly's eyes narrowed. "No talking."

One of my hands formed a fist in frustration but I didn't make a sound.

A voice from the radio cut in. "Okay, Sheila, stand by. We're calling Todd now."

The phone rang three times before a sleepy, gravel-laden voice answered. "Who's this?"

"Todd, it's Sheila."

There was a pause like Todd might have been trying to figure out who Sheila was. "Yeah?"

"Here it comes." Dr. Kelly's hands paused. "Turn it up a bit more."

"I'm breaking up with you. You never pay any attention to me, and I think I can do better," Sheila said.

The radio hosts snorted in glee and then silence reigned as they waited for Todd's reply.

"All right."

Sheila gasped. "Th-that's it?"

"Yeah. That's it. I'm going back to bed now." There was a click and the radio exploded in laughter.

Sheila sniffled. "He didn't even try to change my mind."

"Our phone lines are still open. We've got one more pair of tickets for a lucky guy or gal who wants to break up with their significant other right here, right now. Don't go away, we'll be back after this."

Dr. Kelly chuckled as she pulled the drill out and picked up a pointy silver instrument. "Let's make sure I got it all."

I winced as she poked and prodded.

Callie patted my shoulder. "You doing okay?"

"Uh aum finn."

"Try not to talk, please." Dr. Kelly shot me a glare. "A bit more with the drill and we'll get the filling in and you'll be all set."

My eyes squeezed tight, and I tried to ignore the strange, pungent smell that accompanied the whir of the drill on enamel. I vowed I would never have another cavity, even if I had to floss five times a day and never eat jelly beans again.

"And we're back with Friday Cry Day. We have time for one more call and we have someone on the line. Can you tell us your name?"

"Brent."

My eyes snapped open.

Dr. Kelly set down the drill and poked at my tooth. "That did it."

"Good morning, Brent. Tell us whose heart you're breaking today?"

Callie passed the filler material to Dr. Kelly without a word, both listening to the drama unfold on the radio.

The man coughed. "I'm breaking up with my girlfriend."

That voice. Surely there were other men named Brent who sounded like that and made that stupid little cough before they spoke.

"You've come to the right place. So, what's the deal?"

Cough, cough. "We've been together almost a year and I think she expects me to propose soon, but I just can't do it. She's a nice girl and all but maybe she needs to be with someone more... I don't know, boring. Like she is. She's not adventurous. She doesn't argue with me. She's always worried about making everyone happy and—"

"A people pleaser," Callie said with a sage nod.

"—I can't imagine spending the rest of my life with her."

The bottom dropped from my stomach because I knew that voice. I'd heard it order extra onions on his cheeseburger. I'd heard it say my name at midnight when its owner had heartburn and needed an antacid because of those extra onions. It was *his* voice. Brent. *My* Brent.

Dr. Kelly stuffed the filling into my tooth, jamming it in with a sharp instrument and a bit too much enthusiasm. "He sounds like a jerk," she muttered.

That jerk was saying those things about me.

Brent continued. "I'll die of boredom if I stay with her one more day. And it's New Year's. A good time for change."

My heart threatened to burst through my chest, run across the room, snatch up the radio, and toss it out the window.

"Let's get her on the phone right now." There was a pause before the sound of a phone ringing. Under my thigh, my phone vibrated. Tears gathered in the corners of my eyes.

Dr. Kelly's brow furrowed as she pulled her hands out of my mouth, carefully removed the mouth prop and sat back on her stool. "You doing okay?"

Now that I could talk, I didn't want to. Why weren't fillings done under general anesthesia, so I couldn't talk or hear or feel anything?

The ringing again sounded through the radio and again my phone vibrated under my thigh.

"I hope she answers and tells him off," Callie said.

Ring. Vibrate. For Pete's sake, how many times before voice-mail picked up?

A click sounded, and my voice blasted out like a trumpet announcing how pathetic I was. I was going to eat so much ice cream after this. Screw my plan to never get a cavity again. "You've reached Perci's phone. Sorry I'm not in right now. Leave a message and I'll get back to you."

Cough, cough.

"Hi, it's Brent. Look, you're a nice girl and I'm sure you'll make someone really happy one day, but I don't think we should see each other anymore. If you have any questions, you know where to find me."

Dr. Kelly snorted. "What a jackass. Poor girl." She laid a hand on my shoulder and my breath seized, waiting for her to remember my name, to realize I *was* that poor girl. "You're all done. I'll see you in a few months for a cleaning."

Callie moved the tray of instruments and raised the chair. I opened and closed my mouth, trying and failing to shake the numbness. Strangely, that feeling seemed to have moved from my mouth down my throat to my chest.

I shot out of the chair and snagged my purse, moving out of the small open exam room, phone clutched in my hand. My fight response might be underdeveloped, but my flight response was highly tuned. Right now, it urged me to get the hell out of the dentist's office, the city of Houston, the state of Texas, and possibly the country.

Dr. Kelly stood and pulled off her gloves. "Tell your mom I said hi."

I didn't answer because that's when my phone vibrated again—this time with a voicemail notification.

THREE

"One day, you'll need to be the bigger person.
Eat all the cake you can now to prepare yourself."

—MIMI

Ever since I'd graduated from college, I'd lived in a condo in the Brewer Street neighborhood, a corner of Houston undergoing a revitalization. The Lofts was an old, converted cookie factory which, I'm not going to lie, upped the awesome factor. Sometimes, I swore a whiff of long-ago baked snickerdoodles lingered in the hallways.

I grabbed my mail from my box in the lobby and stuffed it in my purse. Skipping the elevator, I trudged up the stairs to offload the things I'd bought at the grocery store on the way home in preparation for a long weekend of being sad and broken-hearted. The fat, sugar, and chocolate food groups were all represented nicely.

Oh, and lettuce and some baby carrots. Mostly because I wanted the cashier to know I was an adult.

The bags bit into my wrist as I juggled them along with my

purse and keys. I paused at the landing to readjust them, leaning against the wall with a sigh as Brent's voice from earlier replayed in my head. *I can't imagine spending the rest of my life with her.*

Last week, he'd sent me beautiful pink roses with a note that read, *Just because. Love, Brent.* Sure, roses were my least favorite flower, but the note? *Love*, it said. Love. I'd obsessed over that word for days. He'd never said it to me. And I'd certainly never said it to him. It hadn't been a case of love at first sight with us, which I wasn't even sure was a thing. My relationship with Brent was built on convenience and prodding from my mother. And, I'd *thought*, mutual respect.

My phone rang from the depths of my purse. I didn't need to check to know it must be my mother. The sound I made was somewhere between a laugh and a sob—there should be a word for that. My mother thought Brent had hung the sun and moon and made the earth rotate. I half expected her to keep him and disinherit me when she found out he'd dumped me.

"He's the one," she'd told me more than once. "I don't think you can do better."

Brent, with his carefully styled hair to hide his ever-widening bald spot. Brent, with that little cough he made before speaking like he wanted to announce his presence. Brent, with his terrible ties and strong dislike of chocolate. (In hindsight, that should have been a clue.)

But he could also be sweet, and I'd thought we were marching toward marriage sooner rather than later. What if my mom was right, and Brent had been my only real shot at marriage and a family of my own?

And he'd traded me for concert tickets.

I bit my lip; I would not cry. A dark tendril of hair escaped my ponytail and fluttered in front of my eyes. I shoved it aside and rubbed my stinging nose.

With a sniffle, I set my bags on the floor and fished my

phone from my purse. After it stopped ringing, I tapped out a group text message to my family and told them my (imaginary) stomach problems would keep me from going to the party at the Loveland Hotel we went to each year for New Year's Eve. Then I shot off a proof-of-life text to my best friend, Mathias, and turned my phone off before anyone could reply.

A door slammed above, and a man appeared, a rush of leather jacket and dark hair as he jogged down the stairs and past me. He was more of an impression than an image, blurred in his haste. No one I'd seen before, but it was a big complex; I didn't know everyone. Still, he paused a few steps past me, turned back toward me.

"Hey," he said. "You okay?"

I straightened, oddly touched that he'd asked. "Oh, um, I'm fine."

His head tipped to the side. He waited half a second before heading back down the stairs, throwing a hand in the air in a wave.

When I pushed into my dark little apartment a minute later, I dumped everything on the kitchen counter and flipped on the lights. There were many boring things about me, but my apartment wasn't one of them.

The tiny dining area held a square chrome-and-turquoise table surrounded by four mismatched chairs. Bold, whimsical prints along with small, framed photographs—a Mayfield family photo, a few of Mimi and me, my sister and I—nestled on the shelf I'd installed along the long, exposed brick wall. A few candles here and there, a vase or two for fresh flowers, a leopard-print fleece blanket (a gift from Mimi) thrown on the chaise, my spoon collection displayed in the hanging wooden cabinet.

If it was bright, bold, striped, checked, floral, or whimsical, I wanted it here. But I hadn't gathered all these things to impress anyone. I'd wanted a sanctuary, and it wasn't lost on me that my little apartment was everything I was too afraid to be.

Sal, my betta fish, gazed at me peacefully from his spot perched on a giant, overturned flowerpot acting as an end table in the living room. I hurried over to greet him.

"This has been a horrible day." I picked up a can of fish food and sprinkled a dusting in his bowl. "I mean, *really* bad. I know you weren't a big fan of Brent." Brent had been forever moving Sal's bowl to another table or the kitchen so he could set up his laptop in the living room. "But it was nice to have someone."

I plopped on the chunky red couch I'd gotten for a song at a thrift store. Exhausted from the day's events, I allowed the silence to soothe what it could of my battered heart. Sal's tail fluttered in a wave of reds and blues and purples as he drifted to the side of the bowl and peered out with one round black sympathetic eye.

I pressed a finger to the glass. "Thanks, pal. I can always trust you to have my back."

Sal smiled, or I like to think it was a smile. Sal and I were close, and he seemed to get me in a way a lot of others didn't. For example, he never told me what to do or judged me. Or if he did, he kept it to himself.

After changing into more comfortable clothes which featured a lot of elastic and stretch material, I curled in the floral-covered papasan chair closest to the patio window in the living room. On sunny days, light shone through the glass door and provided the perfect reading spot. Today wasn't sunny. Today, it was gray and nasty.

Kind of like Brent's heart.

Ten minutes later, which I spent thoroughly examining the many ways that my life was a disaster, Mathias showed up unannounced, bearing gifts of red wine, fruit, and a small dartboard.

"A dartboard?"

"Hold on." From his pocket, he produced a crudely cut-out

picture of Brent's head and slapped it on the board. "I printed it off Facebook."

"And the devil horns and goatee?"

Mathias grinned. "I added those. I think it suits him. You like?"

"Totally."

This was why Mathias was my best friend. He was like the brother I never wanted but couldn't live without. We'd met several years ago when Phee had had a decent shot at the Miss Texas title. Our mother had hired Mathias's mother as her coach, who used her powers to guide young, hopeful women to their full pageant potential. Mrs. Jorgenson had been Miss Texas 1978 and her mother had been Miss Texas 1953. Mathias, unable to follow in their footsteps, had been dragged into the family business nonetheless.

He mostly kept busy as a photographer, but he also helped with the soft skills—public speaking, social media, and marketing—and he traveled a lot to meet with clients for photo sessions and sometimes, damage control. But his knowledge of double-sided tape and Preparation H was well-honed, and he could step in to solve a wardrobe malfunction or a hair crisis when needed. Furthermore, his arsenal of pep talks was legendary. As were his romances with beauty queens.

But he was still always pining for one beauty queen in particular. Namely, my sister.

Mathias dumped it all on the counter, put his hands on my shoulders and leveled a steady blue gaze at me. "Brent is an asshat. Remember that."

"I mean, maybe—"

"Nope. He's an asshat. You are not the problem here. He is." He wrapped me in a tight hug and rested his chin on the top of my head. I melted against him, enjoying the knowledge that if nothing else, I always had him. Plus, he smelled good. Mathias took care with his appearance. His outfits—skinny jeans and a crisp white t-shirt today—might scream casual, but they were always calculated to impress. "God, you're short."

With a snort, I stepped back. "Thanks."

"That's what I'm here for, to remind you of your vertical deficiencies."

"I mean, thank you for, you know, being my friend."

"Like I said, that's what I'm here for." He started pulling open cabinets to get what he'd need to make sangria. "Now, we have some drinking to do."

By the time the knock on the door came an hour and a half later, Mathias and I were delightfully buzzed and well on the way to regretting it in the morning.

I glanced through the peephole. My sister was wearing a long mauve dress with lacy three-quarter sleeves. Her shiny blonde hair was twisted into a sophisticated bun—a picture of elegance.

I pulled open the door. "Hey, what are you doing here?"

Phee brushed past me. "Are you kidding? I called you fourteen times after that stupid radio stunt Brent pulled."

She rested her hip on the counter and turned the full strength of her bright blue eyes on me. People always did stupid things like assume my sister must be only slightly smarter than a piece of cheese because she was a pageant girl. But they were very wrong.

"Are you okay?" She squeezed my shoulder gently.

"It's... fine," I said, and tugged at the t-shirt I'd thrown on. It had a chocolate stain on the front already and the night was young.

"It is most certainly *not* fine."

Mathias breezed into the kitchen. Reaching between us, he grabbed his cup from the counter. "Nice outfit, Phee. You going to a dance at the senior center or something?"

I had to admit the outfit would have been more appropriate if my sister was a sixty-five-year-old grandmother and not a twenty-four-year-old woman. But in the last year, Phee had changed a lot. Mostly it had to do with her new boyfriend—*the* Joel Allen, news anchor at KKRE and all-around jerk. Phee worked there too, as the weekday traffic reporter for the morning news. She woke up at 3 a.m. every day, got to the station and spent five hours wearing impossibly tight dresses while pointing at squiggly lines on a street map and flashing her winning pageant smile. Her fancy-schmancy journalism degree hard at work.

Phee never complained about her job but sometimes I thought she hated it, just a little bit. It was hard to tell with Phee. She'd learned early on to smile and act the part.

"For your information, Joel picked out this dress."

"Oh, right, Joel. Say, did he ever get those butt implants he was thinking about?"

"Shut up, Mathias."

He grinned. "Ouch, the kitten has claws."

"Whatever. It's New Year's Eve. Those of us with dates..." I sucked in a breath. Phee startled and turned to me. "Oh, geez. I'm sorry, I didn't mean that. I just meant, um, I'm going to the New Year's Eve party."

"Nice save," Mathias said, grinning as he adjusted his glasses. The dark frames gave him the air of a debauched professor, which was probably what he was going for.

Phee refused to take the bait, keeping her eyes on me. "I'm meeting Joel there. I just wanted to check on you. I was worried."

Joel, Mathias mouthed behind her back and pretended to gag. "Nothing to worry about, she's in good hands," he said.

She gestured toward the various snacks and alcoholic beverages lined up on the counter. "I can see that."

The strange tension between Mathias and Phee hadn't always been this way. When they'd first met, Mathias had been fresh out of college and hadn't yet discovered the delights of highlights and manscaping, but he had discovered Phee. According to Mathias, the feeling had been mutual. Then Phee had ghosted him without explanation. Sometimes, I thought all his primping since was for the sole purpose of catching my sister's attention. If that was the case, so far, it hadn't worked.

"I should get going," Phee said.

Mathias shrugged and ruffled his dirty blond hair. "You don't want to keep the ladies at the junior league waiting, right?"

Phee rolled her eyes but refused to acknowledge him. "I'm glad you're okay and that you aren't alone. If you want to talk or anything..."

Her voice trailed off and the look she gave me was almost hopeful. My relationship with Phee was complicated. Three years younger than me, I'd fallen in love with her like everyone else. As a child, I'd claimed her for my own and carted her everywhere. She'd look at me with those giant blue eyes, and I'd vow to do anything to keep her happy. I was her protector, her champion, but I wasn't sure we'd ever been sisters. Not in the "we-tell-each-other-everything-while-braiding-each-other's-hair" kind of sisters. The bigger she'd grown, the less she'd needed me, until it was safe to say she'd far surpassed me in all areas.

What good was an older sister a girl couldn't look up to?

"Thanks," I whispered, feeling tears prick the backs of my eyes.

"Wait. Does Mom know?" she asked.

I shook my head, dread settling in my stomach. "I don't know. She called, but I didn't answer."

"I'll feel her out tonight and let you know." With a regal tilt of her head, Phee headed toward the door. "See you at lunch tomorrow, right?"

I nodded.

She wheeled to pin Mathias with a hard stare. "And you too, I suppose."

"Nope. I have plans." He waggled his brows just in case we didn't understand what kind of plans.

Phee rolled her eyes.

"Have fun with *Joel* and the family." Mathias winked and headed for the bathroom tucked in the hallway.

Phee's eyes followed him, a wistful expression skipping over her face. "Are you sure you're okay? I could stay," she said. "Joel would understand."

No, he wouldn't understand, and neither would our mother. This party was Mom's yearly chance to show off her beautiful, successful daughter. And me. "I'll be fine. Have fun."

At the door, she turned quickly and wrapped me in a hug. "Love you, Perci."

I hugged her back, the tears welling up again, but I blinked them back before they could fall.

FOUR

"Pass the jalapeño poppers." Mathias nudged me with a shoulder. Groaning, I leaned forward and pulled the plate onto my lap. He took one and shoved it in his mouth, washing it down with wine straight from the bottle.

"Nothing goes better with pity than jalapeño poppers." Mathias stuffed a second one in his mouth and talked around it. "Soothes the soul."

We were sprawled on my couch, watching television and the clock tick down to midnight. "This is a much better way to spend New Year's Eve than at some stupid party where I have to smile and pretend I'm having fun," I said.

I hiccupped and thought of the sensible black dress with the cap sleeves and matching velvet jacket hanging in my closet. My mother had picked it out and all but forced me to promise I'd wear it to the party. I hated that dress. But I would have shown up in it anyway. Like I did every year as part of my daughterly duties.

"But we're missing our chance to bask in the presence of the *great* Joel Allen." Mathias snorted. "He picked that dress for Phee? It was hideous. I wanted to snatch that thing right off her."

I choked on a slug of wine. "I bet you did."

He frowned, his dark blond eyebrows forming a V. "That's not what I meant."

"Uh-huh. You keep telling yourself that." I grinned. "I wish you two would just make out and get it over with."

With a groan, he dropped his head to the back of the couch. "I can't believe I'm doing this."

"Spending New Year's with your lame-o friend?"

"You aren't lame." He twisted his neck to look at me. "I can't believe I'm about to tell you this. And tomorrow I'm going to blame it on the alcohol. Remember about two years ago, when your dad had that cancer scare?"

Two years ago, Dad had gone in for a biopsy and the results had come back inconclusive. So, he'd had to go back in for more tests. All of us had been on pins and needles waiting for the results.

"Phee showed up at my apartment one night. She was crying so hard, and she looked so, I don't know, not put together." His gaze grew unfocused. "Her hair wasn't even done. You know how she never lets anyone see it down unless it's been straightened."

It was my mom who liked Phee's hair straightened, actually. But I didn't correct him.

"Anyway, she came in and ended up staying the night."

I shot up, tossing a handful of potato chips on the floor in the process "You slept with her?"

"Not like that. We just slept, that's all. I put her to bed after she calmed down and then she asked me to stay with her."

"So, no sexy times?" I asked. Not that I was all that interested in Mathais or Phee's love lives, but I'd always secretly hoped the two of them would find each other. So many times over the years, I'd been certain Phee reciprocated Mathias's feelings. Then someone shinier (and older and more powerful) would come along and she'd get distracted.

"No sex, just sleep. But in the morning, she got out of there like my bed was on fire." He sat up and set his elbows on his knees, dangling his hands between his splayed legs. "I almost," he slid his eyes toward me, "told her how I felt."

"Maybe she feels the same way?"

He snorted. "I know my place. I am firmly in the friend zone. She probably sees a giant blinking sign and skulls-and-crossbones when she's around me."

"That's really sad."

Mathias leaned over and kissed my cheek. "You smell good, and you have great skin and you're smart and you make me laugh. Why can't I love you?"

I blinked.

"I mean, I love you but I'm not in love with you." He took a deep swig of wine and wiped his mouth with a grimace. "I sound like a character in a cheesy romantic comedy."

"We'd be adorable. We could call ourselves Percias."

Mathias's nose crinkled. "Sounds like a foot disease."

"I love you, too."

Life would be a lot easier if the two of us could fall in love. We'd tried it a couple of years ago. Our "relationship" had lasted all of seventeen seconds. Mathias had asked if he could kiss me. I'd said yes and what happened next was the most awkward, disturbing kiss of my life. We'd broken apart and agreed to never speak of it again.

Besides, he had met Phee first, and, like a lost baby bird, he'd imprinted on her. I'd asked him once what this magic was my sister held over him and he'd shrugged and said, "I wish I knew."

On television, the host's voice cut through my thoughts: "... most common New Year's resolutions? Anyone want to take a guess?"

Another host, an ultra-thin girl who starred in some ultra-popular angsty teenager show, hummed. "Losing weight?"

"Correct. That includes working out and eating healthier. Next guess?"

"Psft." I tossed a balled-up napkin in the general direction of the television.

Every New Year's, I made a deal with myself to lose forty pounds and get bikini-ready. I knew how to lose weight—the basic principles weren't rocket science—but I could never quite do it for more than a few pounds before I gave up.

I slugged back more wine and chased it with a handful of chips. Some of them made it in my mouth, others down the front of my shirt, and one definitely disappeared into my bra. Saving it for later.

Mathias's head flopped onto my shoulder. "What does that asshole have that I don't? Joel Asshole Allen. That's his new name."

"I like it. It suits him."

The third guest, the lead singer of a pop group, squinted. He had on more eyeliner than I wore in a year. "A new hobby?"

The host nodded, full-wattage television smile in place. "That's also on the list."

Hobbies? Let's talk about hobbies for a minute. I'd tried those too. From the time I could walk, Mom had thrown me into various and sundry hobbies, hoping one would stick—ballet, art classes, piano, soccer, Girl Scouts, flag team. I stank at all of them. As an adult, I'd tried others—cooking, a second language, gardening, soapmaking, and one disastrous afternoon, woodworking.

Something was wrong with me. Normal people could find one measly thing they were good at. But not me. I'd made all these resolutions and still never turned into a better version of myself.

"I think I'm broken," I said, cuddling the bottle of wine to my chest like it was my firstborn. "That must be the problem."

Mathias slung an arm around me. "You aren't broken."

"I think I am." I banged the bottle down next to Sal's bowl. He stared at me with compassionate, unfailing love. "My mother thinks I am. Know what I got for Christmas?"

He shook his head.

"A gym membership renewal, Spanx, and a new black suit. It's a size too small, but I can't tell her. Then I'd have to admit my real size and she'd tell me if I tried a little harder, it would fit. And you know what? I do try, I try a lot, but somehow, it's never enough."

The voice from the television droned on. "Any other guesses? Popular New Year's resolutions?"

"Oh, I know! I know!" Ultra-Thin Girl hopped up and down. "Dating!"

I groaned and flopped sideways, so my head rested on the arm of the couch. "Yet another resolution I've failed at."

On my list of Things I Was Good At, failure beat out everything else.

I'd been failing my whole life. I'd failed to arrive on my due date. I'd failed kindergarten the first time. I'd failed college biology. Twice. I'd failed to lose weight. I'd failed to keep my boyfriend happy. I'd failed to make my mother proud.

I'd failed.

I always failed.

I was a failure.

That old familiar friend of mine, defeat, joined the pity party, settling in my stomach like a rock. "It doesn't matter how hard I try, I'm never good enough."

The tears surprised me, sliding down my cheeks before I could stop them. Mathias noticed and pulled me up, pressing my face into his chest. I sniffled, breathing in the comforting smells of clean shirt, cologne, and a hint of jalapeños.

Mathias cupped my shoulder and pushed me up. His blue eyes glared down at me. "Look, you're going through a hard time. It won't always be like this."

I scrubbed the wetness from my face, not quite meeting his gaze. Best friend or not, there were some things I worked hard to keep hidden. Sometimes, even from myself.

He stood and paced the living room. Somehow his white shirt remained crisp and his dark-wash jeans appeared freshly laundered. Even when he was wallowing and drinking, he still looked like a movie star. I adjusted my oversized t-shirt and tried to ignore the salsa stain that had joined the chocolate ice cream splatter.

Mathias paused and stuck his hands on his hips, feet shoulder-with apart, a little like a warrior set to do battle. "You know what I tell the pageant girls?"

"Hold your breath, it makes your boobs stick out?"

"I tell them no one will believe in them if they don't believe in themselves." Crouching in front of me, he cradled one of my hands in his. "That's the problem. You don't think you're good enough, so no one else will. You can't please everyone, so you've got to stop trying." He shot to his feet and darted into the kitchen. "I have an idea."

"No more ideas. Or talking. Or thinking." I stretched out on the couch and hugged a pillow to my stomach.

"Four... three... two... one... Happy New Year!" Screams and shouts poured from the television over a pitchy pop version of "Auld Lang Syne." I clicked it off. All that happiness messed with my pity party.

"Happy New Year, Sal." I blew a kiss at the best fish a gal could ask for. "And you too, Mathias. Wherever you are."

"I'm right here." Mathias's face hovered over me, waving a small notebook. He smacked my legs until I lifted them and laid them on his lap after he sat. "We're going to write New Year's resolutions."

I threw an arm over my eyes. "Oh, good, more things for me to fail at."

"Resolutions that are impossible to fail at, like..." The rapid click of his pen filled the silence. He muttered under his breath and scribbled on the paper.

My brain sloshed like a ship caught in a hurricane when I sat up. "What are you writing?"

"Number one: You will not try to lose weight."

I huffed a laugh. "What?"

"You aren't allowed to diet, watch what you eat, take a hot yoga class—"

"Taking a hot yoga class is never gonna happen." Okay, it had happened once. I was still trying to forget.

"—count your carbs or skip dessert because you're worried about the calories." He pointed the pen at me. "Got it?"

"I'm gaining weight just thinking about it."

He tsked. "You'll be fine. Now, number two: You will not try to be more confident."

"Huh?"

"There will be no more trying to be more assertive and speaking your mind."

"So, no more self-help books?"

"Nope."

"What about the that daily email I get?"

"What's it called?"

"'Steps to a More Confident You.'"

He scowled. "No, definitely not. Unsubscribe immediately."

"Really?" I asked, and it was hard not to hear the hope in my voice. These were resolutions I could actually keep.

"Why not?" He shoulder-bumped me. "If none of it's working, then maybe it's time to stop trying so hard."

A smile spread across my face as I turned to him. "I think I like it. They're like anti-resolutions. What else you got?"

Mathias tilted his head back and stared at the ceiling. I joined him. After a moment, he jerked and began writing again. "Number three: You will not put more effort into your job."

"I won't?"

"No more working late at the last minute or taking on extra work because people ask you to. No more being the person everyone takes advantage of."

"I can do that." Maybe. Work was complicated.

"Let's see. Number four?" He hummed and then his eyes lit up. "You will not date. Take a year and be you. You go from one long-term relationship to another. You never just have fun. Plus, you can use it as an excuse the next time your mom tries to set you up."

That idea had real merit.

He raised a hand. "And speaking of your mother, number five: You will not try to be a better daughter or sister."

I snorted. "Are you kidding? I'm terrible as it is."

Tossing the notebook down, he turned to me. "That's just it. You put so much pressure on yourself to be what they want you to be, you forget to be you. Stop trying to please everyone else." His hand cupped my cheek. "You are amazing. Maybe if you try this, you'll see you don't need to be anyone but yourself. You'll believe it, so you'll be it."

The earnest way he said those words, the unabashed fierceness burning in his eyes, I almost did believe it. If this was how he built up the pageant girls, I totally understood why he was so sought after.

"Promise me you'll follow these?" He ripped the paper from the notebook and handed me the sheet.

Bold, concise print filled the page, listing out each of the resolutions Mathias deemed the answer to my life's woes.

PERCI'S NEW YEAR'S ANTI-RESOLUTIONS

1. I will not try to lose weight.
2. I will not try to be more confident.
3. I will not put more effort into my job.
4. I will not date.
5. I will not try to be a better daughter and sister.

"I promise," I said, with the knowledge that oaths made under duress or the influence of way too much wine didn't count.

I stood and took a moment to steady myself before grabbing the sheet from his hand and marching to the refrigerator. There, I hung it with a magnet Mom had slyly stuck on the last time she'd visited. It read: NOTHING TASTES AS GOOD AS THIN FEELS.

My mother was not subtle.

The list stared back at me, taunting me with its five little sentences that summed up my entire life. It would be nice to live my life the way Mathias imagined it, to not worry about anyone else's expectations. But all the little things that made me *me* had never, ever been enough. Maybe some of us weren't meant for greatness.

An impossible dream, that's what it was. By the time I made it back to the couch, Mathias had sprawled across it. "Don't think you're getting off so easy. What's your resolution?"

He shifted, revealing a thoughtful expression. "I'm going to do it."

"Do what?"

"I'm going to tell Phee I'm in love with her."

Seemed like both of us were dreamers.

FIVE

"Dull women have immaculate homes.
And, honey, I'm a terrible housekeeper."

—MIMI

"You ready for this?" Mimi asked as I pulled up to the curb in front of my parents' house.

"No, I'm not." I turned off the car and rested my forehead on the steering wheel. Our family Christmas dinner this year had been pushed to a New Year's Day lunch because of Phee and Joel's schedule.

I stared at my parents' house, a stately three-story with a brick façade and a partial wraparound porch in the West U area of Houston. At over a hundred years old, the house contained five thousand square feet of spacious bedrooms, more bathrooms than I could count on one hand, and a butler's pantry. I still wasn't entirely sure what a butler's pantry was, but it was a crowning jewel for my mother.

It wasn't home, though. My parents had purchased this right before I started high school. Before that, we'd lived in a modest three-bedroom house in a cookie-cutter, middle-class neighborhood. Phee and I had shared a room. On the doorframe between the dining and living rooms, tiny lines marked our height measurements throughout the years. The backyard had a trampoline and playset, and the sprinkler in the front attracted all the neighborhood kids regularly.

Back then, Mom had been a regular mom. She'd yell at us for dragging dirt in the house, and didn't seem to mind that none of the kitchen appliances matched. At bedtime, she still read us stories and it was she who scrubbed the toilets and made dinner each night.

It had been perfect, mostly because it was imperfect.

Then Dad's business exploded, and my parents moved to this big house in the nice neighborhood and imperfections were no longer an option. They had a reputation to uphold.

Mimi flipped down the visor. "Well, honey, there's no way of getting out of it. Hitch up your big girl panties." She fluffed her hair, then dug through her purse for her lipstick, a shade of blinding orange red. "Do you know what this color is called?"

It was such a Mimi sort of color that I felt my shoulders lose some of their tension, happy she was here with me.

Six months ago, after experiencing shortness of breath, Mimi landed in the emergency room. Mom had rushed to Eagle Pass in the middle of the night. After years of huffing her way through a pack a day, the smoking had caught up with her.

The doctors told her she needed to quit immediately, and after another scare a few weeks later, involving a suspicious spot on one of her lungs, the decision was made for Mimi to sell her little trailer and move to Houston to be closer. There'd been talk of her moving in with my parents and she'd flatly refused. So, we'd found her a small one-bedroom apartment in one of those complexes for the fifty-five-and-older crowd.

"Red?"

"'Fireman's Bait.'" She waggled her eyebrows.

I laughed despite my dark mood. "Let's get this over with."

Mimi patted my leg. "This is all just one of them life moments. It will pass, it will."

My mother answered the door, perfect and tasteful in a cream-colored sweater dress that skimmed her body. Although she would never admit it, my mother was a Perkins through and through. Just like Mimi and me, she was naturally short and curvy with dark, heavy-lidded eyes and equally dark hair. The difference was that she had figured out how to win the battle against genetics. With the joint efforts of her personal trainer, a Pilates instructor, a strict diet of ice cubes and lettuce, and, I suspected, a plastic surgeon, she remained thin and elegant.

I guess we had the potential to look alike. If I lost fifty pounds, got blonde highlights, and a personal shopper, we'd practically be twins.

"Mama, what are you wearing?" Mom said, a hint of annoyance in her perfectly modulated voice. When I was very young, she'd had a Southern twang a country singer would be jealous of. But then a woman began coming to our house to give her elocution lessons and beat that accent right out of her. Nowadays, she only slipped when she and Mimi got into one of their "discussions."

A smile stretched across Mimi's face as she adjusted her dress—orange leopard print with a tie at the waist and flirty slit in the back. She strutted past my mother on spiky black heels. "You like it? I got it off that Home Shopping Network."

My mother sighed in annoyance and plucked the pie I'd brought from my hands. She leaned forward and kissed my cheek, wrapping me in the soft fragrance of her perfume. "Thank you for picking her up." Taking a few steps back, she inspected me. "You look very nice. That's the suit I got you for your birthday, right? But"—she frowned; there was always a "but" with her— "we might need to get you a new hair straightener."

I bit my lip, equal parts embarrassed and annoyed. "Mine works, I might've just missed a piece or two."

"Nothing for it now. Come on."

Mimi and I trailed behind her as she made her way to the kitchen. "Your father is finishing up the turkey in that deep fryer. Don't know why he insists on cooking it that way. But don't worry. I got a turkey breast for those of us watching our figures." She winked at me.

I didn't reply because it would be useless. Plus, she was right, I could stand to lose more than a few pounds.

Mimi dumped her purse on the small table in the eat-in kitchen. "I'll definitely be having me some fried turkey. Did you get what I need to make the sweet potato casserole?"

"Mama, do you really need to make that? It's not very healthy."

Hands on her hips, Mimi shot daggers at her daughter. "Bobbie Jo, this is the holidays. We have traditions."

My mother scowled. "Roberta."

"Your birth certificate says otherwise."

"And the federal government says differently." It did as of fifteen years ago, when she'd legally changed it.

Mimi slipped an apron on and tied it with sharp movements. "I don't much care what the government says. You came out of my body, I named you, and that's what I'm calling you."

With a growl, my mother ripped open a cabinet and slammed down a package of marshmallows, a bag of brown sugar, and a huge can of yams. "There. Make your damn casserole."

Mimi opened her mouth to reply—surely something that would only annoy my mother—when a scratching noise at the back door sounded, followed by a sharp bark that sent a chill up my spine.

"Can you let Pericles in, please?" my mother asked, gesturing at me with a bundle of artichokes.

The back door was tucked at the end of the kitchen next to a small dining table. I opened it and Pericles paused, his black eyes staring at me from under a fringe of fur like he could see my soul and found me lacking. I shivered.

When my mother sent Phee off to college, she'd lamented her empty nest and filled it with Pericles—part standard poodle, part demon. Mom doted on him. Pericles had a full wardrobe and was only allowed to eat a homemade diet with ingredients like scrambled organic eggs and rice and sweet potatoes that Mom culled from the canine cookbook she read with religious fervor. But it was his eyes that bothered me the most; the dark, bottomless pits followed me around the room like one of those haunted paintings. I secretly called him Scary Perry when Mom wasn't around.

I turned away and made a gagging face at Mimi. She grinned.

Mom produced a treat and Scary Perry took it gingerly between his teeth. He trotted past me and settled in the dog bed in the corner, turning three times before lying down to survey us humans with haughty disdain.

Mom wiped her hands on the towel and went about rinsing and drying off the artichokes. "Where's Brent? Is he coming later?"

I gnawed on a fingernail nervously. So she hadn't heard anything about the break-up yet. Of course, she'd ask. A whole person *was* missing.

"I wish you'd stop that. It's such a bad habit."

Cocking a hip, Mimi squinted at my mother. "Ya know, you sucked your thumb till you were seven. I thought that thing was gonna shrivel up and fall off, you had it in your mouth so often."

"What does that have to do with anything?" Mom asked.

I knew. Mimi had swooped in to distract my mother and save me. On my list of the Best People Ever, Mimi was numbers one, two, and three.

Mimi shrugged. "You're the one who brought up bad habits. I thought this was sharing time."

"Mama, sometimes I think—"

"Auld Lang Syne" chimed through the house; Mom had a fancy, programmable doorbell with songs for every season.

"That might be Brent right now," my mother said.

"I'll get it." My voice sounded shrill.

Mimi muttered under her breath as I passed. "Big girl panties, honey. Big girl panties."

Scary Perry yipped in agreement.

I answered the door slightly winded from running out of the kitchen and, okay, away from my mother. The door revealed my sister and Joel Allen, although they didn't acknowledge me. It would have been hard to, given they were tangled in a fully involved kiss. Both my sister's red dress and Joel Allen clung to her like second skins. I averted my eyes and counted to ten, waiting for them to come up for air.

Finally, Phee pulled away with a giggle and dabbed at her mouth with the back of her hand.

Joel Allen pointed at the awning above and winked. "Mistletoe."

"Lucky me," I muttered, and stepped aside for them to enter.

Joel Allen nodded a greeting as he passed me in a cloud of cologne and male ego. He had thick dark hair (plugs, Mathias said), a year-round golden tint to his skin (spray tan, Mathias said), and a perma-smile full of ultra-white teeth (veneers, Mathias said).

But the worst thing about Joel Allen was the way he treated my sister. His casual comments about her clothes or hair or intelligence or weight; the stories he told that made her the butt of the joke. She wasn't a person to him, but a status symbol, a beautiful woman he could show off to his friends in the "I still got it" way of divorced men in their thirties.

But even worse than that was how my sister changed around him—a doting, wide-eyed girl who seemed to have misplaced her backbone.

"Persephone, dear, who is it?" my mother asked. She strode down the hallway, Pericles's toenails tapping on the hardwood floor as he trailed behind. From the kitchen, Mimi belted out an off-key version of Dolly Parton's "Jolene."

I gritted my teeth at the sound of my full name. Back in college, my mother had been a Classics major, and she fancied herself a bit of an expert. The way we heard it, she and Dad had made a deal—she would get to name the girls, and the boys would be Dad's territory. Mom had hit the jackpot. And, thus inspired by her love of ye olde Greeks and Romans, we were named Persephone and Phoebe. Even Pericles got in on the action, being Mom's third child. Even if he was a boy.

"Roberta!" Joel Allen announced in the deep, boisterous voice he used in and out of the newsroom (also fake, Mathias said). He hugged my mother, who giggled against his shoulder.

She greeted Phee next and stood back with a smile. "You look beautiful. I'm so glad you're here. We're just missing Brent now. Where is he? You don't think something happened, do you?"

I licked my lips and shifted from one foot to the other as I weighed my options. "The thing is—"

"Brent's coming?" Joel Allen rocked back on his heels and tucked his hands in his pockets. "That's funny. I thought he dumped Perci."

My mother gasped. Phee sucked in an audible breath and nudged Joel Allen with her elbow to shut him up. He didn't listen.

"Man, that break-up was brutal." He slapped a hand on my

shoulder. I flinched and edged away, eyes plastered to my mother's face.

"I see." She dried her hands on the dishtowel she'd pulled from her shoulder. "And everyone knows about this?"

My chest tightened as that familiar sense settled there, the one I got every time I disappointed my mother. I was twenty-seven years old and should be long past the time when I took so much stock in my mother's opinion, but the truth was, I did. Unfortunately, her approval was slippery, and I'd never managed to capture it like my sister had.

"Heck, the entire city knows about it. He did it live on the radio. I like to listen when I'm on the elliptical. That morning show's hilarious," Joel Allen said.

On the list of People I Despise, Joel Allen was now numero uno. Even before Brent.

Mom's jaw tightened with what I could imagine was outrage, anger, probably disappointment, and more than a little frustration. I watched her wearily, waiting for her to ask what I'd done. How had I screwed up again? But instead, she snapped the dishtowel in the air and hooked it on her shoulder. The sound made me wince.

"Gravy's done," Mimi bellowed from the kitchen. "Let's eat. I'm salivating more than a dog at a skeleton convention."

Without a word, my mother turned and stalked away.

SIX

"Always choose kindness.
Unless the other person's a jackass.
Then all bets are off."

—*MIMI*

My survival plan for this meal: Keep busy. Stay quiet. Do not make eye contact.

I rushed to help set the table, bringing in gold-rimmed dishes of mashed potatoes, Mimi's sweet potato casserole, green beans, buttered buns, seven-layer salad, creamy homemade macaroni and cheese, and real cranberry sauce. Then there was the food my mother deemed "healthy." Baked artichokes, riced cauliflower, low-carb rolls that tasted like cardboard, and butter substitute. She made sure to not-so-subtly set them close to my seat.

On the last run, balancing pitchers of sweet tea and ice water, I paused at the entry to my mother's prized butler's pantry, which was little more than a small connecting room between the dining room and the kitchen for extra storage and counter space. Phee and Joel Allen stood side-by-side with their backs to me, shoulders pressed together as they filled glasses of ice.

"I wish you hadn't said anything," Phee was saying. "Perci was going to tell Mom when she was ready."

Joel Allen shrugged. "I thought everyone knew. It was a pretty public break-up."

Phee turned, hitching a fist on her hip. I shrank back and held my breath, hoping they wouldn't notice me.

"Still, it wasn't for you to say. She's my sister, and Brent is a jackass."

He cupped her shoulder, lowering his voice. "Can you blame him? You're the one who got all the hot genes in the family. She's like... a chubby little mouse."

My heart thudded, surely loud enough for them to hear.

"Shut up." Phee grabbed a glass in each hand and ripped her shoulder away from him. "Perci is going through a hard time right now and you only made it worse. You can be a real jerk sometimes, you know that?"

"Calm down. I didn't mean anything by it. Mice can be cute." His voice dropped lower, and he leaned in like he planned to distract her with a kiss.

"Perci, what are you doing, just standing there? Get a move on." Mimi hip-bumped me as she strode by with a wink.

My sister whipped around, eyes huge.

The pitcher in my hand shook. "I... I'll go put these down now." I scurried past them into the living room. A chubby little mouse on the run.

I set the pitchers on the sideboard and sank into my seat next to Mimi, across from Phee and Joel Allen as they joined us. My sister met my eyes with her cautious ones. *I'm sorry*, she mouthed. Her idiot boyfriend fanned out his napkin and smoothed it across his lap like he hadn't just compared me to a rodent.

On my list of People Who Should Die a Painfully Long, Torturous Death, Joel Allen was also number one.

From my pocket, I pulled out my phone and shot a text off to Mathias even though I knew he had plans.

Me: *Joel Allen is a jerk.*

I was surprised to see the three small dots indicating Mathias was typing his reply.

Mathias: *You spelled ASSHOLE wrong. How's dinner?*

Me: *Just started. Can I leave yet?*

Mathias: *Is Phee there?*

Me: *You know she is. You want to know what she's wearing.*

"Persephone, I hope you aren't texting at the dinner table," my mother said. I jerked my head up and caught the searing glare she directed at me.

With a guilty expression, I slid my phone under my thigh just as it vibrated. "Nope, of course not."

"Make way, make way." My father emerged from the kitchen. Daddy carried an oversized platter, a golden-brown turkey displayed in all its deep-fried glory. He did a victory lap around the room, pausing to kiss each of his girls on the cheek before setting his trophy at the head of the table. "Let's carve this puppy up."

I loved my father with his twinkly blue eyes and dark gray hair and belly that had blossomed over his belt in the last few years. He was a handsome man, charming and hardworking. Growing up, his appearance at home for anything more than a quick bite to eat and a few hours of sleep had been rare. He'd built Mayfield Home Mortgage from the ground up—brick by bloody brick, to have him tell it.

Not that he'd been purposely absent, but work came first. My mother had been the one who chauffeured us and attended every parent–teacher conference, music program, art show, band practice, mathlete competition, pageant performance, and informational meeting.

Dad carved. Plates were piled high with food. My leg bounced under the table as I waited out Mom's silence. It was just a matter of time.

"Did you know," my mother began, eyeing my plate with raw determination, "there are four hundred calories in a cup of macaroni and cheese and only fourteen in the same amount of cauliflower?"

"Oh, it's the holidays." My father grinned at me. "Eat what you want, Cupcake."

He always called us by our nicknames. I was Cupcake, Phee was Princess.

No comment.

"That's right, Craig, my boy," Mimi said. "You tell the old drill sergeant to lay off. She needs to remove the stick shoved up her—"

"Mama!" Mom shot Mimi a glare that would have cowed a lesser woman.

Daddy cut in. "Ladies, let's enjoy ourselves. Everything looks delicious, and I'm ready to dig in." He flashed his dimple and reached for the mashed potatoes.

That was Daddy. While Mom was the enforcer, Daddy was the softie, the bleeding heart, the peacemaker which sometimes —okay, most of the time—meant he bowed to my mother's demands just to placate her. He smiled and nodded and tried to cut off the arguments and disagreements to keep the status quo, and he was very good at it.

I had learned from the best, after all.

"Of course, dear."

Mimi smiled sweetly but she dumped an extra spoonful of mac and cheese on my plate and piled on a roll for good measure.

My phone buzzed again. While Joel Allen engaged most of the table in his favorite topic, himself, I slid it out and read the text Mathias had sent.

Mathias: *I'm going to do it.*

Me: *Do what?*

His reply didn't come right away, so I tried to look interested in the conversation. Phee pressed into Joel Allen's arm adoringly and shifted her food around but never took more than two or three bites. I squinted, trying to decipher what she saw in him. Aside from his position at the station, I wondered what the draw was. But Phee had developed a thing for men in positions of power—that professor at university, a lawyer fifteen years her senior, Joel Allen.

The phone buzzed again.

Mathias: *I'm going to tell Phee how I feel.*

Me: *When?*

Mathias: *Now.*

I gasped, and the phone slid from my hands. My mother glared at me in warning. When she looked away, I casually leaned over and picked the phone back up.

Me: *What do you mean, now?*

Mathias: *I'm five minutes away from your parents' house.*

My mother interrupted my next text, which would have said something like, *ARE YOU INSANE?*

"Are you certain Brent broke up with you?"

My face heated, probably almost the same color as the cranberry sauce, and I slid the phone under my thigh. "Yes, I'm certain."

"What's this, Cupcake?" my father asked, a forkful of turkey halfway to his mouth.

"Apparently Brent broke up with our daughter."

"On the radio," Joel Allen added. He flinched, and I thought Phee might have pinched him. I would have preferred a fork to the thigh.

Dad's eyebrow hitched. "Brent?"

"On the radio." Mom tossed a cloth napkin over her half-eaten dinner. "Just embarrassing." She waved a hand at my father. "You'll talk to him, Craig. I'm sure this is all a misunderstanding."

Dad nodded and stuffed a roll in his mouth. "I'll talk to him. We'll get it straightened out."

My stomach dropped. *No, no, no. Absolutely not.* "Please don't. It's fine."

"Fine?" My mother pushed up from her chair. "You two were perfectly suited. What do you think went wrong? Is it the weight, or...?"

Joel Allen cut in. "He said she wasn't any fun and he couldn't imagine spending his life with her."

I eyed the gravy boat with longing. Could a person drown another person in gravy? Maybe if they were really, really motivated.

"What does that even mean?" Mom threw her hands in the air. "Wasn't any fun? Well, you can change that. You'll have to work a little harder, of course, but we'll come up with a plan..."

I cut her off, my voice wobbling. "Mother, he broke up with me to win concert tickets. Leave it alone. Please?"

She stared at me for a long moment and her face softened. Rounding the table, she stopped at my chair and leaned over to hug me. For a second, tears gathered behind my eyes as I clung to her. All too quickly, it was over.

"All right." Straightening, she smoothed her dress and snatched my plate and Mimi's, even though we weren't finished, and stalked into the kitchen. "Let's get the table cleared. We'll have dessert in the living room."

Joel Allen smiled at me across the table—the same fake, awful television smile he'd use on some poor soul whose house burned down in a freak toaster fire. Pity smile. "Never know, Perci. Maybe Brent'll invite you to that concert."

My sister smacked his shoulder. "Shut up."

That's when the doorbell rang. "I'll get it."

I hustled down the hallway. Mathias was dressed to kill in a tailored navy suit. With a glance behind my shoulder, I pushed him onto the porch and closed the door behind us. "What are you doing?"

"I need to do this. I was on a date tonight with... I can't even remember her name. I should remember her name, right? But I didn't care because I was thinking about Phee, and then I thought about Phee with Joel. And I thought, why am I waiting to tell her? This is it. I'm doing it." He leaned in, his eyes full of both yearning and nerves. "Tell me this is the right thing to do."

I opened my mouth to reply at the same time the door opened behind me. "Mathias, I didn't know you were stopping by. Don't you look handsome," my mother said and nudged me aside to give him a hug. "Come in. You're just in time for dessert. It's been too long since we've seen you."

"Of course, Mrs. Mayfield."

She giggled and swatted his shoulder. "Roberta, dear."

I rolled my eyes at their backs. Mathias knew exactly how to charm her. Why had I never mastered that trick? She pulled Mathias into the living room, and I marched back to the kitchen to help with dessert.

It was there Phee caught me alone. "Mathias is here?"

"He sure is," I said, nerves bubbling in my stomach. Should I tell her? What would a good sister do?

But Phee had other things on her mind. "I'm so sorry. Joel doesn't think sometimes before he speaks." She hugged me, but it felt awkward. "He really is a good guy."

I couldn't imagine she truly believed that. But it turns out, she did. Because forty minutes later, in front of our entire family, and the guy who had come to lay his heart at Phee's feet, Joel Allen proposed to my sister.

She said yes.

As soon as I dropped a tipsy Mimi off at her apartment, I called Mathias. He'd smiled and nodded and congratulated the happy couple with everyone else. He'd complimented Phee on her ring —a pretentious princess-cut diamond that must have cost more than my four years in college. I hated it. Mathias had been great at lying his way through the rest of the evening, but I knew it had to have been killing him and it was killing me too.

I was going to be *related* to Joel Allen. *Gross.*

"Are you okay?" I asked when he answered.

"I'm fine. Why wouldn't I be fine?" Mathias said. In the background, I heard music and the indistinct murmur of voices.

"Things didn't go exactly as you hoped tonight."

He snorted.

"I'm sorry, Mathias."

"I waited too long. Missed my chance," he said, and I thought his voice slurred, which was strange. I'd never met anyone who could hold his liquor as well as Mathias.

"My sister is an idiot."

"Maybe, but she's an engaged idiot now." He sighed, and I heard the clink of ice cubes in a glass.

"Do you need me to come get you?" I asked, my heart breaking a little for the sadness in his voice.

"Nah, I took an Uber."

I waited a beat, but when he didn't speak, I cleared my throat. "So, what now?"

"Oh, that's easy. Now I have a new New Year's resolution."

"What's that?"

He laughed, although it wasn't a happy one. "I'm going to fall out of love with Phoebe Mayfield."

SEVEN

*"Home is where you hang your hat
    and eat ice cream straight out of the carton with a
spoon."*

—MIMI

It was almost 5 p.m. by the time I arrived home.

"Longest day ever," I said to Sal as I fed him.

Sal fluttered in understanding. Why couldn't more people be like my fish? The world would be a better place.

I rubbed my tired eyes as I wandered back to the kitchen. The mail from yesterday still sat on the counter—bill, advertisement, bill, late Christmas card. At the last two envelopes, I paused and frowned. Mail for the neighbor again. It wasn't uncommon. The two apartments on my floor were numbers 207A and 207B and our mail was often tangled in transit.

About two months ago, I'd started getting packages and forwarded mail from New York for one Nate Russo, apartment 207B. I'd never met him, though I knocked on his door at least twice a week. A dark-haired teenage girl who spoke in grunts and eye rolls always answered and took the mail with an indifferent shrug.

I slipped out the door, padded barefoot down the linoleum hallway before halting at Mr. Nate Russo's door, and knocked.

The door swung open. "Yes?"

I took in the bare feet, worn jeans and paused at the white undershirt, so tight I imagined it was one deep breath away from busting at the seams. Not that I was complaining. Broad shoulders, sinewy arms, tapered waist.

The view was distracting.

"Can I help you?"

I blinked and dragged my eyes up to his face. Sadly. "Um, hi."

"So..." he said, tilting his head. I guessed he wasn't quite six feet tall and was somewhere around my age. But he wasn't handsome; the harshness of his face prevented that. It was as though God had forgotten to sand his edges—severe cheekbones, a brutally straight nose, eyebrows like dark slashes, one bisected by a small white scar, and a jawline of the warrior variety. Except for his eyes, which were a strange, murky mix of browns and greens and golds.

"So?" Without thought, I brought my thumb up to gnaw on the nail and whacked myself in the face with the envelopes in my hand. My ears went hot.

His lips pressed together in either annoyance or amusement —I couldn't quite tell. "You knocked on my door."

He was right, of course. Straightening, I took a deep breath and did what I usually did when I was nervous—I talked. A lot.

"I'm your neighbor." I held up the envelopes. "I got these by accident. It happens a lot, actually. I bring mail over at least twice a week. There's always a girl here who answers and rolls her eyes a lot." I paused and leaned to peek around his shoulder. Maybe she was in there now. He looked too young to be her father and much too old to be her boyfriend. "I hope you've been getting it. With our apartment numbers being so close, it makes sense. I'm A, you're B, so you see, it's bound to happen. Get it? See? The letter C?"

"I get it," he said, not quite hiding the half-smile. His eyes tracked the mail I waved in the air. I froze, and he snatched it from me. My hands fluttered like drunk butterflies for a moment before I put them down.

"Thanks," he said with a nod.

"No problem. It happened sometimes when Mrs. Duboniski lived here. She didn't get a lot of mail. Mostly cat magazines. Oh, and the Victoria's Secret catalog, which I thought was a little odd since she was in her seventies. Anyway, I usually bring it over when I get home from work. But I came home early because I had a... thing."

"A funeral?"

"What?"

"I'm sorry. It's none of my business. The black clothes and your eye make-up. You look like you've been crying."

Crap. My clothes. Today, I'd worn a boxy black pantsuit—a gift from my mother. *Black is slimming, dear*, she'd said.

"Well, my boyfriend broke up with me over the radio for concert tickets yesterday and my mom found out about it today after my sister's boyfriend... no, wait, fiancé now, told everyone, and then my best friend's heart was broken and, um, it's been a bad couple of days."

Why was I telling him this?

Those murky eyes squinted at me in a way that communicated he might be questioning my sanity. *Ditto, buddy.* "Wow. I'm sorry."

I should have slapped a hand over my mouth. But did I? Of course not.

"By the way, my name is Perci. If you need anything, just knock. I'm home every night, watching TV, baking, eating, sometimes I break out a jigsaw puzzle if I'm in the mood." I bit the inside of my lip. Hard.

The corner of his mouth quirked and now I was certain he was going to laugh. "Got it."

"You know, I have something in the oven. I should..." I spun on my heels to bolt.

"I hope your day gets better," he said, kindness in his voice.

"Yeah, thank you." I sidled toward my door with a little wave. "Happy New Year, or happy holidays or, um, have a good night if, you know, you don't celebrate." I paused, waited a beat, but he said not a word.

Right.

I scurried to my apartment. In the bathroom, I cringed at the dark circles under my eyes from wayward mascara and the wild splay of my hair. No wonder he'd thought I'd just survived a tragedy; I looked tragic. After scrubbing my face, I grabbed a cupcake and sank into the papasan chair, curling my feet under me.

A patch of waning sunlight shone through the patio door. The outdoor space was only enough for a chair and a string of Christmas lights I'd strung along the banister. I plugged them in, and the lights twinkled back at me cheerfully.

Just then, a bright red cardinal landed on the railing. It wasn't unusual to see them year-round, but its presence on my porch was strange. They tended to stick to trees. The tuft of feathers on its head waved gently in the wind. Its head tilted to the side and it locked eyes with me, as though we were friends, and it was stopping by for a chat. I'm not sure why I did it, but I waved.

It waited a beat and then flew off in a flurry of feathers.

EIGHT

"A wolf in sheep's clothing is still a wolf.
  'Cept now he has to dry-clean his coat."

—*MIMI*

The morning of my first day back to work post-holidays and post-break-up went something like this:

6:30: Drag myself out of bed. Step gingerly onto scale. Cringe and swear off all food except kale for the rest of the day.

6:35: Fret about what to wear. Settle on one of the many black suits my mother has gifted me. Straighten hair and apply make-up. Scowl in the mirror.

7:05: Drink coffee. Give myself a pep talk: *You can do this. There's nothing to worry about. Go in, do your job. You got this.*

7:15: Debate calling in sick.

7:20: Stare into Sal's unblinking eyes of love. Feel mildly braver.

7:25: Haul myself to my car.

7:30: Stop at my favorite donut shop. Buy fifteen donuts— one dozen for my co-workers.

8:15: After fighting my way through traffic, arrive at work, three donuts heavier and fifteen minutes early.

8:30: Sit in the parking lot in my car until the last possible moment and pray for an apocalypse-sized meteor, spontaneous combustion, or alien invasion. None of that happens. Unfortunately.

As Mimi would say, "You can't avoid the elephant in the room, 'specially when you're the elephant."

When I graduated from college, a freshly minted business degree I hadn't wanted in hand, I'd taken my first job at a small start-up. With only five employees, it was a mad scramble of disorganization and flailing hope. To be on the ground floor of something new filled us all with mindless excitement, even if the product was a little questionable.

Turbo-Loops were marketed as the latest craze in outdoor games for kids. It involved an enormous slingshot and children wearing vests with bull's eyes printed on them.

Okay, so a lot questionable.

My mother hated that job. "It's a ridiculous idea. Someone will shoot their eye out."

Seemed like parents agreed with her. The ensuing bad publicity led directly to the demise of Turbo-Loops and my job.

Next, I found employment as an executive assistant to the vice president of a car rental company. The hours and pay were good, and I got along well enough with my co-workers. I might have stayed there for the next thirty years if I hadn't accidentally sent a lovely bouquet of anniversary roses along with a scandalous little note written by the boss-man to his wife instead of his mistress.

I was asked to clean out my desk.

For the record, he's divorced now, and his wife cleaned him out.

"You've gotten all that out of your system now," Mom said. "Your father has a job waiting for you."

And so, I broke down and took a position at Mayfield Home Mortgage, where dreams go to die.

Namely, my dreams.

The company had five branches now, but I worked at the flagship office in the Energy Corridor off I-10. Although I'd made my way through several positions, I was now working as a loan officer.

Here's what I did: when a person wanted a mortgage loan for one reason or another, I dissected their finances, asked them seven thousand questions, and made a judgment call based on what I'd learned. And hopefully, in the end, a deserving couple got to buy the house of their dreams.

That was number one on my list of Things I Liked About My Job. It was the only thing I liked about my job. It was a short list.

Balancing the box of donuts, I pushed open the door. Miss Ruby hunched over her desk, pecking away at the computer one finger at a time. *Hunt, peck, hunt, peck.* Repeat. She paused and tilted her head toward me, hands frozen clawlike above the keyboard, and peered over tiny half-glasses.

Ruby mainly answered phones, kept up with her online dating profiles, and barked at people to take a seat in the waiting room. She excelled at all three. At the end of this year, she was finally retiring. It would be strange to not see her sitting at this desk.

When I was very small, Mom had been Dad's Girl Friday. She'd worked side-by-side with him, dragging me along to the office. I'd spent hours doodling on the backs of discarded mortgage applications and climbing into empty copy paper boxes. When he could afford it, Dad had hired Miss Ruby as his first official employee.

I plastered on a smile. The box of donuts slid sideways, and

I mashed it to my chest. "I brought treats. You know, to say welcome back."

Miss Ruby's lips pressed together in a thin line. "I heard what that boy did."

No need for her to clarify what she meant.

With a suddenness that startled me, she stood and slid around the desk, surprisingly spry. Pausing in front of me, she seized the box and tossed it on her desk. "He sure done you wrong. I'd like to snatch him bald-headed for the way he treated you."

She wrapped her arms around me in a rib-cracking hug, pinning my arms to my sides. Before I could respond in kind, she pulled back and retreated to her desk.

I blinked, fighting with a strange urge to both cry and blush at once. "Um, thank you."

With a curt nod, she was back to hunt-peck-hunt-pecking. "Now, get those donuts off my desk."

With a grin, I did what she asked and took them to the small kitchen in the back of the building.

Okay, fine. I took one back to my desk to eat.

I enjoyed the quiet of my office for fifteen minutes before my officemate appeared. Marianna Ortiz, she of the booming voice, arrived in a whirlwind of wild black curls, muttering under her breath.

"Stupid traffic... stupid drivers..."

Marianna held entire conversations with herself, rattling off rapid-fire while she tapped away at her computer or reviewed paperwork. A bit older than me, she'd recently divorced and currently hated all men past, present, and future, save her two little boys who were equal parts adorable and troublemaker.

"The traffic this morning," she sighed. "Some days, I dream

about getting out of my car and explaining to those people how to drive."

"I believe that's called road rage. Highly discouraged."

She flopped in her chair. "Speaking of killing, I want you to know whenever you're ready, I'll help you bury his body."

Again, no need to clarify the *he* in this scenario. It was laughable how my own parents hadn't been so clearly on my side as the people I worked with. In some strange way, it made me feel both seen and unseen.

"Got it."

"I cannot believe him. He couldn't—"

Marianna's phone rang—thank the stars—before she could continue that statement. Frowning at the number, she answered, her tone already belligerent. Must be the ex-husband. I checked my email, trying hard not to listen in on a heated discussion about "agreements" and "they're your kids too" and "you're so selfish." Abruptly, she yanked the phone from her ear and pressed the *end* button.

"I miss being able to hang up on someone like we used to," she said.

"Didn't go well?"

Marianna slouched in her seat, her long legs stretching out in front of her. "No. Something came up and he can't take the kids tonight for their visit."

I nodded in sympathy, not quite making eye contact. "That's tough."

Leaning forward, she rested her arms on her desk. "The thing is"—a crooked smile flashed across her face—"I have a client interview this afternoon at five and I need to pick up the boys at four, so..." Her voice trailed off, a hopeful note hanging in the air.

Mathias's voice played in my head. *Stop letting them take advantage of you at work.* I should do that. Of course I should. But Marianna's dark eyes were pleading, and she'd mope and sigh and mutter under her breath all day if I didn't volunteer.

"Fine. Yes, I'll take the interview for you."

She blew me a kiss. "You're the best."

"No big deal," I said with a shrug. What did it matter anyway? I didn't have a boyfriend or kids to rush home to. Pity party, table for one.

"Perci!" Miss Ruby bellowed. "Client's here."

A few years ago, Dad had installed a fancy phone system with intercom capabilities. Miss Ruby flat-out refused to use it. "My voice is plenty loud all by itself." She was not wrong.

Still, I could have cried tears of joy at the sound of her. My chair almost toppled in my haste to stand. "Coming."

"He's a pig, you know. That's exactly why—" Marianna railed on while I gathered my paperwork. With a wave, I slipped out of the office.

Mike and Shelly Granger were waiting in the small conference room, sitting side-by-side at the oversized round table. Their file informed me they'd been married for five years, had a two-year-old daughter, and another on the way. No credit cards, no car loans, no school debt. No credit history to speak of.

"It's nice to finally meet you," I said, shaking hands with them in turn.

"Yes, us too." Mike nodded and wrapped a long arm around his wife's shoulders. "We're eager to start looking for a house."

Shelly patted her belly. "Baby will be here in three months. We'd love to be settled by then."

I slid into a chair across from them. "How exciting."

Mike grinned and tapped his phone. He presented a photo of a tiny girl with crooked red pigtails and a gummy smile. "This is Celine, and this one"—he patted his wife's belly—"is a boy."

Shelly rolled her eyes. "He has to tell everyone. It's bragging rights, or something. Like he's wholly responsible for the baby being a boy."

He kissed her cheek, a wicked gleam in his eye. "I definitely enjoyed getting him in there."

His wife gasped and slapped his chest. "Michael!"

A laugh tumbled from me before I could stop it, which covered the stab of pure, unadulterated longing nicely. What would it be like to have someone tease me with devilish charm? To make me feel like I was the only one in the room with a brush of his fingers? I'd never had that with Brent, or anyone.

More than that, what would it be like to be married and have a household of babies? I knew it wasn't exactly politically correct to admit my secret longing to find a nice guy, settle in a little house in the suburbs, and make lots of babies. I wanted to join the PTA and know all the names of my children's friends and plant flowers in the front yard and plan vacations to national monuments. At night, I wanted to curl up next to a man who made me feel beautiful and loved.

As strange as it sounded, I wanted to be my mother when I grew up.

We spent forty-five minutes discussing their situation. I took them through a checklist of information I would need and learned more about the state of their financial affairs.

"We have enough money to make a small down payment—a gift from Shelly's grandma. I have a job lined up too." Mike passed over a letter of intent from a local engineering firm, his face earnest.

Shelly worried her lip. "Do you think we'll be approved? We've worked really hard to stay out of debt, and both of us grew up in apartments. Owning a home is our dream."

Some parts of my job required approving people who didn't deserve to own a doghouse, and yet, I didn't have a choice. If they looked good on paper, they were approved. Numbers didn't lie. I gathered documents, wrote a report, gave my informed opinion, but in the end, the final decision came from my boss. And I wasn't exactly on his list of favorite people, nor was he on mine.

But at that moment, I decided to dig in my heels. Barring me discovering that they ran an illegal alpaca farm or robbed banks to make ends meet, the Grangers were getting that home loan.

Without warning, the door opened, and the interloper coughed. "I apologize for interrupting."

I pulled in a breath and waved. Like a moron. "Did you need something?"

Like a heart?

"I apologize for interrupting. I have a meeting to get to, but I hoped we could talk over lunch today."

"Gosh, I'm sorry. I promised I'd eat with Ruby today." That wasn't exactly true, but Miss Ruby terrified him, so I knew he wouldn't argue.

"Then tomorrow?"

My hand curled into a fist. "I need to check my schedule."

He smoothed the flap of thinning hair atop his head. "Could you squeeze me in for coffee, perhaps?"

"I'm not sure."

His eyes narrowed.

Mike shuffled a few papers on the table, drawing my attention. For a moment, I'd forgotten they were there. Smiling sweetly, I held out a hand à la Vanna White. "I'm so sorry. Mike, Shelly, this is Brent Tompkins, he's the vice president of Mayfield Home Mortgage."

Oh, and my ex-boyfriend.

NINE

"If it ain't broke, don't fix it.

If it is broken, make damn sure fixing it's worth the trouble."

—MIMI

Two days later, I found myself sitting across from Brent at a café two blocks from work. As I explained to Mathias via text messages, I was here under extreme duress.

Me: *I agreed to have lunch with Brent.*

Mathias: *Do you enjoy torture?*

Me: *My mom made me do it.*

Mathias: *You have mommy issues.*

Me: *I KNOW!*

Brent Tompkins, golden boy of Mayfield Home Mortgage and my mother's favorite son, perused his menu with agonizing slowness although we'd been to this restaurant many times over. I'd never noticed before how long it took him to order.

His eyes rose above the edge of the menu. "Thanks for agreeing to meet. Do you know what you want?"

I nodded and turned to look out the window. A barrage of Texas-sized trucks passed, luxury cars stuffed between them.

A server with red-framed glasses and a hurried smile paused at our table. "Ready to order?"

"Perci?"

I ignored Brent and turned to the waitress. "I'd like a garden salad with house dressing on the side. No croutons. And a water, please."

That's not exactly what I wanted, but I was always careful about what I ate when I was with Brent, even now, when it didn't matter. A spark of anger lit in my chest. Why did I care what he thought of me? I glared at him while he ordered a cheeseburger with fries.

The waitress took our menus and raced off to put in our order.

Brent set his elbows on the table and tented his fingers. "I thought it would be a good idea if we talked."

I guzzled half my water and set it down with more force than I intended. "Go ahead."

He cleared his throat. "I hoped we wouldn't have any hard feelings."

"We?"

Red bloomed across his cheeks. At least he had the decency to look embarrassed. "This"—he waved a hand between us—"didn't turn out as either of us expected."

I stared at him.

He continued. "Perhaps we thought this relationship was

heading in a different direction. But after some deep soul searching, we found it kinder to end it before we went further."

Kinder? Sort of like when someone shoots a horse in the head instead of fixing its broken foot. "So, *we* decided breaking up on the radio was the kindest thing to do?"

"I didn't think you'd mind," he said with a small, uncomfortable smile.

"You *what?*" I hated the crack in my voice.

"I thought you'd understand."

"I'd understand?"

He fussed with his tie, an abysmal shade of mustard yellow with bright green stripes. His ugly ties were not ironic; he thought they looked professional. I used to think that was kind of cute. "Perci, that's who you are."

"What does that mean?"

"You don't seem to mind anything I do. Why would this be any different?"

A strangled gasp escaped me, and I turned toward the window again, unable to answer as a sharp pain wrapped around my sternum. My eyes caught on a homeless man who stopped to pick through a garbage can, a cart holding all his worldly possessions at his side.

The server slid our dishes on the table. A thick silence grew between us. Brent dug into his hamburger. Mustard dripped from the sandwich and landed on his tie, blending in with the color. I didn't tell him. Let him figure it out. I wasn't responsible for pointing those things out anymore.

"Because I didn't argue with you?" I asked my salad in a quiet voice. "Because I'm not fun? Because I'm boring?"

Swallowing, he wiped his fingers on a napkin. "I didn't think you cared all that much about this whole relationship."

I paused, dissecting his words. Was that true? I'd cried more than once since the break-up. But had it been over Brent? Did I miss him? Did I miss us? Or were my tears because of how he'd embarrassed me? Or because this relationship was another failure in a long list of my failures? Was it because I didn't like how he'd done it and the words he'd used?

Worse, was it because everything he'd said was true?

The sounds of the café—forks scraping against plates, the rise and fall of chatter—echoed loudly in my head. My eye caught on an older couple sitting in a corner booth. The woman, her hair in tight, steely-gray curls, was reading a paperback novel. She pushed her half-eaten plate across the table to the bald man buried behind a newspaper. Without looking, he pulled the plate closer and touched her hand, their fingers tangling for the briefest of seconds. I couldn't be sure, but from my seat, it didn't look like they'd spoken a word to each other.

An overwhelming urge to cry settled in my throat.

I pushed my food away without taking a bite. A salad would not fix this sadness; that required chocolate. "I cared about you, Brent." Maybe not the way a girlfriend should care about her boyfriend, but I'd expected better from him. "And how does that make it okay to embarrass me on the radio? For concert tickets? Did you think about me having to tell my parents and how it would embarrass them?"

He pressed a hand to his forehead. "It was because of your mother..." Clamping his mouth shut, he shook his head.

"My mother?"

"She came to see me a few weeks ago when you were out of the office and asked me when I planned to propose." He spread his hands out in front of him. "She asked me if I needed help picking out a ring. I guess I panicked."

For a moment, my vision grew hazy.

"I caught the radio show and..." His brow creased, the corners of his eyes pulled down. "Look, I'm sorry. Perhaps I didn't handle this in the right way, but I'd like us to look past this. People break up every day. We can still be professional at work."

Part of me didn't want to be professional. Part of me wanted to go to my father and demand he fire Brent. But I knew how that would turn out. It wasn't that he loved Brent more; it was that he always did what was best for the business, and Brent was good at his job.

But a bigger part of me couldn't stand one more second sitting across from him. "Whatever you want."

He exhaled in relief. "I appreciate it."

I flagged the waitress. "Can I get a to-go box for this?"

Her gaze darted between us, first at Brent eating his fries like a starved man at a church potluck, and then at me as I gathered my purse and slid to the end of the booth. "Sure thing. Need anything else?"

A pillow to scream into? A million gallons of ice cream? A backbone to tell Brent exactly how I felt?

"My treat," Brent said. "Order whatever you want."

"You know what? I'll take a banana cream."

"A slice?"

My eyes skipped again to the window and the homeless man. "I'll take the whole pie."

She nodded. "Okay."

I snatched a menu from the table next to us and thumbed through it. "And I'll take a double cheeseburger, an order of fish and chips, and a milkshake. Chocolate. As big as you can make it."

Grinning at me, the waitress slipped her notepad in her pocket. "I'll meet you up front with your to-go bag."

On the walk back to the office, I handed over the pie, the cheeseburger, the fish and chips, and the salad to the homeless guy. The chocolate milkshake I kept for myself, even though my appetite, like any feelings I might have harbored for Brent, had fizzled entirely.

TEN

"Never look a gift horse or a politician in the eye.

    Both of 'em usually want something you aren't willing to give."

—*MIMI*

The next week, Dad called me into his office. Tucked in the back of the building, it looked one paper stack away from an episode of *Hoarders*. Boxes lined one entire wall, six feet high, all with labels written in hasty black marker. Stacks of papers and files covered his desk. A very dead houseplant drooped from the cabinet in the back corner. Photos of the family covered the only available wall. Not one picture frame was straight.

Sometimes I thought Dad liked to be fenced in, like a barrier from the outside world. It was a source of comfort, even if it gave everyone else an eye twitch. In his office at work, he was also free from the watchful eye of my mother.

"Have a seat, Cupcake."

I dumped a stack of books from one chair to another and

slid into the freed seat, staring at his salt-and-pepper head as he scribbled a note. "What did you need?"

He finished writing and peered over his half-moon reading glasses. "I wanted to see how things were going."

"Fine."

"And you and Brent?"

Oh, that. Brent and I had danced around each other all week, only speaking when necessary—and I made a point that it was never necessary. My father seemed oblivious to any awkwardness. I tried to pretend it didn't matter. The thing was, it was starting to matter. A lot.

"Like I said, it's fine."

"You'd tell me if it wasn't fine, wouldn't you?"

"Sure." No, I would not. On a list of Things I Didn't Want to Talk to My Father About, my relationship with Brent was at the top.

"Is there a chance the two of you could get back together?"

I sighed. "Daddy."

"Sorry, I know. Your mother asked me to ask you and you know it's just easier..." He waved a hand in the air. "Never mind. I just want to know that you and Brent can work together without any issues."

I forced a smile. "Of course. Not to worry."

He stood and rounded the desk, almost tumbling a group of shoeboxes stacked on the floor. "Cupcake, you know I love you and I'm always on your side. But business is business, and Brent is great at his job. I don't want to lose him."

I rose and stuffed my hands in my pockets. "I understand."

"That's my girl."

Was I? I wondered once I was back in my office and digging into my emergency supply of chocolate. I know Dad loved me, but I also knew Mom was "his girl," not me. He'd always take her side over mine. If she wanted Brent and me back together, then so did Dad. Even when Mom wasn't in the room with me, her presence was like a dark cloud. With a sigh, I bit into the chocolate, but it tasted more bitter than sweet.

Despite the tension, the best part of my week was that I completed my review of the Grangers' finances and was happy to recommend them for a loan. I pulled my report together and sent it off to Brent on Friday afternoon for his approval.

I'd just returned from lunch—orange chicken, fried rice, wonton soup from the place down the street—when my phone buzzed.

"Go out with me tonight," Mathias said in place of a normal greeting.

"Hi. I've had a good day, only one Brent sighting. Thanks for asking."

"Did you hear me?"

"I'd probably hear you better if you asked nicely."

He snorted. "Perci Mayfield, would you do me the honor of going out with me tonight so we can have a couple of overpriced drinks?"

"See? How hard was that? What's gotten into you?"

"I—" He paused, and the background noise changed. So did his voice, dropping low. "Phee called me this morning. She asked if I'd do the photography for the wedding."

"What?"

"After I got off the phone with her—"

"Did you say you'd do it?"

He ignored me. "I thought getting drunk and finding someone to make me forget her seemed like just the thing. Besides, that was my New Year's resolution, anyway. What better time to start than now?"

The New Year's resolutions. I'd avoided looking directly at the piece of paper hanging on my fridge. Something about them made me uncomfortable—like being judged about how I was— or wasn't—living my life every time I walked into the kitchen. They taunted me: *I will not try to lose weight. I will not try to be more confident. I will not put more effort into my job. I will not date. I will not try to be a better daughter and sister.* I'd tried to throw it away more than once and couldn't bring myself to do it.

"Fine. Let's do it," I said. "You didn't answer my question, though. Did you say you'd do it?"

He sighed. "Of course I did."

I dropped my forehead on my desk. "Is that a good—"

"Be ready at eight. I'll pick you up."

I sighed. "Fine."

"And Perci, wear something that doesn't look like you're going to a funeral?"

ELEVEN

"You lie with dogs, you get fleas.
  You lie with liars, you get crabs."

—*MIMI*

Mathias arrived promptly, took one look at my outfit—a pair of wide-legged black pants, white button-down, and cardigan—and marched me back into my bedroom. Then he spent twenty minutes complaining about the state of my wardrobe.

"I wish you'd let me take you shopping." He held up a shapeless dark wool suit—thanks, Mom—and grimaced. "What is this?"

I opened my mouth to answer.

"That was a rhetorical question. The answer is the same for everything in this closet. It's sad." He shook his head and pulled out a dark purple pencil skirt from the deep recesses of my closet. "This isn't hideous."

I crinkled my nose, remembering when I'd purchased it during a shopping trip with my mother. In a rare act of rebellion, I'd refused to buy it in black or brown. That shade of purple was gorgeous, deep, sultry—the opposite of me. When I got home, though, I hid it in the very back of the closet, never even took the tags off. "Why can't I keep on what I'm wearing?"

He shoved the skirt in my hands. "Put it on. Take off that cardigan. Where did that even come from? The Mister Rogers' Collection at Target? Keep the shirt but tuck it in."

I rounded on him in horror. "But then people can see my butt."

Instead of answering, he glared at me with the steely-blue eyes of a man who'd reached his limit. I didn't argue further.

The SoHo was a new, trendy bar located close to downtown. It was more club than bar with a wide, central dance floor and pulsing music played in thirty-minute intervals. Clubs were not my friend. On a list of Reasons I Didn't Like Clubs, number one was the dancing. All that writhing and gyrating. The casual way people flitted from one person to the next. The sweat.

No, thank you.

I perched at the bar on the far end with an unobstructed view of the whole place. Mathias had parked me here before surveying his options. He worked the room before settling on a petite brunette with a pixie haircut and muscular shoulders. The exact opposite of Phee.

The bartender hovered ten feet away. I tried to catch his eye and when that didn't work, I waved my hand in the air to get his attention. I was certain he saw me, but he turned and ambled toward a group of giggling college-aged women.

Someone bumped my shoulder and a deep voice muttered, "Sorry."

"It's okay," I said.

Although the guy next to me didn't say any more, I could feel the weight of his gaze on me and when I looked, my mouth dropped open. It was him, my non-handsome neighbor, Nate.

In a dark green t-shirt and heavily worn jeans, he was clearly not going out of his way to impress anyone. His head tilted and his eyes honed in on me.

"Hey, it's me, Perci. Remember? I live down the hall from you."

An eyebrow hitched over a murky-colored eye. "I remember."

I propped an elbow on the bar and set my chin in my palm. Nate turned toward me, leaning against the counter like he had all the time in the world.

"Has anyone ever told you that you have weird eyes?" I said.

A corner of his mouth quivered. "Has anyone ever told you you don't have to say every thought out loud?"

"Yep. Diarrhea of the mouth. I'm afraid it's a chronic condition." I grimaced. "I really need a drink."

He grinned.

I leaned over the counter. "Hey, can I get some help? Please?"

The bartender shot me a look that could only be described as a pitying sneer. I guessed the answer was no. I sat down hard on the stool and crossed my arms. Nate glanced between the bartender and me. He frowned, the lines of his face sharpening. Which should have been terrifying but instead, caused my heart to flop against my ribcage.

He turned and stared down the bartender. "Yo."

Three seconds later, the bartender appeared in front of us. Nothing on Nate's face moved except one dark eyebrow, the one with the little white scar I'd noticed before. He stared; the bartender stared back. The air got a little tense. It was... weird... and kind of hot.

The bartender blinked first. "What can I get you?"

Nate held out a hand toward me. "You first."

"Oh, okay." I ordered a mojito and Nate, a beer.

He handed over his credit card and waved me off when I

tried to pay for my portion. He glared at the bartender until he set our drinks in front of us. "That guy is not getting a tip."

"You didn't have to do that." I grinned.

He shrugged, a smile tugging at the corner of his mouth. "No big deal. You have a face like mine, you learn to use it to your advantage."

"I like your face. It's very nice." I took a swig of my mojito, trying to ignore the amused light in Nate's eyes.

"So, you come here often?" I asked, wincing at what sounded like a cheesy pickup line.

"First time. Here with a couple of guys from work." The sound of his voice, deep and low, sent a tingle up my spine.

"Always good to hang out with friends after a long week of... of..." My voice trailed off as I glimpsed someone familiar in the crowd. My hand tightened around my glass.

It was Brent.

And he was not alone.

Why was he here, of all places? He'd never once asked me to go to a place like this. I guess he thought I'd be too boring to say yes.

I hunkered down, using Nate as a shield, but couldn't resist studying the woman on Brent's arm. About my height, her blonde hair was pulled into a ponytail, accentuating high cheekbones. She wore a pink dress of the short-and-tight variety. And she was curvy. Like me. Maybe a bit heavier—the hips, the boobs, the thick waist—it was all there on display.

That last detail felt like a dagger in my chest. A small part of my brain had believed Brent had broken up with me because of my weight. Somehow, believing he'd broken up with me over that had made the whole situation easier. But if it wasn't the weight, then maybe all those other things he'd said were true. I was the problem. *Me.*

I slumped in my seat, downed the rest of my drink, and

slammed the glass on the bar. Brent absolutely could not see me.

Nate frowned. "Are you okay?"

My eyes darted to him and then drifted right back to Brent. He moved closer, and I held my breath. The woman was young enough she might still need a babysitter. She giggled at something he said. He put an arm around her and kissed her. An inappropriate-in-public kind of kiss. *We just broke up two weeks ago!*

"I'm fine," I said with a weird little panicked laugh. "Just great. I have a drink. I'm having pleasant conversation with my neighbor. I'm at a club with all these people. I'm just taking it all in, you know."

Nate's eyes darted from my face to what was holding my attention in the crowd and then back to me. "Is that concert ticket guy?"

"What? How did you...?" Then I remembered telling him that day on his doorstep when I'd looked like I'd lost my way coming home from a funeral. Why did I have to talk so much?

A floor-pounding pulse of music returned. The lines around Nate's eyes crinkled as he leaned closer. He smelled good, not the manly, foresty scent I'd expected. Instead, it was sweet, fruity. "Is he going to be a problem? I can hang out for a minute."

"No!" I took a deep, calming breath. "I mean, no. Thanks for offering. Everything will be fine. We're fine. I'm fine. It's all—"

"—fine. Got it." Drink in his hand, he pushed back from the bar. "If you're sure?"

I nodded, sneaking tiny glances at Brent and the nearest exit.

"I'll see you around then."

"Sure thing, and thanks again," I said, but he'd already wandered off.

I ordered another mojito from the now very attentive bartender—thank you, Nate—and hunted the dance floor for Mathias. He and the little brunette were currently tangled in the PG-13 sort of dancing that was one gyration away from an R-rating.

That was my mistake. I took my eyes off the enemy, and he attacked.

Brent appeared beside me, arm wrapped around his date. "I didn't expect to see you at a place like this."

I took a long swallow of my second mojito. "Yep. You know me. I like to get out and have fun. I'm a fun person. Fun all day, every day. I am a fun machine."

His gaze darted into the crowd and back at me. "Are you here with someone?"

I ignored him and held out my hand. "Hi, Brent's friend. I'm Perci, Brent's former girlfriend. You might have heard him dump me on the radio."

"I'm Candy," she said with a smile.

"Of course you are. How did you two meet?"

"Brent was at the job fair last week at the University of Houston. He asked for my number."

"That's great." I slugged back more mojito and debated ordering another.

"Are you here with someone?" Brent asked again.

I wasn't a liar by nature. In fact, given my propensity to nervous rambling, I was a terrible liar. But, right there, in that moment, with rum coursing through my veins, staring at the man who'd dumped me nine days ago (yes, I was counting), I decided lying was the perfect solution. The very best idea I'd had in ages.

"Yep."

Brent's eyes narrowed. "With that guy who was here a few minutes ago?"

"That's him." Another sip. I waved the bartender over for the next round o' mojito.

"He's here? With you?"

I hated the question in his voice, the utter disbelief that someone like me could be in this place with a guy like Nate. My back straightened. "Yes, he's here with me. He had to run to the bathroom."

The overhead lights turned into strobing multicolored flickers that beat in time to the music. My stomach resented this.

Brent smirked. "Looks like he got lost."

My eyes tripped around the room until they landed on Nate. He stood at the edge of the dance floor, a leggy redhead standing a little too close. She threw back her head and laughed.

"He seems nice," Candy said, all big, innocent eyes.

"Yep, I sure know how to pick 'em." I stood, wobbled, and leaned against the bar to hide it. "Be careful with this one, Candy. He gets bored easily."

She nodded, her expression serious. "Yes, ma'am."

Ma'am? I snorted, and willing my legs to behave themselves, strolled past Brent and his schoolgirl date, past Mathias who appeared to be closing the deal with the brunette, and past Nate and his redhead.

Outside, my back pressed into the brick of the building, I texted Mathias to tell him I had a headache and called for a ride.

The tears didn't come until I got home. I was pretty proud of myself for that.

TWELVE

"Hell hath no fury like a woman
   who is pissed off at her man."

—MIMI

From: Brent Tompkins <brent.tompkins@mayfieldhomemort-gage.com>
To: Perci Mayfield <perci.mayfield@mayfieldhomemort-gage.com>
Subject: (re): Approval for Mike/Shelly Granger

Perci,

After careful consideration, I don't feel it is in the best interest of Mayfield to approve the Grangers for this loan. Please let them know with our condolences.

Thanks,

Brent

I stared at the email which had arrived Monday during my mid-morning snack (carrots and hummus to offset the kolaches I picked up on the way to work). Frowning, I reread it three times. But no matter how many times I read it, the words stayed the same.

Never once before had Brent overridden me. While I might not love my job, I was good at it. This had to be a mistake. I'd walk myself to his office and get this all sorted.

Brent's office door was closed. I knocked and waited, gnawing on my thumbnail.

"Come in."

I pushed the door open and stepped in. Brent leaned back in his chair stationed behind his ultra-large desk. The first time Mimi had visited Mayfield, she'd taken one look at Brent's desk and rolled her eyes. "Big desk syndrome."

He tapped his fingers impatiently, but it was the other man in the room who spoke first.

"Good morning, Cupcake."

"Hi, Daddy."

Sweat beaded on my forehead. Why was it so hot in here? "I received your email about the Grangers. I think there might have been a misunderstanding."

"There's no misunderstanding. I don't think they're a good risk." Brent ran a hand down his tie—a hideous shade of orangey-red.

Frowning, I took a step forward. "Look, I took my time with this couple. I've never been wrong, not once in three years."

"Everyone gets it wrong once in a while." His smile was smug.

A zing of something hot raced down my back. "Except I didn't get it wrong this time."

"What's going on here?" Dad asked.

Brent shrugged. "Nothing serious. A professional disagreement."

"He won't approve a loan for a couple I vetted. I know they're a good risk. They deserve this loan."

Daddy shifted in his chair. "Well, Cupcake, Brent has more experience than you and I expect you should defer to him on this. That's his job."

My mouth dropped in disbelief as I stared at my father. He nodded; my shoulders slumped.

"Is there anything else?" Brent asked, his smile now a smirk.

Without replying, I slid from the room and back to my desk. Marianna shot me a concerned look.

My desk felt strange, foreign. But it was all the same—same stapler, same computer, same fake houseplant. A photo of Mimi and me in the corner, taken when I was in high school. Mimi's smile lit up the picture, her red velvet dress this side of too short. The girl in the photo wore a tent-like t-shirt and stood just behind Mimi.

I still took photographs that way, trying to find the least conspicuous place, hiding in plain sight.

Why did I do that?

I pulled up Brent's email again. Heat settled on my chest and moved up my neck to my face. My hand curled into a fist.

"You okay over there? Your face is all red," Marianna said.

"I'm fine."

Before I could lose my nerve, I clicked to print the email and then shot off a text.

Me: *I think I might be about to do something stupid.*

Mathias: *Do you want me to talk you out of it or let you do it?*

Me: *I'm doing it.*

I tossed the phone on my desk without waiting for a

response. The printer spit out a single sheet of paper and I snatched it up.

Channeling Mimi in all her brassy, high-heeled glory, I marched down the hallway. I imagined it was her hand crumpling that email into a ball. Without knocking, I threw open the door to Brent's office and flinched when the wood bounced against the wall. Swallowing an apology, I stalked forward. My father and Brent craned their heads in my direction.

Red-hot, righteous anger coursed through me. It felt good. "Why did you deny the Grangers?"

Brent stood. "I already told you—they aren't a good risk."

But my brain heard something else entirely. *She's so boring. She's not adventurous; she doesn't argue with me. She's always worried about making everyone happy. I can't imagine spending the rest of my life with her.*

"That's not true, and you know it. You feel invincible now." I gestured toward my father. "Break up with the boss's daughter? Humiliate her? Who cares? Everyone knows my father does what's best for business, right?"

Hurt flashed in my father's eyes. "Now, hold on."

"It's my job to make these decisions," Brent said. "I'm your supervisor for a reason."

My eyes narrowed and again, other words scrolled through my brain. *I'll die of boredom if I stay with her one more day.*

Heat radiated from my chest, moved to my gut, and burned through my veins. I'd never been this angry in my life. This new fire in my belly almost overwhelmed me with its strength. "You're a... a... jerk!"

Okay, so my fightin' words were underwhelming; I was new at this.

"Cupcake."

I wheeled around. "Stop calling me 'Cupcake.' I have a name, Mr. Mayfield."

Daddy's brow creased in concern. "This isn't like you at

all." He pulled his phone from his shirt pocket. "Let me call your mother and—"

"No! This is New Perci. Get used to it."

Of all things, Mathias's face rose up in my mind now: the pain in his eyes while he stood by and watched Joel Allen propose to the woman he loved, the sadness as he watched his chance slip away. A zing of panic snaked through me. Was this my chance? Would I let it slip away?

Brent rounded the desk and put a hand on my shoulder. "Maybe you need to get a drink of water and calm down."

Glaring at him, I ripped my shoulder away. "No, I am not calming down. I quit."

My father climbed to his feet. "Now, don't do that."

I stalked to the door. "Yes, I quit."

Arms crossed, Brent glared at his feet; lines creased his forehead. "Let's talk about this. No need to make a scene."

"You didn't seem to have any problem making a scene before. It's my turn now. You don't get to treat people like this and expect to get away with it."

Brent's hands dropped to his hips. "You're blowing this way out of proportion."

My fist tightened around the wadded-up email. It flew out of my hand and slammed into my former boyfriend, former boss, and current jerk's forehead.

"I quit."

By the time I arrived in the lobby of my apartment building carting a box of everything I'd packed up from my desk, the adrenaline had been replaced with What-In-God's-Name-Did-I-Just-Do? panic. While I waited on the elevator, any lingering hint of bravado puddled at my feet.

Clutching the box under one arm, my purse in the other, I

attempted to call Mimi first. No answer. Then Mathias. Again, no answer. Phee was next. Nope.

"Does no one answer their phone anymore?" I tossed it in the box and yanked the ponytail holder out of my hair, which splayed around my shoulders in all its frizzy wonder.

Someone behind me cleared their throat.

I jerked in surprise and turned to find Nate. He wore scruffy jeans, a long-sleeved white t-shirt under an orange reflective vest, and heavy work boots. Dirt was smudged on a cheek, a sleeve, and the toes of his shoes, although his hands with their long fingers and blunt nails were scrubbed clean.

Next to him stood a child. He had a kid? Just not a teenage one.

She was around eight, I thought, and a girl, although it was hard to tell. Because of the outfit. A long-sleeved sunshine-yellow t-shirt clashed with camo-colored leggings. Bright red rain boots splashed with bumblebees completed the look. But it was the mask that really threw me off.

Dark, unblinking eyes peered at me through an oversized plastic owl mask. Two sprouts of brown hair shot out from either side of her head. The effect made her look wise beyond her years and super weird.

But it worked for her. And those boots were kind of adorable. I gave her a tiny smile. "Nice mask."

Her pigtails bounced with her nod. "Thank you. My teacher wouldn't let me wear it today, even though today was Wear Your Favorite Thing Day, and this is my favorite thing. She said if I didn't take it off, she would call my daddy. So I didn't and then he had to come pick me up."

Nate sighed.

"Oh, wow. Way to stick to your guns."

"I didn't have any guns. Just my great horned owl mask." She rose on her tippy toes. "What's in your box?"

"Let's just say I stuck to my guns today too and now I don't have a job."

"Rough day?" Nate asked, and all I could do was nod in response.

The elevator opened, and I stepped in first. Nate followed, the little girl trailing behind, big round eyes peering at me with interest.

I jostled around to hit the button for the second floor and in the process sent the box careening to the floor. "Hot spit and monkey vomit!"

A giggle escaped the little girl. "Ew."

"My grandma says that sometimes." I stared at the things scattered on the floor. This had to be a metaphor for my life—my phone, a red stapler, a framed photo, a bag of emergency chocolate, the romance novel with the half-naked man I kept in my desk drawer to read at lunch, my self-respect. My throat tightened, and the tears were right there, awaiting one tiny sob to start the whole messy ball rolling.

I felt Nate's razor-sharp attention but couldn't bring myself to look his way. The elevator jerked to a start. I knew I ought to pick up my things, but I felt frozen to the spot.

Nate bent over and tossed all my things back in the box. He stood, box in arms, eyes pointed at the metal doors.

"Thank you," I said and held out my hands.

He didn't relinquish the box. Or speak. It wasn't a creepy, angry silence; it was like he understood how fragile I was at that moment.

"Okay, then," I whispered.

The elevator stopped, and I stepped out and dug my keys from my purse. Nate trailed behind me and the little girl behind him. I opened the door to my apartment. "I guess I'll take that now."

He handed it to me, fingers brushing mine.

I forced myself to meet his eyes—they were more green than brown today. "Thanks."

"No problem. That's what neighbors are for." He smiled then. It slid across his face from one blink to the next, but not before I noticed the way it softened all his sharp edges. It was the nicest thing I'd seen all day.

The little girl gave me one long, last, assessing look from behind her mask. Finally, she raised her hand and waved as they walked away.

THIRTEEN

"There's more than one way to skin a cat.
  Whichever way,
  you gotta kill the cat first."

—MIMI

I got ahold of Mathias a few hours later. In that time, I'd changed clothes; dumped my box of stuff in the closet; eaten a bowl of cereal, two slices of banana bread, and apple slices (for fiber) slathered in peanut butter; and had just enough time to really work up a panic.

"What was I thinking?" I asked from my prone position on the shaggy black rug in the living room.

"This is a good thing," Mathias said over a barrage of background noise. He was traveling again this week, somewhere on the East Coast.

"Where are you?"

"Dinner."

"By yourself?"

"Nope."

"Blonde or brunette?"

"Redhead. I'm branching out. She's in the bathroom. I'm going to talk fast, so listen up. I'm proud of you."

I scoffed. "Don't be proud of me. I quit a perfectly good job. And I've disappointed my father and when my mother hears about—"

"Stop it." His voice took on an authoritative edge and my spine straightened in response. "That job wasn't good for you. You'll find a new job, a better one. Time to stop worrying about pleasing other people. Remember?"

"But I have bills to pay. I... I have a fish to feed."

"Sal can take care of himself. Hold on." His voice muffled as he spoke to what I guessed was a waiter. "As I was saying, this is your chance to reinvent yourself."

"Reinvent myself," I repeated.

"Tomorrow, you'll feel better about this."

"Tomorrow? I don't have anywhere to go tomorrow." I rolled on my back and stared at the ceiling. "I don't have a job."

"Sleep in, watch some bad reality television, go on a walk."

My voice climbed an octave or three. "Go on a walk?"

"Hey, she's coming back. I gotta go."

"Well, thanks for your crummy advice."

"Perci Mayfield. Time to take charge of your life. You can do this." The words cracked through the line; they carried weight that found its way into my brain. Maybe, just maybe, he was right. Maybe I could do this, become this new person who didn't care what others thought, who wasn't concerned about making them happy all the time.

It was time to start living like New Perci.

I woke with a jolt the next morning, heart racing at the thought of being late to work. Then all of it came back to me at once. No work today.

I was New Perci and New Perci was unemployed.

"What was I thinking, Sal?"

The World's Best Betta Fish swam about serenely.

"I think I'm having an early midlife crisis here. Tell me I'm going to be okay."

He nodded. Okay, fine, I know he didn't nod in the traditional sense, but I could tell he was listening. Did other people have emotional support fish? They should.

After dressing, I made pancakes. With chocolate chips. And whipped cream. I piddled around, read a little, watched television. I ignored five calls from my mother, two from my father, one from Brent, but answered when Mathias called. By afternoon, I feared even Sal was bored with my presence.

Having reached my limit, I went for that walk Mathias had suggested. The air was cool and dry, a small breeze adding a bite to the mix. Rain overnight had left behind its mark in the small puddles dotting the sidewalks. I'd never, in the almost six years I'd lived at The Lofts, taken more than a handful of walks. It surprised me now, as I strolled the sidewalk, how adorable this area was.

The Brewer Street neighborhood had been built just after WWII and it showed in the line of tiny brick storefronts, most with bright awnings. Big box stores and chains had been kept at bay, leaving the mom-and-pop shops to thrive.

There was a quaint little café named Rita's anchored at the corner. Three little tables with wide white and red umbrellas squatted out front. I made a mental note to come back for lunch soon. On the next block, I discovered a florist called Sunshine Flowers. Out front, a woman with curly auburn hair scribbled on a blackboard set on the sidewalk under a blue and white awning: A PEONY SAVED IS A PEONY EARNED. —BENJAMIN FRANKLIN

I laughed when I read it.

The woman smiled. "Nice day for a walk, isn't it?"

"It is," I said, feeling lighter than I had in the last twenty-four hours. Maybe Mathias was right. A walk was just the thing.

Three storefronts down was Fancy, a vintage clothing store. It was the one shop I had visited a handful of times, drawn in by The Dress displayed in the front window. It was knee-length with a sweetheart neckline, nipped in at the waist, with off-the-shoulder cap sleeves and a full skirt. Dark red with a matching bow in the back, it resembled something a 1950s housewife would wear to a cocktail party. It just needed a string of pearls and high heels.

I loved it. I wanted it. But I couldn't bring myself to go inside and try it on. If it didn't fit, I'd be devastated.

Eventually the streets narrowed, and oak trees and small homes lined the way. It was the last house on the corner that caught my eye—bright yellow, surrounded by a white picket fence. In front, a sign read: MISS MARGE'S PRESCHOOL AND DAYCARE. From my spot on the sidewalk, I could see the enclosed backyard contained a wooden play structure with a miniature slide and two swings. Right now, a passel of children ran wild, climbing and chasing, giggling and shrieking.

A ball sailed over the fence and landed near my foot. I retrieved it and eyed the playground until I saw a tiny girl with uneven pigtails staring at me.

"Is this yours?" I asked.

She popped her thumb in her mouth and nodded, making her pigtails bounce in the most adorable way. I tossed the ball back, and she rewarded me with a blinding smile.

With a little wave, I turned and walked around the corner. The yellow house had a cobblestone walkway leading to a bright red door, a large window to the right of it. I could make out a desk behind lacy sheer curtains. Something else caught my eye. There, taped to the window was a HELP WANTED sign.

My heart sped up at the sight of it. I told it to chill out. I couldn't get a job at a daycare. For one, my experience with kids was limited to watching *Toddlers & Tiaras*. For another, my mother would have the fit to end all fits if I did. I could already hear her lecturing me.

Besides, I was going to have to face facts. I had a bit of savings to get me through a couple of months, but woman could not live on reality television alone. Money was important to my survival. The truth was obvious—it was inevitable I would end up back at Mayfield Home Mortgage. Once I worked up the courage to grovel, my old desk would be waiting for me.

I'd been a rebel for a whole twenty-four hours, and I was already losing my confidence. So much for New Perci.

My phone vibrated—*MOM CALLING*. I sent it to voicemail, where I imagined she left a lengthy diatribe about my common sense, my duty to the family, Brent, and probably my hair.

But, as it turned out, of all people, it was my mother who forced me to call Miss Marge's Preschool and Daycare about that job.

FOURTEEN

"It's the thought that counts,
but math never was my strong suit."

—MIMI

On my list of Reasons I Hated Mother/Daughter Brunches, number three was my mother's supernatural ability to calculate caloric value for any food in mere seconds. Number two, I hated brunch. Why would I want to combine two meals into one? Give me breakfast *and* lunch any day. And the number one reason? My mother used the guise of a friendly meal to meddle. She expected a full account of my accomplishments for the month, and this naturally presented the perfect opportunity for her to offer her opinion.

My accomplishments this last month? I'd kept my fish alive.

We made plans to meet at a little restaurant close to Phee's apartment inside the Loop. I'd dressed carefully—navy pants, ivory blouse, sensible shoes. I'd straightened my hair, applied make-up, prayed for a quick death.

My mother had already been seated when I arrived. I

waved and made a beeline for the table. When I was in high school, I remember a friend complaining about how her mother "just didn't care." My mother was the opposite: she cared. Too much. Mimi once told me my mother thrived on other people's messes. "When she thinks someone needs her, she's like a mosquito at a hemophiliac's convention."

That might be okay if her methods weren't both swift and soul-crushing.

At the table, I shrugged off my coat and slid into a seat.

"Hello, dear," Mom said, not taking her eyes from the menu in front of her.

I smoothed my hair with a nervous hand and smiled. "How are you?"

"Poor Pericles has a cold. I had to take him to the acupuncturist this morning." Yes, my mother paid for someone to stick tiny needles in her dog. "In fact, we may have to cut things short today so I can pick him up. Poor baby."

"I'm sorry to hear he's sick." God didn't even strike me dead when I said that either.

She set the menu aside and tapped her phone laying on the table. "Plus, I'm expecting a phone call from the garden club. The yearly fundraiser is coming up, and I think the board has finally come to its senses and let me head it this year. Last year's event was so predictable. A garden tea for a garden fundraiser? Really? I think Sarah Ingram called that one in." Leaning in, she lowered her voice. "Personally, I think Sarah has a bit of a drinking problem."

A server interrupted to set glasses on the table, for which I was endlessly thankful. I was sure I was about to hear every questionable thing Sarah Ingram had ever done, in alphabetical order.

Although better Sarah was under scrutiny than me.

"There's an iced tea for you. Unsweetened." Mom gestured to the drink in front of me.

I swallowed a sigh. Drinking unsweet iced tea, which was basically tinted water, practically demanded I turn in my Texas resident card, move to someplace like California, and start consuming coconut water without irony. I took a sip. "Thanks."

"I'm glad you arrived before your sister. We need to discuss your job situation."

"No, we don't. Everything's fine. I've been doing lots of things around the house, like..." Rearranging my spice cabinet didn't seem like it would impress her. I let the sentence hang.

"If you just called your father and explained you made a mistake, it could all be worked out." She patted my hand.

I was still working on a reply when Phee arrived, looking traffic-girl-ready in a form-skimming blue dress only slightly bigger than a band-aid, and matching high heels, hair teased in a way that would make Mimi jealous. A man stopped her as she passed his table, his face splitting in a dazed smile. She chatted him up, laughed at a joke, swatted him playfully on the shoulder.

As I watched, a little girl of perhaps ten approached Phee for a picture. A minute later, an elderly woman in a wheelchair stopped her. Phee crouched and listened, then embraced her. Nowadays she couldn't go anywhere without being recognized. In fact, lately I'd noticed Phee elicited more attention than Joel Allen. I wonder if that bothered him. I hoped it did.

Phee kissed my mother's cheek before sliding into her seat. "Sorry about that."

The waitress arrived and took our orders. Phee ordered a cup of fruit. That was it. I felt my mother's eyes on me as I ordered a house salad, no croutons or cheese—so basically lettuce, with salad dressing on the side.

"You know, a vinaigrette has seventy calories per table-spoon, and that dressing has twice as much," Mom said, giving me a pointed look over her glass of tea.

I hated vinaigrette.

I smiled grimly at the waitress and changed to the vinai-grette. My mother nodded in approval.

"You'll never guess what happened," Phee said when the waitress left, her eyes bright. She practically bounced in her seat. "You know my producer at work, Chuck? Big guy, always smells a little like pizza?"

I remembered him. Phee set me up on a blind date with him once. She wasn't lying—he did smell faintly of pizza—pepperoni and onion, to be exact.

"He called me this morning, and it turns out Grace Michaels, the weekend anchor, has a stomach bug and can barely get out of bed and Sandy Jones, who's the backup weekend anchor, is in Oregon for her grandmother's funeral." She looked downright giddy.

"That's sad," I said.

Phee waved a hand. "Of course, very sad. I sent flowers." The glimmer of excitement in her eyes didn't dim. "He asked me to anchor the evening news this weekend. He said this could be a trial run and maybe I could do it more if this goes well."

This was Phee's dream. She'd majored in broadcast journalism. Being a traffic girl was a stepping stone, she'd told me once. It was anchoring, maybe making it to a national news program, doing *real news*, that was her goal.

My mother gasped and put a hand on Phee's arm. "This is wonderful. What does Joel think?"

Phee's smile slipped for half a second before returning with extra wattage. "I haven't had a chance to tell him. I'm just so excited."

Our food arrived. Mom and Phee chatted about work. I shrank into my seat, trying to be as inconspicuous as possible while choking down dry, tasteless tortoise food. The more Phee talked, the less I'd have to. This plan had worked for me on many occasions.

Between breaths, Phee stole a carrot off my plate. When we

were kids, we'd done this with our dinner plates when no one was looking. She loved green beans and chicken; I loved all things bread and peas. I'm not sure we ever ate an entire meal on our own once we figured this trick out.

"This is fantastic, Phoebe. I'm so proud of you," my mother gushed, a cat-in-cream smile settling on her face. She pulled out a compact from her purse and flipped it open to check her teeth in the mirror and reapply her make-up.

Phee snatched up a cucumber slice and popped it in her mouth. I was tempted to push the whole plate toward her and give up the illusion that this meal was even a little satisfying.

The compact clicked shut. My mother turned, brown eyes burrowing through my forehead and into my brain. I shivered. "Persephone, can we discuss your situation now? I'm concerned."

I twisted my fingers in my lap. My mother had a way of making me feel seven instead of twenty-seven. My eyes drifted around the room and landed on a small girl tugging at the neck of a stiff white dress with a Peter Pan collar. Her mother gave her a stern look, and the girl wilted. It was like looking in a mirror—my mother and I in almost any conversation we'd ever had since the beginning of time.

"I'm fine."

"Is that so?"

"Yes."

"Your father isn't fine. Leaving him like you did put him in a bind. You've had time to get this all out of your system." She leaned forward. "Don't you think you need to get over this silly disagreement and get back to work?"

I had expected nothing less. Those voicemails and text messages and emails (and probably a billboard somewhere) she'd left all week had followed the same theme: Perci is wrong. Perci needs to fix this.

But I wasn't wrong. And besides, New Perci wouldn't take

this. New Perci would speak up for herself. I straightened. "I'm not going back there. Not when I can't do my job."

"Of course you can do your job, don't be silly."

Phee patted Mom's hand. "Maybe we should let her talk." She flashed me an encouraging smile. I tried to return it, but my mouth wouldn't cooperate.

"What's to talk about? She needs a job, doesn't she?" Mother sniffed, but delicately because she was a lady. "And this attitude toward Brent."

"We are *not* talking about Brent," I said, my voice firm.

My mother's jaw snapped together. "I have raised you girls to be go-getters, to make a name for yourselves."

I knew what was coming next.

"Just look at Phoebe. She's set goals, and she has a rewarding career to show for it."

If I looked good in a skintight dress, maybe I'd have a rewarding career too. I winced. That was unfair to Phee, who was so much more than how she looked. But Mom, whether she realized it, had labeled her the Pretty Daughter.

I was the Failure.

"What are your goals? What have you accomplished with your life?" my mother demanded.

My chest tightened, and my cheeks heated. I didn't want to be the Failure anymore. New Perci wasn't a failure. Right?

"What have *you* done, Mother? What have you accomplished with *your* life?"

This wasn't a wise thing to say for three reasons. One, it was mean and petty, and I didn't want to be either. Two, my mother may have never held a job outside the home, but she'd spent countless hours volunteering with the PTA, the Rotary club, the church, heading fundraisers, and spearheading donation drives. Before Miss Ruby, she'd been Dad's do-it-all woman at the office. Her contributions were plentiful even if she never got paid a dime, and I respected her for it. And three, my thoughts about my mother usually always stayed just that: thoughts.

Phee's eyes bulged. My mother appeared momentarily flummoxed, a little like her favorite kitten had just scratched her.

"I see your attitude hasn't improved since you stormed out of your father's office. You know I love you and want the best for you. Sometimes you need a nudge in the right direction."

"I told you, you don't need to worry about me. I... I need..." What did I need? What would the New, Improved Perci Who Didn't Care About Making Her Mother Happy say? "You don't have to worry about me. I already have another job."

Yep, New Perci was a liar.

Mom's eyes narrowed. "A new job? I haven't heard a thing about this."

I nibbled the inside of my lip. In for a penny, in for a lot of trouble, as Mimi liked to say. "I got a job working at a daycare around the corner from my house."

A yawning silence stretched. The waitress paused at our table, took one look at my mother's face, and scurried off without a word.

Phee frowned. "I didn't know you wanted to work with kids."

Yeah, me neither. "I think a change would be good."

"This is ridiculous. You already have a job with your father." Mom unlocked her phone and slid it across the table. "Call him now and tell him you'll be back to work Monday."

I stared at the phone, a heaviness settling in my stomach.

I will not try to be a better daughter... Mathias had written that on my list. New Perci didn't do what her mama told her just to keep the peace.

I grabbed my purse and hugged it to my chest. "I'm not going to do that."

"Persephone."

My hands shook as I stood. "It was good to see you."

I rounded the table and pressed a kiss to my mother's cheek. The comforting scent of her perfume and face moisturizer assaulted me.

"I don't like this," Mom said, softening slightly.

"You don't have to like it, Mom." I straightened. Pride pushed my shoulders back, firmed my voice. "But I'm doing it, anyway."

"Good luck with the new job," Phee said, and when I looked at her, she winked.

With a nod, I turned and made my way through the crowd, feeling my mother's eyes bore into my back. I didn't turn back. No, I didn't. With a fledgling confidence I didn't know I had, I kept right on walking.

FIFTEEN

"You could go on a wild goose chase,
or you could let the goose come to you."

—MIMI

Mimi came over to my apartment on Sunday afternoon to give me a cooking lesson. "One of you girls needs to know how to make food that sticks to a man's ribs," she explained.

Naturally, I was the right choice since I also liked food that stuck to my ribs.

She buzzed around my kitchen wearing an apron that read, YOU CAN TOUCH MY BACON ANYTIME.

"Did you get what we needed for the cobbler topping?" she asked, opening the fridge and moving things around until she found the Bud Light I kept on hand for her. She cracked it open and chugged half the can. "Yep, that hit the spot."

I shuffled around her and dug through the cabinets for the ingredients. "Can you get the butter out of the fridge?" I asked.

But when I turned around, Mimi was standing there, beer

can in hand, squinting at the refrigerator like she expected it to propose.

"Mimi?"

"Sugar, what's this here?" She pointed with the can to the list of resolutions hanging there.

Cheeks warming, I tried to grab it. "Oh, that's nothing."

Mimi put a hand on my wrist and stopped me. "What are you doing? I was reading."

She took a long pull of her beer and cocked her head. All her hair was scraped back into a high ponytail, a black bedazzled hair clip and a lot of hairspray holding it in place. Her eyes moved across the list once and then again, muttering a word now and then.

"It's not a big deal." I tugged on her arm. "Come on. This cobbler isn't going to make itself."

"We'll get to that. I want to know about these resolutions of yours."

I hesitated. "It's something Mathias came up with."

An eyebrow arched with interest. But instead of pushing me for answers, she turned to the island where all our baking items were spread out. She pulled the pot of peaches from the stove and set it in the sink, where she flushed out the boiling water and added ice. "We need music."

I produced the radio I kept for her from under the sink and plugged it in.

"You start peeling the peaches when they cool, and I'll find us something to listen to. Good music makes—"

"—good food," I said. Classic Mimi-ism.

Mimi fussed with the dial before settling on a George Strait song. We worked together for the next ten minutes, me following Mimi's instructions, Mimi breaking into the occasional dance routine when the spirit moved her.

"I like those resolutions of yours," she announced once the cobbler was in the oven.

I scoffed. "I'm not taking them seriously."

"You sure about that?" Her eyes narrowed as she surveyed me. "Is this why you quit?"

"No? Yes? Maybe? It's not like that." And then I told her all of it, about the lunch with Mom and how New Perci had lied through her teeth about having another job, and about how I was not going back to work at Mayfield. I thought. Probably.

"Good."

"Good?"

She took my hand and squeezed it. "You've been dressing like a widow and acting like you're dead. Just lying around and letting people walk all over your grave."

I imagined my black-clad body draped on the floor with one of those chalk outlines drawn around me. Mimi did have a way with painting the word pictures. "I guess I don't know how to act any other way."

"Sure, you do. You got a backbone—you just need to remember how to use it."

The oven timer went off and Mimi took the cobbler out and set it on the island to cool.

"I hardly think a bunch of resolutions is going to make that happen." Nevertheless, I turned and stared at the list.

Mimi patted me on the cheek. "Maybe not. Or maybe Mathias is smarter than you're giving him credit for. Seems to me, he knew exactly what he was doing when he wrote these."

On Monday, I set my alarm, weighed myself, winced at the number, showered and dressed. I spent the next hour updating my résumé, then pulled on my tall black boots and trekked the four blocks to Miss Marge's Preschool and Daycare.

My steps were lighter as I made my way to the little house on the corner. The *HELP WANTED* sign still hung in the window. I pulled out my phone and punched in the phone number before I could second-guess myself.

Someone answered after the fourth ring, sounding breathless and as warbled as a warped record. "Miss Marge's Preschool and Daycare, how can I help you?" In the window, I could make out a squat, round form edging around the desk.

"Yes, hi. I saw your 'help wanted' sign."

"Thank goodness. My son told me to put an ad online, but I told him the internet's full of weirdos. I always use the window sign and it always brings me someone just right for the job. Now, what's your name?"

"Perci. Perci Mayfield."

Through the window, I saw her sit and thumb through a book on her desk. "Perci, you say?"

"Yes, ma'am." Feeling restless, I paced the sidewalk, keeping the window in my line of vision.

She chuckled. "Polite, I see. That's a good thing. Do you have experience with kids?"

I sucked in my bottom lip and contemplated how to best answer. "I like them a lot."

That was probably accurate. Babies were awfully cute.

"All right then, when would you like to come in for an interview?"

A grin stretched across my face. "Anytime. You just let me know when it's good for you."

"Since I expect that's you walking back and forth on the sidewalk, how about now?"

I froze. The woman stood at the window. She waved; I waved back.

"Now would be good."

A woman in her sixties, Miss Marge had short gray hair, a friendly smile and patient expression. After I filled out an application, she ushered me inside the little room with the window that overlooked the street. A big desk took up most of the space, the top neatly organized. She hardly glanced at my application, instead watching me with steady green eyes.

Her questions weren't rocket science. Was I available to work early mornings? Yes. Did I have a criminal record? No. Did I have physical restrictions? No.

"You're hired," she announced.

"I am?"

"My gut says to take a flyer on you. I always trust my gut." She pointed a pen in my direction. "You'll need to pass a background check."

"That won't be a problem."

"You can start next Monday." Her salt-and-pepper eyebrows arched. "That work for you?"

I fumbled with my purse strap. "Um, yes, of course. That would be great."

Miss Marge leaned back in her chair and settled her hands on her stomach. "The kids might eat you alive, but maybe you'll surprise me."

"What?" I asked, not quite sure I heard her correctly.

She shook her head, a smile touching the corners of her mouth. "We'll see you on Monday."

SIXTEEN

"Silence may be golden,
but duct tape is silver and it's real cheap."

—*MIMI*

"Miss Perci, will you be my valentine?"

The tiny voice belonged to a tiny little boy, not quite three, but already a heartbreaker. He extended a misshapen paper heart covered in great clumps of glue and glitter. His giant blue eyes gazed at me with innocence despite the red marker on his shirt, hands, the table, and his face.

Crouching, I pinched the corner of the heart to avoid the glitter and smiled. "Julian, of course I'll be your valentine. I'd be honored."

A grin spread across his face. Before I could blink, he pressed a sloppy kiss to my cheek and ran off in a trill of giggles.

Since I'd started working at the daycare, I'd already learned a thing or two about kids. For instance, they were gross. I'd been sneezed on, peed on, spit on—accidentally, but no less disgusting—and on one occasion I hoped to never repeat, puked on. I'd been covered with paint, marker, glue, and glitter. I'd found something—food, art supply, a used band-aid—in my hair each day when I got home. I'd started bringing a change of clothes to work, just in case. But the kids were also adorable, liberal with their giggles and smiles and hugs, and worth all the changes I'd had to make for this job.

For example, most days, I woke up and got myself to work by 6 a.m. After figuring out what my new paycheck would look like and another panicked call to Mathias, I made a plan to walk to work.

"You can no longer afford luxuries. Like gas," Mathias had said.

There were other cost-saving efforts in place. I packed my lunch and I'd limited myself to donuts on Fridays only. Between the walking and the kids, it was all I could do to drag myself to the grocery store these last couple of weeks. Turns out, a woman *could* live on peanut butter sandwiches alone.

But it was worth it. Sometimes I found myself smiling so big, my cheeks hurt. I'd somehow become one of those people who was excited to wake up and go to work.

With a grin, I added this valentine to my growing stack. After work, I planned to take them all home and hang them on my refrigerator, so I could smile every time I saw them.

"You're staying until six tonight, right?"

I jolted from my thoughts and found Miss Marge standing in front of me. "Yes, ma'am."

Amanda, one of the other teachers, had begged me to work closing on Valentine's Day for her, and I'd agreed. It wasn't as though I had a hot date waiting in the wings, although my mother had attempted to set me up on no fewer than three blind dates. I'd avoided her calls and texts with ninja-like stealth. Besides, it would give me a chance to work on setting up the accounting program I was trying to talk Miss Marge into. A trial run, of course.

Miss Marge grinned. "Good."

"I figured I'd set up that laptop for you tonight."

On my first day of work, I'd discovered Miss Marge was old school. Like old, *old* school. She had a sign-in sheet for parents, an actual pen-and-paper setup. Her records were kept in that book she carried. Any transactions involving money were noted there. An old-fashioned triple carbon-copy receipt book was used when needed. She kept all her expense receipts in a shoebox. And every two weeks, we employees received paper checks.

It made my eye twitch thinking about all that extra work that could be replaced with a simple computer program. A laptop was hiding under her desk, a Christmas gift from her son. She hadn't even taken it out of the box.

It was a joke between us now. I threatened to set up the laptop; she thought I was teasing. "It will make your life so much easier."

"I've always done it this way," she said, holding up the bulging account book and clipboard.

"Sometimes it's better to ask for forgiveness than permission. I'm sure once you see how much easier it is, you'll appreciate it."

Marge shook her head. "All you need to do is make sure the right kid goes home with the right parent. Think you can handle it?"

I grinned, realizing she hadn't said no to my plan. "I'll try my best."

"Make sure the parents sign the kids out here." She held up the clipboard. My next goal was to set up a digital sign-in/sign-out. Baby steps. "By the way," she said over her shoulder as she headed for the hallway, "it's nice to see you in jeans finally."

On the first day of work, I'd shown up in linen pants and a cream-colored blouse. Miss Marge had shaken her head and said it was clear as day I'd never worked with kids. Despite that, she let me stay. It didn't take long for me to be gazing with envy at the leggings and jeans and t-shirts the other teachers wore.

Depressingly, my closet was full of dark, sad suits. Which was why I'd ended up at Walmart one Tuesday evening, buying a few pairs of sensible jeans and solid-colored t-shirts.

"Is that a cat on your shirt?" Mathias had asked when he'd seen one of my new outfits.

I'd grinned. "It's great, isn't it? I got one with puppies on it, too. The kids love them."

He'd rolled his eyes, but he did it with love. "I didn't think it could get worse than the suits. I was wrong."

But I didn't care what Mathias (and I'm sure my mother) had to say about my new clothes. I liked them.

By quarter to six, there were four kids left. Michael and Sarah were a set of twins whose mother was always the last to arrive. Julian, my little valentine-giver, was also still there. The fourth child, a little girl with dark hair, was curled in one of the beanbag chairs with her nose in a book. She wore a long-sleeved t-shirt with a giant eagle flying in front of an American flag, purple-and-blue striped leggings and a pale pink tutu.

"She's a new one," Amanda had said with a snap of her gum as she'd packed up to leave for the day. She always worked the closing shift and knew more of the school-aged kids. "Her dad is kind of hot. But she's weird."

Weird was okay. I was weird. I made my way to her side of the room. "Good story?"

Huge dark eyes rose above the top of the book. "Uh-huh."

"What's it called?"

"*The Complete Guide to Earthworms*. My daddy got me the whole entire series and I'm going to read every one of them." She flipped the book around, so I was staring at a close-up of a slimy brown worm. "Did you know worms have five hearts?"

"Five? Wow." Also, gross.

Eyes sparking, she nodded. "And they can reproduce all on their own." She turned the book around and flipped through the pages. When she found the one she wanted, she climbed to her knees and held it five inches from my face.

I scratched behind my ear. "How old are you?"

She giggled. "I'm eight but Daddy says I'm very mature for my age and sometimes he lets me stay up to 8:30 because he says mature people can handle it. And when I get to stay up, Daddy lets me watch an extra episode of *The Bird Show with Duke Crosby*. It's my favorite because birds are my favorite. There are one hundred and seventy-three episodes and all of them are about birds."

"I've never seen it."

"Do you like birds?"

I mean, I didn't have strong feelings either way. "Sure."

"I love them. They're awesome. For instant, did you know a group of owls is called a parliament?"

I shook my head.

"And most hummingbirds weigh less than a nickel."

"That is tiny."

"And did you know peacocks are the boys, peahens are the girls, and peachicks are the babies?"

"I did not."

"Peafowl are very interesting," she said with a serious nod of her head. "Do you have a favorite bird?"

I said the first bird that came to mind. "Flamingos are pretty cool."

"Oh, they are. Do you know why they're pink?"

"There's a reason?"

"'Cause they eat shrimp all the time and it makes them pink."

"You're like a walking bird encyclopedia, aren't you?"

"My favorite bird is a cardinal. Guess why?" She crooked a

finger at me and lowered her voice to a whisper. "Cardinals are the most specialest birds. 'Cause when you see one, it means someone in Heaven is visiting you."

I thought of the little red bird I'd spotted on my patio weeks ago. Strange that those few seconds had made an impression. Oddly enough, I'd seen one again today. "Guess what I saw today at my lunch break? A cardinal, sitting right out in the yard." It had stayed long enough for me to notice it before it flitted off.

Her head jerked up, eyes round. "Really? I saw one today, too!"

Smiling, I took a small step forward. "I'm Perci, by the way. What's your name?"

"Lilah," she said, and held out a little hand. "Daddy says I should always shake hands when I meet a new friend. I like you. You're my friend now."

Grinning, I shook her hand. "It's very nice to meet you. I'll let you get back to your reading."

With a distracted nod, she went back to her worm book. I stared down at her head an extra beat. The entire exchange was a little dizzying, like driving too fast over a speed bump or watching a familiar movie dubbed in a foreign language. But I couldn't shake the feeling that I'd just made a lifelong friend with an eight-year-old.

The twins' mother arrived first, signed them out, and rushed them off in a flurry. Julian's grandmother was right behind her, a cheerful woman with a smile she'd passed on to her grandson. A few minutes before 6:30, the front door opened, bringing in a sharp rush of cool air. I poked my head around the doorway and froze. Nate was standing in front of the counter.

Nate Russo. As in my neighbor. The one I seemed to

embarrass myself in front of every time I met him. Why would he be here?

My cheeks heated. In fact, I think the temperature rose at least fifteen degrees. I cleared my throat. "Hi?"

He was clothed in the same beat-up jeans, long-sleeved work shirt and boots. His hair looked damp. In one of his hands, he clutched a bright red gerbera daisy. I wanted to sigh in pleasure at how delicious he looked.

I blinked. *Delicious?* Where had that come from? Thank the stars he couldn't read my thoughts. His eyes sharpened on my face like he was trying to, anyway.

"What are you doing here?" he asked.

"I work here. What are *you* doing here?" Nervous laughter, bordering on crazy, slipped from me.

Chill out, Perci. And then it hit me—the little girl who'd been with him in the elevator that day. I'd never seen her face because of the mask.

From behind me, Lilah squealed. A tangle of skinny legs and dark hair rushed by. She flung her arms around Nate's waist. "Daddy!"

Nate held up the daisy. "Happy Valentine's Day."

Lilah gasped. "For me?"

"Yeah." He tickled the tip of her nose with the blossom. "Here, you take it."

She did, gripping it with one hand and leaning into his side. "Thank you, Daddy."

Nate pressed a kiss to the top of her head. My insides did a surprisingly accurate imitation of Jell-O.

"Lilah, you didn't tell me we'd met before," I said.

Her shoulders rose to her ears. "I didn't think it was important." She turned to her father. "This is my new friend, Perci. Her favorite bird is a flamingo and—"

"No bird talk for now, please. Let's get going. I've planned a very special meal for my valentine."

"Is it macaroni and cheese?" Lilah dug a fist into her hip. "Again?"

"Excuse me, I said 'special.' It's shells and cheese." He tweaked her nose, and she grinned up at him. "Where's your backpack?"

Lilah raced off while Nate signed her out in Miss Marge's ancient logbook. He leaned a hip against the counter while he waited, his eyes skimming the small area before landing on me. The corner of his mouth quirked. "Nice shirt."

I tugged at the hem of my t-shirt—bright red with an enormous candy heart on my chest that read, *HUG ME*. "The kids liked it."

He nodded and again, I got the impression he was holding onto a smile. "Kids are good judges of character. Lilah seems to like you a lot."

"I like her too. I had no idea you and she were"—I tapped my two pointer fingers together in a supremely awkward gesture—"related."

His grin reached his eyes and confirmed he did have a dimple in his left cheek. "We are indeed."

Lilah rushed into the area, dragging a backpack with a giant owl on it. Pausing in front of her dad, she dug around until she pulled out a folded piece of construction paper. "Happy Valentine's Day!"

Nate took it with reverence, like it was a priceless piece of art. He studied the card before he flashed Lilah a wide smile that made my chest tighten. "I love it."

Her face beamed. "And guess what else?"

"What?"

"I saw a cardinal today, and so did Perci."

Nate's face changed in an instant, his brow crinkling. "Lilah."

"I saw it at recess. It was right there at the fence, and I saw it again when I got back to my class and looked out the window. I think it followed me. Do you know why?" A note of excitement slipped into her voice.

"I know you think you know why."

"But it's true, I swear."

I fiddled with the logbook on the counter, wondering what this was all about and why it felt like I'd just walked into a weirdly intimate discussion. Finally, I couldn't take the tension. "Sounds like that little guy liked you."

"She." Lilah grinned.

"She?"

"I know who that bird was."

I frowned, remembering how she'd whispered that cardinals were visitors from Heaven. "Who do you think it was?"

She turned to me, dark eyes shining. "It was my mommy."

SEVENTEEN

"A gentleman never kisses and tells,
his lady's smile does all the talking."

—MIMI

"Would you help me with something?" Mathias said.

"That depends," I said into the phone on my walk home
from work. Skipping around a mud puddle from a storm last
night, I paused in front of the little boutique and stared longingly at The Dress in its window. I bet New Perci would work
up the courage to try it on.

"I'm giving a series of talks at Hope House and—"

"What's Hope House?" I plopped on a bench in front of a
bakery. The wind had picked up in the last few minutes,
bringing a patch of ominous clouds with it.

"It's a non-profit. They support women getting back on
their feet with classes and help with jobs and interview skills.
Stuff like that."

"That sounds interesting." A bird perched on the bed of a
pickup truck parked on the street in front of me. Its red feathers

ruffled in the wind—another cardinal. Lilah's dark eyes as she'd announced that the cardinal she'd seen was her mother flashed in my head. My chest tightened to think of the hope in her voice.

"I'm glad you said that. I need you to teach a class for me there tomorrow night."

"Teach a class?" I pulled out a package of peanut butter crackers from my purse and tossed one on the sidewalk, then took one for myself. The cardinal side-eyed me before hopping to the ground and snatching it up.

His voice took on an impatient tone. In the background, I heard an announcer give updated flight information. "Yes, a class."

"Like, in front of people?" The cracker I'd started eating congealed in my throat.

"It's not a big deal. When I presented last month, there were three women. I have a PowerPoint presentation. You show up and talk them through it and you're done."

On my list of Things I Never Wanted to Repeat, number two was public speaking. The last time had been in college in a required communications class. I had dropped my notes, crawled on all fours to pick them up, couldn't figure out how to reorder them, and started crying in the middle of explaining the benefits of conflict management to a class of fifty people. I scraped by with a C in that class, probably because the professor felt sorry for me.

"It's a couple of women, four at the most. You don't even need to answer questions. Just be a warm body who knows how to run a computer and read stuff off a screen."

The sun dipped behind angry gray clouds and the branches on the oak tree across the street bowed under the increasing strength of the wind. A gully-washer, as Mimi called them, was imminent. My cardinal tilted its head and took off for safety.

"That's all?" Standing, I slung my purse on my shoulder and hurried toward my apartment.

"That's it."

The background noise grew louder and now I was certain I heard an announcement for a Tallahassee flight. "Are you headed to Florida?"

"Something came up." He lowered his voice. "A photo surfaced of a Miss Florida contestant from a couple of years ago and we have to go do some damage control."

"How bad is it?"

"Let's say it appears clothing was optional at that particular event. She's topless."

"Yikes. How do you spin that?" A drop of rain plopped on my nose.

"She was protesting breastfeeding laws? I don't know. We'll figure something out." I imagined him running fingers through his hair in frustration. He hated clean-up situations. "I have to run, they're boarding. Listen, thank you for doing this. I promise I'll make it up to you."

"But I didn't—"

"I'll email you everything you need. Text me and let me know how it goes."

"I don't know if this is such a good idea. I'm not great at this kind of stuff."

No reply.

"Mathias?" I pulled the phone away to stare at the screen. He'd hung up. Water splashed on my arm.

Stuffing my phone in my purse, I half jogged, half trotted down the sidewalk. But I'd only made it a couple of yards before the skies opened. Within seconds, the rain had drenched my hair. I shoved it out of my eyes and hightailed it down the street. At the next intersection, I had to wait for the cars with a green light, my shoes growing soggier by the minute.

A faded red pickup truck honked and I jumped. The

window rolled down and Nate's face appeared. He smiled and my stomach flipped. "I thought that was you. Are you going home?"

"Yes."

Thunder ripped through the air. He popped open the door.

"Get in. I'll take you."

Despite the chill from the rain, my face heated, pleased and embarrassed and, okay, a little excited. I hesitated. "Are you sure? I'm going to get your seat all wet."

"Come on. It'll dry." He moved back from the window, and I climbed in. "Here, give me that." I handed him my purse, my fingers brushing his. I shivered—and not from the chill of the rain—and crossed my arms over my chest.

After setting my purse in the backseat, Nate pulled into traffic and stopped at the end of the block at a red light.

"I'm sorry if you have to go out of your way."

"It's only a couple of blocks. Not a big deal."

"Were you on your way to get Lilah?" It was almost four in the afternoon, around the time I usually walked home unless I stayed later to close.

He shook his head. "Nah. I'm going grocery shopping before I pick her up."

"Oh. That's smart." A sheet of rain pounded on the front window. So much so, Nate had to slow down a little because it was hard to see through it. My fingers twisted in my lap with nervous energy. "The weather forecast said it wasn't supposed to rain until tonight."

"The weather changes fast here. It's different from back home."

"New York?"

He tossed me a curious look.

"Your mail," I said.

"Oh, yeah. Well, Houston has good weather for construction. Mostly warm days." Lightning flashed on the not-too-distant horizon. "Except for when we get rained out."

"Is that why you moved here? For the job?"

"Something like that. I knew a guy who knew a guy who could get me a job, and I was looking to start fresh, I guess."

As the truck slid to a stop at the next light, I glanced around the interior—an empty bottle of water in the cup holder, loose change in the ashtray, a few Froot Loops on the floor, a booster seat in the back.

"Nice necklace." I pointed at the macaroni creation dangling from the rearview mirror. It looked like one of the art projects from Miss Marge's.

"Thanks. I've been told pasta really brings out my eyes."

I laughed and made the mistake of glancing at him. The sharp edges of his profile softened into a smile. My breath caught, and I coughed to cover it.

He shot me a concerned look. "Hey, are you cold?" He fussed with a dial and a wave of warmth blasted from the vent. At the next light, he twisted around and pulled something from the backseat. "Here. Put this on and get warm."

It was a sweatshirt. *His* sweatshirt.

"It's an extra one I keep in the car, just in case." When I hesitated, he nudged my elbow. "It's clean, I promise."

"Um, thanks." I pulled it over my head, praying it fit me. After wrestling with it and the seat belt, I found myself swallowed in it. In fact, I had to roll up the sleeves. The front read BRONX COMMUNITY COLLEGE. "Your alma mater?"

He snorted. "For about five minutes."

"You didn't like school?"

"Back then, I didn't like anything that was good for me."

I wasn't sure how to respond and, in my silence, I couldn't help picturing Nate the Bad Boy. I won't lie—it was an attractive thought.

He turned down the final stretch to the apartment complex.

Disappointment pooled in my stomach, almost outweighing the nervousness. It was nice talking to him, easier than I'd expected, and I wanted to keep the conversation going. I groped around my brain for a topic.

"Did you know worms have five hearts?" Yes, that's what I said.

"That so?"

"I, um, yes." *Stop right there. No. More. Words.* "They can also reproduce on their own." My fingers curled around the seat belt strap. "And peacocks are male, peahens are female, peachicks are babies, and peapods are their eggs."

My face flamed, likely a shade of red so brilliant, there wasn't a name for it. Now we could name it Perci Red, and Mimi would get a pair of shoes in that very shade and tell everyone they were named for her granddaughter. "I was kidding about the peapods. That was a dumb joke. I do that sort of thing when I'm nervous."

I felt, rather than saw, him glance at me.

"Not that you make me nervous in an 'I think you might be a serial killer' way. It's more of a... a..." The truck lurched to a stop in front of the apartment complex, saving me from finishing that sentence.

He grabbed my purse from the back. The corners of his eyes crinkled in amusement. No, still not handsome, but I could have stared at him forever. Which I was apparently trying to do.

He cleared his throat. "We're here."

"Oh, right." Pushing open the door, I slid halfway out of the car and turned back. "Thanks for the ride."

He smiled. "No problem."

I hopped out, slammed the door, and took a leaping step before I was yanked back by the sweatshirt I'd just shut in the door.

"Oh, gosh. Sorry," I said when I opened the door.

"Goodbye, Perci." His voice brimmed with laughter, and I felt it in my toes.

I raced into the apartment lobby and out of the rain. Then, like a dope, I stood right in front of the door, my face pressed to the glass like a kid at a candy store and watched him drive away.

EIGHTEEN

"Don't judge a book by its cover.
At least you know it'll be better than the movie."

—MIMI

Hope House was nestled in the outskirts of west Houston in what appeared to be a former grocery store in a strip mall. Everywhere I looked, off-white besieged me. Off-white walls, off-white floors, an off-white couch that looked like it had lived a long, off-white life and needed to be taken out back and shot.

On the wall behind it, a crooked poster displayed the Hope House Rules:

1. No drugs.
2. No alcohol.
3. No fighting.
4. No weapons.
5. No stealing.
6. No nonsense.
7. No giving up.

No one greeted me at the front. After fiddling with my purse strap, rereading the sign, and questioning once again how I'd ended up here, I ventured down the main hallway until I came to a closed door marked OFFICE. I hesitated. I could turn and run now. No one would ever know. Except me. I would know. My grip on the laptop bag in my hand tightened. I had no idea what this presentation was even about. Mathias had emailed only an hour ago, and I hadn't had time to read it.

Old Perci would run. But New Perci would not buckle under the weight of crippling stage fright. Besides, Mathias had said it would just be a few women. It would be like chatting around the lunch table with some girlfriends. I knocked.

"Yeah?" a voice yelled. "Come in."

A woman was hunched over the desk, phone pressed to her ear as she rattled off something I couldn't quite hear, but I thought I caught the words "parole" and "arrested."

"I'm asking you to give her a chance. She's a hard worker," the woman said and held up a finger in my direction. I waited.

"Who are you?" she asked the second her call disconnected.

"I'm Perci Mayfield. I'm here for the presentation. Mathias Jorgensen was supposed to give it, but something came up and I'm taking his place. I figured he would have let you know."

"He did not." Under the weight of her glare, I shifted on my feet. "Is that a cat on your shirt?"

I tugged on the hem. "The plan was to change before I came, but we were short-handed at work, so I had to stay late and came straight here."

She muttered something under her breath, which didn't sound complimentary, and marched toward the hallway. "Come on then. I guess you'll have to do. I'm Stella Martinez, the director here."

I trotted behind her down the hallway. We entered a room at the end with a large screen on one side and several rows of chairs facing it. I walked up the center aisle to the table at the front, counting five rows of six chairs. Thirty people. Nope. No way. "Mathias mentioned it would be a small group."

Her eyebrows rose. "That so? We have..." She thumbed through the papers on a clipboard she carried. "Here is it—twenty-seven signed up. Word got around about it after last time Mathias was here."

Panic blurred the edges of my vision. I leaned a hand on the table, thought about crawling under it. Twenty-seven? "What is the name of this class again?"

With a frown, she scanned me from head to toe. "'How to Dress for Success.'"

The dubious expression on her face had merit. Dressing for success wasn't my field of expertise. A person had to feel comfortable in their own skin for that, and I'd been faking it for years.

But New Perci was comfortable. New Perci didn't worry about pleasing other people. New Perci would face these twenty-seven women head-on. New Perci would kill this.

New Perci was me, dang it.

Plunking the laptop bag on the table, I smiled with what I hoped was confidence. "So, where should I set up?"

The women began arriving thirty minutes later. Some looked too young to drink, others looked old enough to have watched Jesus turn water into wine.

An older woman with frizzy white hair and a wide smile that showed four missing teeth paused in front of me. Her smile dipped into a frown. "You ain't the fellow with the glasses."

"No, sorry. I'm taking over for tonight."

She cranked her head around. "Suze, he's not here."

A round woman with cropped dark hair and a neck tattoo jerked her chin. "Sheeet. Been looking forward to this all week."

The first woman turned back to me. "I didn't get to come

last time, but the word is that one was real entertaining and a looker on top of it. Heard he had a nice ass."

Instead of leaving, she plopped herself in the front row. Crossing her arms, she eyed me skeptically.

A steady stream of women filled the room over the next ten minutes. All found seats; some clustered together, others pulled their chairs off to the side.

One woman caught my eye the second she walked in the room. About my height and size, she seemed to take up more real estate, as though her body was too small to contain her personality. Hair cut short and dyed a neon pink, she strutted to the first chair in the front row. It was occupied, but that didn't stop her. She folded her arms and stared daggers into the occupant's head until she moved.

After sitting, she tipped her chin at me. "Stella said I should have your back."

"Should I be worried?" I asked.

"No. I have your back," she said, like she was speaking to someone with limited brain power.

At seven on the dot, despite my sweaty palms and longing to run, I cleared my throat. "Hi, everyone."

I waited, but the room did not quiet. In fact, the volume grew.

"Hey, ladies, if we could get started."

No response.

"Can we get started, please?"

Still nothing. This felt like a test, and I was terrible at tests. My hands opened and closed at my sides; I rubbed them against my t-shirt.

The pink-haired woman stood, climbed on top of her chair, and faced the crowd. She placed a thumb and finger in her mouth and blew. The high-pitched whistle startled the entire room into silence.

"I don't know about you, but I want to learn somethin'. So,

shut it." Her glare touched on each woman before returning to me. "All right. Say what you gotta say now."

"You teacher's pet, Bria?" a voice yelled.

Bria made an obscene gesture that garnered hoots of laughter before climbing off her chair.

Twenty-seven pairs of eyes swung my way. I swiped at my forehead, grimacing at the sweat. "Thank you."

"Well, get on with it," Bria said. "I got things to do."

I got on with it.

It wasn't the worst presentation ever, but I wouldn't be winning any prizes. The slide show moved quickly, but it was the interruptions and arguments that delayed us.

For example, the impassioned discussion about what size hoop earring was desirable in a work environment. Silver or gold lip ring—which was classier? Were five-inch heels appropriate for an office job? After a heated debate over whether belly shirts were okay to wear to an office party almost resulted in a fistfight, I felt it prudent to call it a night.

"Thank you for coming. If you have any questions, feel free to come up afterward and ask."

Please don't. Please don't. Please don't.

As the crowd dispersed, I gathered my things. My eyes locked on the door, and I hurried toward it like I'd seen a sign for free ice cream. But halfway to the exit, a solid form with neon-pink hair stepped in my path.

I stopped short. "Can I help you?"

"I'm Bria." She glared at me like she expected me to argue.

"Thanks for your help earlier." I swallowed. "Did you have a question?"

An awkward, stretching silence followed in which I suspected I was being studied carefully. This close, Bria didn't look old enough to be a high school graduate. Tattoos snaked around both her arms—one looked to be a saint of some kind, driving a sports car. The pink hair fell to just below her ears, which had four piercings each.

"Yeah. Can I get the PowerPoint emailed to me? I feel like I missed stuff."

A strange, breathy laugh fell out of my mouth. "Oh, sure. I can do that." I rummaged through my purse and found a paper and pen. "Write down your email address."

Her upper lip lifted as she snatched it from my hand and began to write. "Where do you work?"

I smoothed a hand over the spot of green paint on the hem of my t-shirt—finger-painting day. "At a daycare. But I used to work at a mortgage company."

Her expression disbelieving, she handed the paper back. "You left an office job to work with a bunch of snotty kids? Man, that's stupid."

Maybe my mom planted her.

"I like it."

Her chin jerked up. "I want an office job with good pay. And dental." She flashed a smile, revealing a gap between her front teeth. "I need me an orthodontist."

"What do you do now?" I asked and took a step toward the door. She followed.

"Fast food," she muttered. "Not too many people want to hire someone who just got out."

My steps slowed. "Got out of where?"

"The slammer. Lockup. Prison. Why you think we're all at Hope House?"

Now my feet came to a complete halt. "Prison?"

"Hope House helps us with stuff—jobs and stuff, so we can be"—she raised her hands and made air quotes—"'productive' members of society. No one wants to give us the time of day." She shrugged. One of her bra straps slid down, and she hoisted it back up. "Besides, I got goals."

I wondered what she'd done to land her in prison. Was I allowed to work that into the conversation? Something like, *Hey, nice to meet you. By the way, did you murder someone?*

"Goals are good."

"So," Bria said, lip ring winking in the light. "You coming back next week?"

Nope. "I'm not sure."

Her shoulders slumped before she straightened, a hard, unreadable expression in her eyes. "Yeah, I understand."

Then she walked away.

NINETEEN

"Never ask a woman how old she is,
  how much she weighs,
  or if she's pregnant."

—*MIMI*

February 19 was my twenty-eighth birthday, a day I dreaded for one reason: Family Birthday Dinner. It would be the first family meal since New Year's Day, and I wanted to be anywhere else.

I rushed home after work and shuffled through my closet. After some consideration and trying on four different options, I settled on a pair of high-waisted black pants, a dark green blouse, and black heels. I suited up in my armor of Spanx—thank you, Mom—and gave myself a cursory look in the mirror.

The woman staring back at me looked fine.

Just fine. Not good or great. Just fine.

"You, Perci Mayfield, are twenty-eight years old today. Is this as good as it gets?" I smoothed a hand over the blouse. "Green looks terrible on me."

True enough, it washed me out. But my mother thought it

was "just enough to add a little color, but to hide all the trouble spots."

New Perci didn't have to listen to her mother, right? New Perci could wear whatever she wanted.

I slipped the shirt off, tossed it on the floor, and searched my closet again. In the back, I found it. A couple of years ago, I'd been appeasing my vintage clothing addiction by window-shopping on eBay. I hadn't been able to resist a 1950s-style blouse with a high neck, three-quarter sleeves and a shape that flared at the waist. The best part? Whimsical slices of watermelon dotted the fabric. I fell in love, paid way too much money for it, and hung it in my closet.

I could hear Mom now. "Don't you think something classic would be better suited for you?"

But I loved this shirt, and New Perci was not a people pleaser.

Daddy answered the door when I arrived. In one hand, he gripped a stack of paperwork, which he'd clearly been working on. "Cupcake!"

After the Big Scene at work, Dad and I had talked a few times. Somehow, we'd reached an amiable compromise—he wouldn't bring it up, and neither would I. Just the way things had been done for years in the Mayfield family. "Hi, Daddy."

He pulled me in for a hug. I caught a whiff of his aftershave and the peppermints he always had in his pocket. "What are you doing here?"

With a shake of my head, I took a step back. "Dinner tonight, remember?"

"Oh, that's right. It's Phoebe's birthday."

"Nope, the other daughter."

He had the decency to look sheepish. "Happy birthday."

"Thanks." I hung my purse and coat in the hallway closet,

smoothed a hand down my shirt, and gave the watermelons a secret smile.

"Mom's in the kitchen." He lowered his voice. "She's been extra sensitive today."

I snorted. Extra sensitive? Maybe I should have worn a suit of armor and earplugs. "Thanks for the heads-up."

But he was already wandering back to his office. I marched down the hallway, past the row of family photos that started at my birth and ended with our group picture taken this New Year's, Joel Allen smiling his stupid newscaster smile with an arm around his new fiancé. A foul taste hit my mouth at the thought of seeing him this evening.

Earlier this week, I'd begged Mathias to come with me. "Please. My mom loves you. She's always nicer when you're there."

He'd hesitated. "It's not a good idea. Besides, you'll be fine."

"No, I won't."

He shook his head and mustered up a smile. "Phee and Joel will be there. I just can't. Besides, I'll take you out for a special birthday dinner if you're good."

In the kitchen, Mom bustled around, put together like she was modeling for an article titled, "Style Tips that Take You from the Kitchen to the Yacht Club." In the corner, Scary Perry lifted his head and stared in his black, soulless way.

"Oh, good, you're here." Wiping her hands on the towel hanging from her apron pocket, she rounded the island and pressed a kiss to my cheek. Her mouth started an upward turn, paused, and froze. "This shirt?"

Old Perci wanted to shrink under her assessment. New Perci straightened her spine. "It's vintage. I love it."

"Patterns can be difficult to pull off, especially... fruit." A tiny muscle in her jaw ticked, but she kept her half-smile locked in place. "Well, why don't you set the table?" She marched into the dining room, and I followed, feeling a tiny bit smug and a lot confused. She hadn't said anything remotely critical.

"Remember, fork, knife, spoon," she said, like she hadn't drilled it into me by the time I was six along with: no elbows on the table, napkin in your lap, and the salt and pepper are like an old married couple; they stay together until the bitter end.

"Got it."

After fussing over the centerpiece, she turned and watched me. "Your hair... There's something different."

I smoothed my hair self-consciously. "I got highlights."

Last week on a whim and without an appointment, I'd showed up at The Hightower, a fancy full-service salon Mom and I had been going to for as long as I could remember. For years, Jacque, who told everyone he was from the south of France but was actually from Jersey and who, you guessed it, was also Mom's stylist, had been cutting my hair into a sensible chin-length bob. Each day, I straightened out the natural wave even though it added an extra thirty minutes to my morning routine. "This makes you look thinner," he'd insisted. My mother agreed.

But last week, Jacque wasn't available; Alisa was.

Alisa had purple streaks in her hair and rolled her eyes when I explained how Jacque always cut my hair. "A bob like that hits you in the absolute wrong spot. You should totally grow it out."

"Really?"

She narrowed her eyes and spun the chair I was sitting in, running her fingers through my hair. "Yes, and highlights would look awesome. They'd brighten up your face and make you look younger."

Wide-eyed, I stared at myself in the mirror. "I look old?"

With a shrug, she pulled a hair color swatch book from a drawer. "Thirty-five isn't old or anything. But you could look younger."

Thirty-five? But I wasn't even thirty yet. I hadn't found the love of my life. I still couldn't use plastic wrap properly. I secretly liked to watch cartoons on Saturday mornings while eating a giant bowl of sugary cereal. *I was not old.*

"Do it," I'd said. "Do the highlights."

Alisa had been right. The lighter color did brighten my face and make my eyes sparkle. I'd stopped straightening my hair too, choosing thirty more minutes of sleep instead.

My mother inspected me. "It's different, but... nice. I'm going to go check on dinner. Let me know if you need anything."

"Okay?" My gaze followed her as she walked back to the kitchen. Not one criticism? Not one. Had my mother been switched with an alien?

Phee arrived just before dinner started, gift bag in hand.

"Happy birthday," she said, linking an arm with mine as we headed from the front door to the kitchen. "I got you a very inappropriate gift. Very naughty. Do not open in front of Mom."

"What is it?"

"Chocolate. Fancy, rich chocolate. So. Many. Calories."

I laughed. "I shall enjoy every bite."

"Excellent."

We took a sharp right just before the kitchen into the living room. While I stuffed the gift in my purse, Phee stripped off her coat to reveal a pair of jeans and a simple wrap-style shirt. From the neck up, neither a hair nor an eyelash was out of place, make-up carefully applied, blonde curls slicked back into a low ponytail. It was weird to see her in jeans. Not that she didn't ever wear them, but it wasn't often, and certainly not to a family dinner.

"Where's Mathias?" she asked, fussing with her coat instead of making direct eye contact.

"He's not here. He thought it would be better if he didn't come."

Her head jerked sharply, blue eyes widening, before she adjusted her expression to one of cool disinterest. "Oh. Well. I'm... just surprised he wouldn't be here for your birthday."

"I heard you asked him to do the wedding photography and he agreed."

"It seems like a good idea. He is a photographer." She flopped back on the couch, stretching out her long legs in a decidedly unladylike manner. I shot a look toward the doorway. Had I been the one in that pose, it would be guaranteed to bring my mother and her look of disapproval like a siren song. Somehow Phee never got caught.

"It's just that you two kind of have a history." I watched her closely for any tell. But Phee was good at hiding things when she wanted to.

She shrugged. "That was a long time ago. We're both adults. Besides, it's been the easiest wedding decision I've made. Do you know what it's like planning a wedding with Mom?"

"Terrifying?"

"She has a *book*, Perci. A giant wedding book with color swatches and seating charts and wedding cake toppers. It's like Martha Stewart threw up bridesmaid dresses and printed napkins."

I sat next to her. "Really?"

"Oh, yeah." She patted my knee. "Don't worry. There's one for you too."

"Goody." I cringed, thinking of the Mom of the Bride version of our mother.

"Girls, where are you?" Mom called from the kitchen.

"Coming," we both shouted back, although neither of us moved.

Finally, Phee rose and smoothed a hand down her waist. "Do I look okay? I was doing an interview for a story I'm working on and forgot to bring a Mother-Approved Outfit to put on after."

I stood with a hum of concern. "You know what Mom says about jeans. They're only for farmers and..."

"...soccer moms who've given up."

"But I think you look great. Very comfortable." *Unlike me and these damn Spanx.* "Maybe she won't notice."

Phee snorted and hooked her arm through mine. "You always were the optimistic one."

TWENTY

"Drinkin' your sorrows away
only works till the beer runs out."

—*MIMI*

On my mother's list of Favorite Sayings, number three was, "I might lose the battle, but I always win the war." Clearly, she had declared war on me. This was the reason I found myself sitting around the dinner table with my family and Brent.

When he'd arrived, a victorious light shone in Mom's eyes, and I realized I'd been lulled into a false sense of security. "I hope you don't mind."

What could I say? I hid in the bathroom and texted Mathias.

Me: *Please save me. Mom invited Brent. BRENT IS HERE.*

Unfortunately, Mathias did not come to my rescue, nor did I contract bubonic plague and subsequently die.

A knock on the door jarred me. "Someone's in here. Be right out."

"It's me, sugar. Open up."

I yanked it open, and Mimi slipped inside. She plopped down on the lid of the toilet. "You hiding?"

"Why would she do this? Why would she invite Brent?"

"You know your mama. She has to be in everyone's business. Like that as a kid too. Bossy and too smart for her own good. Always thought she could solve the world's problems. You know, she ran for class president her senior year in high school because she actually wanted to make positive changes to the school? Had this speech she wrote and rewrote and practiced a hundred times until it was perfect."

"Did she win?"

"'Course not. The kid whose older brother bought the beer for all the parties did." Mimi dug around in her purse and pulled out a pack of cigarettes and a lighter. "I will say this about Bobbie Jo, she always could pick herself back up and find a new cause." She stood, climbed on the toilet, and opened the tiny window above it. A whoosh of cool air followed. The lighter flickered red as she lit a cigarette.

"I just wish I weren't one of her causes." I crossed my arms. "And you are not supposed to be smoking."

She pointed the glowing end of the cigarette at me. "Now, it's just the one. And lower your voice. If your mama hears, there'll be no end to her nagging."

Slumping against the door, I slid to the floor, a feat of epic proportions considering half of my body was wrapped tighter than a mummy in those Spanx. "I don't need her to fix my life. My life is fine."

Mimi dangled her smoking hand out the window and leaned over enough to catch her reflection in the mirror. I tensed at her balancing act, ready for her to fall and break a hip. "You might think that, but your mother doesn't. Mamas want their chick-adees settled. Most of us let them find their own way, maybe with a little proddin'. But your mama wants it done *her* way."

"I can't sit through an entire meal with Brent and Joel Allen and my mother." My stomach clenched at the thought. Maybe I did have the plague. One could only hope.

Mimi took a drag of her cigarette and frowned. "Time to use that backbone, Perci Mayfield. I swear, you are right on the edge of starting to live your life. I might have to shove you off."

I rested my chin on my knees. "I don't want to go back out there."

"Too late for that. If I had to miss bingo night at Our Lady of Perpetual Sorrow with that hottie bingo caller—"

"Isn't he a priest?"

"Priests can be hotties." With a grin, she mashed the end of her cigarette on the brick ledge and chucked it in the yard before closing the window. From her purse, she pulled out a miniature bottle of perfume which she spritzed liberally, then mouthwash, and gave her mouth a swish.

I clambered to my feet, wincing as the Spanx cut into my waist. "Let's get this over with."

Mimi linked arms with me. "That's my girl."

We marched into the dining room where only two seats remained—one next to Joel Allen, the other next to Brent. I turned to Mimi in horror. In the end, I sat next to Brent. Better the devil you've kissed and lived to tell about, I guess.

I made it through most of the dinner with no cause for alarm. If I pretended Brent didn't exist, he almost didn't. Well, except his right elbow, which bumped into my arm over and over. And if I faced forward, I was met with the fake-smiling face of Joel Allen.

So, I stared at the tiny watermelons on my shirtsleeve and counted the minutes until I could leave.

"How are things?" Brent nudged me again with his elbow as

he cut up his meatloaf—my favorite childhood meal. Except Mom had made a healthy version with low-fat ground turkey to "cut the calories." And the taste.

I shrugged. "Fine. How's Candy?"

"Oh, good. We're keeping things easy."

"What does that mean?" I tipped my face toward him. A small spot of gravy dotted his tie, which was a ghastly shade of grayish-brown. I stared at it.

"We aren't exclusive, you know?"

"So, you're seeing other people?"

He shrugged. "Something like that. What about you? You seeing anyone?"

An image of Nate, that small smile on his face, popped into my head. Where had that come from?

"Brent," my mother said, from her reign of terror at the head of the table. "It's so nice you could make it. How's work?"

"It's good. Thanks for inviting me, Mrs. Mayfield." He smiled.

"You know you're like a member of the family." Mom's eyes cut to me. "Isn't that right, Persephone?"

Brent settled his arm around my shoulders with a laugh. "It sure feels that way."

I tried to shrug him off, but he didn't take the hint. Mom beamed at us. "Such a lovely couple."

"Mom, we aren't a couple," I said.

Her laugh tinkled like a bell and my teeth gnashed in response. "You never know, dear." She turned to my sister. "Honey, have you two set a date for the wedding yet?"

Joel Allen stopped shoveling food in his mouth long enough to answer. "We're thinking next March."

"Wonderful. That gives us plenty of time to plan." Mom set her fork down. "We've got to find a venue. What do you think about Daddy's club? Or maybe that place your cousin got married a few years ago. What was it called?"

No one answered. I stuffed a spoonful of what Mom called "cauliflower mashed potatoes" in my mouth. (Only sixty-six calories per serving.)

"Well, no mind, we'll figure it out. It'll need to be big enough to accommodate a large wedding, of course. How many guests, do you think?" Mom paused for a sip of wine and plowed on. "At least three hundred? Oh, we must go dress shopping immediately. Won't that be fun?"

Phee straightened, her expression uncertain. "I'm thinking something small and intimate."

"Of course, for the ceremony. But the reception needs to be huge," Mom said, excitement in her eyes as if it were her wedding. "Two local celebrities marrying? We'll have quite the guest list, I'm sure."

"Mom," Phee said, a note of resignation in her voice.

My mother pushed her plate aside and went to her happy place—meddling in her children's lives. "Let's go dress shopping soon. We'll make a day of it—all us girls. Your sister will be a bridesmaid, of course. What colors are you thinking? Perci looks best in black, which won't do for a wedding." Her gaze locked on me like a missile with a target in sight. "You know, honey, you have a year. We'll get you on a diet and—"

"I can give you the name of my personal trainer," Joel Allen chimed in.

Kill. Me. Now.

"You know I'm sitting right here, don't you?" I asked, fingertips turning white from gripping my glass of water too tightly. "And it's my birthday."

Phee frowned. "Geez, Mom. Stop. Perci looks good in a dress right now and in lots of colors. She doesn't need to lose weight."

Pressing my lips together, I pushed the food around on my plate. Brent's arm still lay across my shoulders like a weight.

The Spanx felt suffocating, pinching my body into strange shapes.

Mom leaned back in her chair, her expression earnest. She was, you know, *helping* here, after all. "It's something to consider. Wedding photos do last forever, and you don't want to embarrass yourself."

The room went silent. I wanted to disappear. Mimi reached for her iced tea, took a slow sip, and set it down with a thunk.

"Did you know, Bobbie Jo here used to carry around a few extra pounds? Chubby little thing when she was little." Eyes narrowed, she turned to her daughter. "Now, you're skinny and a bitch. Eat some cake, honey. We'd all appreciate it."

My mother's face turned a very unflattering shade of red. "Mama! I cannot believe you."

Mimi replied, but her words were white noise in my head. I pushed away from the table, chair legs scraping against the floor. A sharp pain cut through my chest and those damn Spanx tightened around my body. Like a noose. "I have to go to the bathroom."

I splashed cool water on my face, but it was useless. My hands shook with embarrassment, but more than that, anger. I peered in the mirror. Why was I always the target? Maybe I wasn't smart or beautiful like Phee, but I still deserved kindness. The worst part was my mother believed she *was* being kind, helpful even.

Following Mimi's actions from earlier, I climbed onto the lid of the toilet, opened the window and stuck my head out. The cool air helped some, but those Spanx cut into my thighs, my waist, my ribcage. A whole-body suit to suck in all the parts my mother frowned on. I wasn't even certain I could button these pants without them.

Mathias's voice replayed in my mind, reminding me of

those resolutions and that I wasn't supposed to try and be a better daughter. And that's what I was doing, wasn't I? Hiding in the bathroom instead of telling my mom how I felt.

But I was New Perci now, and New Perci had a backbone.

My fingers went to my waist all on their own. They unhooked the first button of my pants and the weight in my chest eased. A moment later, I stood in my parents' downstairs bathroom, stripped to my underwear, the Spanx tossed in a beige heap on the floor.

Yes, that was better. Tension drained from my shoulders, my head cleared, my body relaxed. *Yes, yes.* I straightened, feeling more grounded and pissed right the hell off.

Stop trying so hard. Be you.

The pants didn't quite button without the extra help, but I held them closed with one hand and snagged the Spanx from the floor with the other. Shoulders straight and with as much dignity as a woman whose pants didn't fit could muster, I marched into the dining room.

No one noticed my return.

"Daddy." My voice came out as a whisper. Scowling, I cleared my throat and tried again. "Daddy!"

Okay, perhaps too loud. Having a backbone might take some practice. Six pairs of eyes swung in my direction.

"I would appreciate it if you would try to remember when my birthday is, just once." I nodded and swung around to face the other side of the table.

"Brent, I wish you weren't here. We are never, ever getting back together. In fact..." I straightened, and a mental image of Nate flashed in my brain, of him smiling down at Lilah and how he'd rescued me from the rain and of how he fascinated me without even trying. That image translated into words. "To answer your question, yes, I am seeing someone. His name is Nate, and he's my neighbor."

My mom let out a tiny gasp, drawing my attention.

"And, Mom, do not ever, ever buy me Spanx again." I tossed the offending article of clothing her way. It landed on top of the meatloaf, a leg flopping into the gravy.

"Persephone!"

"Thank you for a lovely birthday dinner. It's one I'll never forget. I'll call you later, Mimi."

Head high, I twisted on my heels, took three steps and tripped over a prone Pericles. He gave me a look that said, *it serves you right*; I gave him a look that said, *I will dance on your grave someday*. Then I hobbled to the front door, Mimi's cackling laughter following in my wake.

TWENTY-ONE

"There's a foot for every shoe,
a hat for every head
And an ass for every saddle."

—*MIMI*

"You did what?" Mathias stared at me with amusement.

"I told them all I was seeing someone." I paid close attention to the off-white wall behind his head. It was a Thursday evening, and we were at Hope House for one of Stella's weekly meetings for volunteers, and apparently, I was now an official volunteer. After Mathias begged me to come back to help with another class, I'd found myself looking forward to it.

Plus, Bria and I had forged a friendship. Maybe friendship wasn't the right word. More of a grudging respect for each other. We'd emailed each other back and forth in the beginning and she'd asked me questions about job applications and advice on interviews. Before long, I was volunteering to help her study for her high school equivalency test to get her GED. In fact, after this meeting, we would be getting together for a torture—er, tutoring session.

Stella shoved a flyer in my hand and then one in Mathias's. I studied it. "Bowling night fundraiser?"

But Mathias wasn't distracted. He leaned closer and whispered, "You lied?"

"I wasn't planning on saying it. It sort of slipped out."

His shoulders shook as he tried to rein in his laughter.

I scowled. "Hey, best friend, you aren't supposed to laugh at me." I pointed at the front of the room where Stella now stood. "Pay attention."

Meetings at Hope House were quick and dirty. Stella didn't like to lecture. She called them "weekly status reports", and strongly recommended all volunteers and any of the ladies who could make it attend.

"One of the women's uncles owns a bowling alley, and he's giving us fifty per cent profit. We can always use money." She jammed her ever-present clipboard under her arm and flicked up a finger as she listed off our deficits. "I have a waitlist a mile long for tutoring, employment counseling, parenting classes, food pantry, all of it. You name it, we could use more of it."

As she explained the details, Mathias leaned over and whispered, "You're a terrible liar. No way your mom bought it."

"She's texted or called me at least twenty-three times a day to remind me she can't wait to meet him." I dropped my forehead to the tabletop. "I told them it was my neighbor."

Stella rapped her knuckles on the same table and raised her voice. "So, invite all your friends. Invite people you don't like. I don't care, as long as they pay."

But Mathias was undeterred. "The construction worker with the kid? I'm sure Roberta is having heart palpitations as we speak."

I groaned. "I haven't even told her that part and anyway, it doesn't matter because I'm not actually dating him."

The door creaked and heavy footsteps crossed the room. I didn't even lift my head. "Hi, Bria."

"What's wrong with you?" she asked as she sprawled in the chair next to me.

"Yes, what is wrong? Please share with all of us," Stella said, arching a dark eyebrow.

"She made up a pretend boyfriend and now her mom wants to meet him," Mathias announced, drawing more than a few chuckles.

I smacked his shoulder. "Shut up!"

Bria snorted. "I know some guys I could hook you up with. My assistant manager at work just got his car out of impound this week and his license is only suspended for another couple of months."

At least someone could joke about this.

"Now that we've gotten all that taken care of, I have a couple of announcements and then you can be on your way." Stella studied her clipboard. "The bathroom on the east side of the building is closed forever, or until I can find a plumber willing to do a little pro bono work. We'll see which one comes first."

Mathias bumped me with his shoulder. "Hey, maybe your new boyfriend can fix pipes. Isn't he good with his hands?"

I shot him a dirty look.

"And last..." Stella said, with a dirty look of her own directed at Mathias. "Ladies, if you haven't turned in your progress reports, I need them by end of day tomorrow. Thank you, volunteers, for all your help. Hope House keeps going because of you all. And that's as sappy as I get."

With that, she stomped out of the room and almost everyone followed. I rose to escape while I could, but a hand clamped on my arm and pulled me back into my seat.

"We had a deal anyway," Mathias said. "You're not

supposed to be dating at all this year. The resolutions. Remember them?"

I hadn't. With a mental note to worry about this whole boyfriend situation later, maybe after I moved to a houseboat on a Caribbean island under an assumed name, I straightened. "And what about your resolution?"

The look on his face could only be described as uncomfortable. His eyes cut to Bria and then back to me. "Can we talk about this later?"

Bria folded her arms and settled into her chair. "Don't mind me. Go ahead."

Mathias sighed. "I kissed her."

"Who?"

"Phee. I kissed Phee."

"You did? When? I thought the plan was to fall out of love with her." Although, if I were honest, I wanted just the opposite for Phee and Mathias. I thought they were kind of perfect for each other. Except for the part about her being engaged to someone else.

"Wait, who's Phee?" Bria asked.

"My sister," I said.

"Her sister," Mathias said at the same time. "We met to talk about engagement photos, and I kissed her."

I fell back in the chair. "What did she do?"

"She slapped me." He looked so hang-dog miserable at those words, I wanted to hug him.

"Daaaamn," Bria whistled. I shot her a quelling look, and she lifted a shoulder. "Sorry, but dude got shot down."

"That's why you wouldn't come to my birthday dinner, isn't it?"

Mathias's fingers sliced through his hair. "I thought it might be... awkward."

"I guess so." I sighed. "Phee is an idiot—"

"Yeah, but she's someone else's idiot."

"—and she's going to marry Joel Allen and you're gonna miss your chance. Maybe you should tell her how you feel. It might make a difference."

He scoffed. "I don't want to talk about this."

Ignoring him, I cupped his shoulders. "She's about to make a huge mistake and you're going to let her. You're always the one giving me pep talks about being true to myself and all that, but it seems like you don't believe a word of it."

"She's going to turn me down," he said, his voice soft.

"I'm with Perci on this one." Bria nodded and stood, slinging her backpack behind her. "I'll wait for you in the study room."

Mathias and I watched her leave before I spoke. "Maybe. Probably. But you have to try. If it doesn't work out, at least you tried."

He blinked. "When did you become so full of wisdom?"

"New Perci says what she's thinking. She goes with her gut. It's kind of nice." I smiled and stood, pressing an affectionate kiss to the top of his head. "You should try it one of these days."

TWENTY-TWO

"Three can keep a secret,
if you're willing to murder two of 'em."

—*MIMI*

Later in the week, Mimi and my mother showed at my door.

"Oh, good, you're home," my mother said. "I worried you might be on a date with, what is his name? Nelson? Nick? Is that it?"

"Nate."

"That's right. I'm not sure why I can't remember his name."

I barely contained my eye roll at that comment. She remembered his name perfectly.

"I tried to stop her," Mimi said as she followed my mother inside. "I swear I did. I wanted to stop at the Walmart and see about getting a new push-up bra, but your mom doesn't like when I talk about lingerie."

I closed the door slowly and smacked my head against it, once, twice. *Suck it up, Perci.*

"Persephone, is this your dinner? A grown woman eating

cereal with marshmallows. Really?"

With a sigh, I stumbled down the hallway and found my mother hovering over my half-eaten bowl of Lucky Charms. I wisely chose not to tell her I'd planned on having a popsicle for dessert. "So, here you are... in my apartment. Surprise."

"I gotta tinkle. Be right back." Mimi made her way to the bathroom.

Mom perched on the edge of the couch. "Your grandmother had a doctor's appointment, so I drove her."

"Could have gone on my own," Mimi yelled from the bathroom.

"Please. Someone needs to take care of you."

"Yeah. Me. Get your own life."

Annoyance scribbled on her face, Mom turned back to me. "Can you imagine her driving in Houston? Terrifying. Anyway, we were in the neighborhood"—they were most definitely nowhere close to my neighborhood—"and thought we'd stop in."

I sat down on the couch opposite her and waited.

She smoothed a hand down her pants. "How are things with work?"

"Excellent."

Her eyes studied my face. "You seem to enjoy working there."

"I love it. The kids are fun, Miss Marge is great. I think I finally found something I'm good at."

Mom folded her hands in her lap, and I could see her fingers turn white as she squeezed them together. I knew whatever came next was the real reason she was here.

"I still don't see how there's any kind of future in being a preschool teacher. I appreciate this period of fancifulness, but you're almost thirty. Why don't you go back to work with your father? The mortgage business may not be your heart's desire, but sometimes we do things because they're the right thing to do, even if we don't want to. Besides, your father misses you."

I squirmed under her sharp, dark eyes, but I held my ground. "I'm not going back to Mayfield."

"Persephone, really. I've never known you to be this selfish."

"Mom."

She snapped her mouth shut at whatever she heard in my voice. "Fine. I hope this job of yours is the right decision."

Mimi appeared from the hallway. "Nice toilet paper you got there, Perci. Always get the good stuff for your lady bits."

"Mama!"

"Bobbie Jo."

With a scowl, my mother said, "Do you know she asked the doctor what was the going trend in sexually transmitted diseases for seniors these days?"

"Got a bunch of free condom samples from her too," Mimi said with a wink. "I'm on a fixed income, you know."

"I have such a headache. I wonder why?" Mom rubbed her forehead and glared at Mimi. "Is your ibuprofen still in the cabinet by the refrigerator?"

"Yes, Mom."

"What's this?" She called from the kitchen a moment later. She was pointing at a flyer I'd hung on the refrigerator—on top of that annoying list of anti-resolutions—for the Hope House bowling night.

"A fundraiser for a place I've been helping with."

"Oh, what sort of place?" Her voice was infinitely polite.

I hesitated. "Hope House. They provide all kinds of services to help women get back on their feet." That wasn't exactly the whole truth, but I was worried about what my mother's reaction would be. Bria had sort of taken root in my heart, and I bristled at anyone judging her or the rest of the women at Hope House.

"I've always said it's important to give back when we can." She hurried over to her purse and pulled out her day planner. I had to admit she had always been willing to help in the community—PTA, donations, fundraising, etc. She could organize a bake sale with her hands tied behind her back. "And I want to support you. I'm penciling it in right now."

I blinked. "Penciling in what?"

"The bowling night."

Trepidation pooled in my stomach. "Do you even bowl?"

"Sign me up too," Mimi said from the living room.

"You all don't have to go."

"I never do anything I don't want to do," Mimi said. "And besides, you know I like to bowl."

"It's settled then." Mom smiled and snapped her planner shut. "I'll be able to see how you're spending your time and help out a good cause. Don't worry, I'll tell Phee."

Phee, too? What was happening?

A few days later, I was still trying to figure out how my entire family had invited themselves to this bowling night when Lilah stumbled upon me inviting Amanda at work. It was Lilah who decided on the spot she wanted to go bowling too. And it was Lilah who asked Nate the minute he picked her up.

"Please, can we go, Daddy?" she asked, playing it up with those big brown eyes.

"It'll be pretty boring. Just a bunch of grown-ups," I said.

Nate gave her a time-honored parental response. "We'll see."

Everyone knew that was code for, *Not a chance.*

I sighed in relief. I already had to juggle my mother, my sister, and my grandmother on Friday night; I couldn't risk my pretend boyfriend who was my real next-door neighbor and didn't know he was my pretend boyfriend popping up too.

That would be awkward. Embarrassing. Ridiculous. A complete failure on so many levels.

So, of course, that was exactly what happened.

TWENTY-THREE

"A good man's hard to find and even harder to keep."

—MIMI

Main Street Bowling Alley sat on the corner of a once-busy thoroughfare; the area, like the building, a little worn out. I showed up early to help Stella set up an information table for Hope House in front of the eight lanes reserved for our event.

"I think that pretty much says it all." I pointed at the sign Stella had hung on the front of the table which read, DONA-TIONS WELCOME. DON'T BE A CHEAPSKATE.

Five minutes later, Mathias found me nursing a Diet Coke, and he wasn't alone. With him stood a Marilyn Monroe looka-like who I later learned once held the title of Miss Cheese Festival and was a current Miss Wisconsin hopeful. Her name was Olivia.

"Is Phee here yet?" Mathias asked.

I side-eyed him as he ran fingers through his hair and fiddled with the collar of his button-down. "Why?"

"No reason."

I hummed and slurped my soda.

Olivia leaned on his arm. "Let's go get our bowling shoes, Matty."

Matty? I mouthed.

With a shrug, Mathias let her lead him away. After that, things got busy. A couple of carloads of Hope House women arrived, Bria one of them. Neon green shot through her hair now, accented by oversized hoop earrings. With a chin lift in greeting, she slunk by and settled at one of the lanes.

Phee arrived next, Joel Allen trailing behind her. "Joel wanted to tag along. Hope that's okay."

I wanted to scream it was not okay, but I smiled instead and introduced them to Stella, who didn't seem all that impressed with their local celebrity and assigned them to the same lane as Mathias.

"I can handle this. Go mingle," Stella said, waving me off.

I slid into a seat next to Phee. Joel Allen sat beside her, a glass of beer in his hand. He raised it in Mathias's direction and with exaggerated movements, wrapped an arm around Phee's shoulders. Mathias played with a loose tendril of Miss Cheesehead's hair, his smile bright.

"How are the wedding plans going?" Mathias asked.

Phee laced her fingers with Joel Allen's and set their hands on the table. A band of light hit her engagement ring and made it sparkle. Joel Allen shot Mathias a grin that showed too many teeth.

"They're fine," Phee said. "After you decided you couldn't do the photography, we found someone else."

"She's done several celebrity weddings before," Joel Allen said, swigging back his beer.

My head swiveled in Mathias's direction. "You quit?"

He shrugged, but the high color in his cheeks belied his attempt at appearing nonchalant. "Creative differences."

Joel Allen smirked.

I wanted to grill Mathias further, but his eyes begged me to do the exact opposite. Besides, my mother and Mimi took that moment to arrive in a flurry of sequins—Mimi's shirt may have had a former life as a stage costume for a Vegas showgirl—and pinched looks—my mother's reaction to wearing *used* shoes.

Mom kissed my cheek. "You look very... colorful."

Mimi marched between us. "I do like those earrings, darling. You get them from the flea market?"

Mom snapped her mouth closed and took a fortifying breath before continuing. "They are lovely."

Lovely?

Mimi nodded, a glint of satisfaction in her eye. "That's what I thought too."

"Thank you?"

"Of course." With a stiff smile, Mom greeted Phee and Joel Allen. "I suppose I must get a pair of shoes now. Used shoes. The things I do for my children." She shuddered and drifted to the counter.

I tugged on Mimi's arm. "What was that about?"

"We had a little talk. She might be trying to keep her comments to herself a bit more." She patted my cheek with a ring-laden hand. "Now, who's ready to bowl?"

A little voice yelled, "Me!" seconds before a slight body slammed into mine. But I wasn't looking down, my eyes focused on the person standing right in front of me: Nate.

"Lies are like cockroaches and the White Pages," Mimi liked to say. "They might be useless, but they'll never go away."

As usual, she was right. For example, my lie was currently smiling at my mother and shaking her hand.

"You told me Nate wasn't coming," Mom said. "And who is this little one we have here?" That last statement was a question loaded with all kinds of things I didn't want to deal with.

"Whoops," Mathias muttered behind me.

I waved at Nate. "You came, and you've met my mom."

"I remembered about the bowling, and I asked and asked and asked until Daddy said yes," Lilah said. With a toothy grin, she adjusted her Wonder Woman headband.

"Daddy?" Mom repeated, one eyebrow crawling upward against all Botox odds.

"Mom, everyone, this is Nate and his daughter, Lilah." I introduced everyone else, their faces varying degrees of curiosity and amusement.

"I see," Mom said in a tone that told me she saw way more than she wanted to. She turned to Nate. "Why don't you join our game? We're about to start another."

"No!" I said, my voice attracting the attention of anyone within a five-mile radius. With a nervous chuckle, I continued in what I hoped sounded like the voice of a completely composed person whose heart wasn't threatening to combust. "I mean, Nate probably just wanted to stop by and say hi. I'm sure he—"

Nate shook his head, his smile confused. "We came to bowl."

"Great." *No, not great.* "I'll help you pick out a ball. Lilah, stay here and talk to Mimi." I didn't give him a second to reply. Instead, I marched over and grabbed his hand. If he was surprised, he didn't show it. I dragged him far, far away from my family. We stopped by the racks of bowling balls lined against the back wall.

"Everything okay?" Nate asked, his eyebrows slashes of concern.

"I can't believe you're here. Why are you here?"

"I thought you invited us?"

"You weren't supposed to come. You said, 'We'll see,' and every kid in America knows that's code for, 'Not a chance.'"

"You know Lilah. She wouldn't let it go." He paused. "I still don't understand why it's such a big deal."

Oh, God. I was going to have to say this. Out loud. To his face.

My cheeks burned. "This is so embarrassing." I shoved a thumb toward my family. Mom crossed her arms. Mathias shook his head. "They think we're a thing."

Nate's head dipped. "What? You're whispering, I can't hear you."

The next breath overfilled my lungs to the point of pain. "My family thinks we're dating."

A hand settled on my shoulder, and I tried hard to ignore how warm it felt. He didn't reply. I wondered what we looked like, our heads close together like this, eyes locked. To my family, we might even look like we knew each other intimately.

"Why do they think that?"

I selected a bowling ball randomly from the wall and hefted it into his arms. He caught it with ease. "I maybe told them we were."

No reply. Just a twitch at the corner of his mouth.

"No good?" I pointed at the ball before taking it back and circling him to inspect the balls on the other side of the wall. "You might remember around New Year's, my boyfriend dumped me for concert tickets. Then I quit my job, which is also the family business, and my mom hated that. I just couldn't take it anymore. So, I threw my Spanx on the meatloaf and I lied and said you were my boyfriend. It just slipped out, I swear." I glanced at him, expecting to see anger on his face. Instead, I saw what looked like curiosity. "I thought no one would ever find out.

"Plus, you've seen my sister. She's kind of perfect. Smart, beautiful, successful, engaged, blah, blah, blah. She's younger than me and I don't have any of those things. I mean, my life isn't bad. I have friends and a great fish and a job I like, but I wanted for my mom to not think of me as such a failure."

I found a fifteen-pounder and hoisted it with both hands. "Here. Try this one."

He took it from me, his fingers brushing mine, and it felt like he'd meant to do that. Which was dumb since I was in the middle of what had to be the most embarrassing moment of my life, and that included the time I walked into my second period class in seventh grade with my skirt tucked inside my underwear. Or the time I'd accidentally walked into the men's bathroom at a Christmas Eve service and got an eyeful of the youth pastor. Or the time I'd face-planted it at my college graduation ceremony.

I couldn't look at him, so I crossed my arms and glanced toward the lane. Lilah waved, and I returned it. "It was stupid and I'm sorry I involved you and I will go over there right now and admit the whole thing to them. I understand if you never want to see my face again."

Slowly, he set the ball back on the shelf. The clink of it fitting into place sounded impossibly loud. This was it. This was when he told me off, and I had to take it. He stared down at me for a long moment, his eyes unreadable, and then something seemed to click. He smiled.

"All right. Let's do it."

"W... what?" I stammered.

"I'll play along."

"No. No, you can't do that."

He tucked a bowling ball under one arm. "We'll play it light and easy. Lilah doesn't need to get confused by all this."

"But why? Why would you do this?"

Grinning, he grabbed my hand and tugged me back toward the group of gawking family and friends. "Why not?"

. . .

Nate proved to be an exceptional fake boyfriend. He stood firm against my mother's daunting interrogation. Although she walked a fine line between politeness and wanting to bleed him dry of information, he kept his answers simple and evasive.

"It's new. We're not telling Lilah right now," he explained, while she was out of earshot.

Mom bought every word.

It was impressive.

As was the way he sat beside me most of the night and played the part of my attentive boyfriend with award-winning realism. How the weight of his arm rested on my shoulders or how my head fit perfectly in the crook of his neck. I remember he kissed me on the corner of my forehead two times when Lilah wasn't looking, and my mother was.

In fact, everyone bought it.

When Phee made fun of my throw, it was Nate who volunteered to help me with my stance.

"What are you doing?" I asked as he stood behind me, barely a breath of air between us.

He trailed his hand down until it rested on top of mine. I shivered. "I'm helping you. It's all in the wrist."

"But you don't need to do this." I sounded like I'd just finished a 5K in record time.

"Yeah, but your throw is really bad," he said, leaning a little closer so his breath skated across my ear. "I'm doing this as a service to the bowling ball."

Danged if I didn't bowl a spare that turn either.

Nate was so good at this, I had to remind *myself* it wasn't real. He was putting on an act, being kind so I wouldn't embarrass myself in front of my family and friends. He was a good guy, a gentleman, a neighbor, a knight in shining armor.

On the other hand, Joel Allen and Mathias seemed to be entrenched in some unspoken competition but with bowling balls. When Mathias destroyed him by over fifty points, Joel

Allen swore and shoved his hands in his pockets. "I need another drink."

"Great idea," Mimi said. "Bring us back some pizza."

"Olivia and I are going to go check out the arcade in the back. I'm on a winning streak. Lilah, you want to come too?" Mathias winked at the crowd, threaded his arms through theirs and the three strolled away.

Mimi plopped in a seat and propped her feet on the chair next to her. Using a cup of ice water on the table, she dabbled drops on her chest. "Hotter than hell in July in this place, doncha think?"

Scowling, Mom sat across from Mimi. "Mama, could you please get your feet off the chair? We are in public." She shot Nate a pointed look. "And we have company."

"'We are in public,'" Mimi repeated in a fair mimicry. "It's a bowling alley, Bobbie Jo. Relax. Besides," she winked at Nate, "our guest might be family someday. Young man, you do look like you work out." She reached for his arm and Nate obligingly flexed it. "Oh, my."

"You like that? I got another one right here," he said with a grin and flexed his other arm, the one right next to me.

"Perci, give that a feel," Mimi said.

I hesitated, unsure where feeling up my fake boyfriend fell on the list of acceptable actions when on a fake date.

Nate nudged my shoulder. "Go ahead. I don't bite."

So, I did. He was solid, lean but muscly and warm under his t-shirt. All those hours doing construction-y things in the hot Texas sun, getting all hot and sweaty...

"Nice," I said, much too loud, and snatched my hand away.

"Strong genes, this one. Strong genes make good babies," Mimi said.

I choked on the sip of soda. *Good God.* Before she had us married with two kids and a dog, I waved Bria over. "I want you to meet someone."

"I do like your hair," Mimi said, eyeing Bria with interest. "You think I could do something like that?"

My mother ignored her and shook Bria's hand. I imagined her taking a tally of Bria's tattoos and piercings, the way her t-shirt was a size too small and her shorts a hair too short. "It's nice to meet you. How do you know Persephone?"

"Persephone?" Nate whispered with a chuckle. "Where did that come from?"

"Never mind," I muttered, eyes on the scene in front of me.

"Through Hope House," Bria said.

Mom's head tilted to the side. "Now, what is Hope House exactly?"

"They help us integrate back into society."

"Where were you before?"

With an exaggerated sigh, Bria cocked a hip. "Prison. Didn't *Persephone* tell you any of this?"

Only those who knew the signs would have noticed the way my mother's eyes narrowed just so, the way her hand curled around the edge of the table, the way the corners of her mouth tightened. "No, she did not."

Joel Allen slid a pizza on the table. "One more coming and drinks, too."

"You look familiar," Bria said, squinting at him. I bit back a smile. She knew exactly who he was. I'd told her all about my family.

Beaming, Joel Allen preened under the attention. "You might have seen me—"

"You that guy who wears the pizza outfit and waves at people on the street?"

Joel Allen's smile deflated, and he sputtered around for his words. "No, I'm the anchor for KKRE."

At my side, Nate snorted.

"Bria, why don't you stay, have a bite?" my mother offered, ever polite.

"Nah, that's okay. I have to get back to our game. Nice to meet you all." She backed away from the table, catching my eye with a smirk.

Mathias, Olivia, and Lilah wandered back in time to eat with us. We divvied up the pizza. Mom passed.

"Three hundred calories a slice," she said, and sent a knowing look in my direction.

"Good point, Roberta," Joel Allen said, aiming a look of his own at my sister.

"I'll take two pieces," I said, holding up my plate, doing my best to ignore my mother's frown.

With a smile, Nate obliged me. "Let me know if you need more when you finish those."

See? Top-quality fake boyfriend material. And he hadn't left my side once. Along with keeping up our charade, it made it impossible for my mother to get him, or me, alone. I needed to be careful. I could get used to this.

"Well, I'm going to see if this establishment has anything resembling a salad." Mom stood and drifted off to the concession stand.

"Since you're all here and Mom already knows, I can tell you the good news," Phee said, pushing her uneaten pizza aside. "Guess who's in the running to get a permanent anchor position?"

Mimi hooted, loud enough for more than a few heads to turn our way. "That's my girl."

"The position will be open sometime this fall. Chuck called me in today to talk about it."

"You'll get it." Mathias shot her a small, congratulatory smile. Phee met his eyes and her cheeks pinked. For a moment, they both seemed to forget anyone else was around them.

"Now, it's not a done deal," Joel Allen said, selecting another piece of pizza like it was a prom date. "Don't want to get your hopes up."

Phee frowned. "Chuck said I was a shoo-in."

"Things happen." He flashed his news anchor smile, all white teeth and lies. "Besides, there are a lot of things going on in our lives right now. Maybe a change at work isn't a good idea."

Phee crossed her arms. "I guess we'll see."

Soon after, Nate announced he had to get Lilah home for bed. I walked with the two of them to the shoe return counter and waited while Lilah ducked into the bathroom next door.

"I can't thank you enough for tonight. I think they actually bought it," I said when we were alone.

"You think so?"

"Totally. In a few weeks, I'll make sure we break up. And don't worry, it will be all my fault." That wouldn't be hard to manufacture. Plus, I would have an excuse to eat more ice cream and Mom would buy it without blinking an eye. Win-win-win.

Nate raised an eyebrow. "I'm just not sure your grand-mother believes us."

I snorted. "Are you kidding? Mimi might cry when we split."

"But just in case," he said.

The back of his hand brushed my cheek. I startled.

"Are they looking?" He gently turned me to face him.

"Who?"

"Your family. Are they looking?" He cupped my cheek, spearing my eyes with his. I glanced over his shoulder.

"Yes," I said, my voice a little breathless.

He smiled. "Good."

And then, right there in the middle of Main Street Bowling Alley under the prying eyes of my family, friends, and most of Hope House, Nate Russo kissed me.

TWENTY-FOUR

*"All a woman needs is a man who treats her like an angel
and kisses like the Devil."*

—*MIMI*

On my list of Things I Did Not Want to Do on a Saturday morning, wedding dress shopping with Momzilla-of-the-Bride was number one. But as I was now avoiding Nate for the rest of my natural life, this seemed like a solid choice. Although it put me right in the crosshairs of my mother. It was a lose-lose situation all around.

"Persephone, what in heavens are you wearing?" my mother demanded as soon as I arrived.

With a frown, I glanced down at the bright yellow peasant top and light-wash jeans. "Clothes?"

Scowling, Mom patted her pale pink blouse, certainly raw silk. "It's not really appropriate attire for wedding dress shopping."

"There's a dress code for wedding dress shopping? I might have to elope."

Not really. I'd always imagined a ceremony in a small church in the country. Instead of a fussy veil, I'd wear a flower crown which my mother would hate, but I would insist on, anyway.

Mother stalked around me and settled into one of the three throne-like chairs covered in ivory satin. "You will not. You know it would break my heart and you wouldn't do that to me."

She was right. I wouldn't do that to her, no matter how angry she made me. I loved her. Maybe that was the point of family. They drove you insane and you loved them, anyway.

"Besides, the Ackersons' daughter... What is her name?"

"Missy?"

"Yes, Missy. She eloped last month. To some gaudy 24-hour drive-thru chapel in Las Vegas. Can you imagine?"

"Oh, I'm sure—"

"Just broke Donna Ackerson's heart. And she married a *mechanic*." She leaned toward me, her eyes taking on the shine that indicated she had gossip and wasn't afraid to use it.

"Mechanic isn't a dirty word."

She ignored me. "I know things like this happen, but your father and I have always impressed upon you girls to make good choices. That's why I stayed home with you, so I could raise you right. I bet Donna Ackerson is wishing she'd stayed home about now."

"Isn't Donna Ackerson a pediatrician?"

"I could have been a pediatrician or a lawyer, but you girls always came first."

A pounding began to take up space in my head as she kept on, enumerating the ways in which she could have made different life choices but gave it all up for Phee and me. Such a martyr. So selfless. So... so... Mom.

When Phee arrived, I took in her full face of make-up, carefully styled hair, pale pink tailored suit, and spiky matching heels. She resembled Newscaster Barbie à la 1986, and I didn't mean that in a good way.

"Wow. That's... an outfit," I said.

Phee glanced down at herself. "Joel picked it out. He said it was a classic."

I stared.

"Is it bad?" Her fingers fussed with a strand of pearls at her neck. Pearls! Was she a sixty-five-year-old grandmother? Actually, Mimi would die before wearing pearls. "Joel says pink is a good color for the camera."

"Joel has a good eye," Mom said.

Our consultant appeared seemingly out of thin air. Her nametag read Sandra, which she pronounced Saaaan-dra, and she was dressed in head-to-toe black. Mom and Phee rounded up several dresses and Phee skipped to the back of the store, slipping behind a heavy white door.

My phone vibrated with a text.

Mathias: *How's it going?*

Me: *Fine*

No response.

I sat in one of the thrones and sipped on a complimentary mimosa—eighty-nine calories for the whole glass. Mother-approved. Beside me, my mom's eyes bore into the side of my head.

"This man you're seeing. The one with the child. What was his name? Norm?"

My foot stalled half-swing and settled on the ground. "Nate."

"Tell me about him. What does he do for a living?"

"Don't worry, he's not a mechanic. He's in real estate development." Construction was basically the same thing, right?

Mom hummed. "Is this a serious relationship?"

Sandra interrupted before I could figure out a reply. "Attention, please. Time for the first dress."

Phee glowed in a mermaid-style dress, strapless with a princess neckline. Tears glistened in the corners of Mom's eyes. A small pedestal stood in the middle of three giant mirrors. Phee climbed atop it. Her hands shook as she smoothed them over her stomach.

My phone buzzed again.

Mathias: *Is she trying on dresses?*

Me: *You want me to send pictures?*

Three little dots appeared and then disappeared.

Face glowing, Phee turned and spread her arms out. "Do you like it?"

Mom stood and circled Phee, angling her head this way and that. "I don't know about the drop waist. You can do better."

"You think so?" Phee glanced in the mirror. "I kind of liked it."

Sandra stepped in. "We have lots of options. Let's go try something else on." She whisked Phee off for round two.

"Try on that ballgown next," Mom called. She stood and wandered the racks nearby for a few minutes before stopping in front of a particularly princess-y dress. "I always wanted a ballgown, you know."

"Why didn't you?"

She made her way back to the chair and sat. "Oh, it was a different time. Your father was finished with school, and we were in a hurry to move to Houston for his job. Mimi couldn't afford a big wedding, anyway. It was a justice of the peace for us."

"Seemed to work out okay though," Phee said, floating into the room in a confection of a dress. The bottom swayed like a bell as she climbed onto the pedestal. Sandra fussed with the tulle underneath and placed a headpiece with a long lace veil on her head.

"Of course it did. Thirty years in September."

Phee gasped. "What if you had a big anniversary party this year? We could do it for you."

Wait. *We?*

"It would take some planning." She turned, the veil twisted, and Sandra muttered under her breath as she straightened it. "We could use Mom and Dad's house. It's perfect for entertaining. We'd take care of everything."

"You girls don't have time to plan something like this," Mom said, but her eyes gleamed. "Phoebe, you have a wedding coming up, and you're busy with work. And Persephone..." My mother, sister, and Sandra all turned to stare at me. "Well, you have your life."

And a fish and a fake boyfriend, thank you very much.

I wiggled in my seat and eyed the entire pitcher of mimosa longingly. It wasn't hard to see where this was going. And it was not good.

"Perci, you *could* do it. I would help, of course, but you could kind of be in charge." Phee stepped off the pedestal; Sandra tsked and grabbed for the veil.

"I could?"

"This will be wonderful." Phee threw her arms around my shoulders. Behind her, Sandra squawked as the dress dragged on the floor.

"Phee." I fought through seven hundred yards of tulle to whisper in her ear. "This is a terrible idea."

"Oh, it'll be fine," she said. "It will get her thinking about something besides this wedding."

Panic throbbed in my brain at the whole idea of planning a party for my parents. I'd screw it up somehow. Pick the wrong flowers or order the wrong appetizer. The tablecloths might not match the china.

"Do you mean it?" Mom squealed. "Oh, I have the best daughters in the world."

The part of me that longed to please my mother perked up at her words. Maybe I could do this. Phee and my mother seemed to have confidence in me.

New Perci smirked. New Perci wasn't daunted. New Perci wasn't scared of messing up.

"This dress does nothing for your figure. Sandra, next, please," Mom said.

Sandra bobbed her head and ushered Phee back to the wilds of the dressing room.

Mom perched on the edge of her chair and rubbed her hands together. "Oh, this will be amazing. We can have hors d'oeuvres and rent linens. And I can make your father get a new suit, finally."

I downed the rest of my mimosa in one gulp, swallowing the strange urge to laugh with it.

Mom left us two hours later to take Pericles to a pedicure appointment, so Phee and I decided to grab a quick lunch at our favorite pho restaurant close by.

"All right, Mom's gone. Tell me all about Nate. I want details. Like what's he like in—"

"Maybe we should order?" I examined my menu with the sort of intensity reserved for the gazes of brain surgeons and teenage boys at the beach. "It looks like it's busy here. Could take a while."

"There's only three other people here. I think we're safe." She grinned. "So, Nate. Not at all what I expected."

I was pretty sure I knew what she expected. "Why?

Because he doesn't have a dad-bod and belong to the Star-Wars-Figurine-of-the-Month Club?"

She let out one of her *Oh Perci* sighs, but she didn't deny it. "Nate does not look like a guy who owns figurines. I can tell he's totally into you. He adores you."

I bit back a groan. I should just tell her. Rip the band-aid off and get it over with. It was just that this secret made me sound so pathetic. Despite his Oscar-worthy performance, the truth was, Nate didn't adore me. He had been kind when I'd thrown this mess at him, and that was all. "I think adore is kind of a strong word."

"Trust me. He likes you a lot."

I knew I should put an end to all this lying. It wasn't good for me. But did I listen to myself? "It probably won't work out or anything. You know me and relationships."

"What does that mean?"

"Just that I never quite seem to meet expectations somehow. Look how it worked out with Brent."

"Nate is not Brent. I know I only spent a couple of hours with him, but it's pretty obvious." She placed a hand on my arm. "Any guy would be lucky to have you. You're sweet, kind, smart, funny. You bake stuff and like kids, and people feel comfortable around you."

I side-eyed her. "They do?"

"Duh." She rolled her eyes. "Besides, it's not about whether some guy wants you. It's whether you want him."

"That's easy to say when you're a ten-foot-tall beauty queen."

"Tell Mimi that. Can you imagine her waiting around to see if some guy decides she's worth his time?" She was right. Mimi would never put herself in a position where a man called the shots.

The waitress stopped at our table and asked if we were ready to order. I pounced on the chance to change the subject.

After she left, I pulled out a notepad from my purse and launched into a lengthy discussion about appetizers for the anniversary party.

"Oh, I had an idea," Phee said. "It would be fun to make a slide show of Mom and Dad through the years and play it at the party on a loop. We could look through all those family photo albums. Mimi must have photos too."

"And by *we*, you mean *me?*"

Phee grinned. "Exactly."

I snorted.

"Do you really think this outfit looks bad?" She adjusted the lapel of her Pepto-Bismol pink suit.

"I wouldn't say bad." Awful would be more accurate.

"Joel insisted it was the right image. Professional but feminine." Her shoulders slumped.

"Hey," I said, touching her hand. "Everything okay?"

"Sometimes it feels like Joel doesn't know me at all. Like this outfit." She bit the corner of her mouth with uncertainty, an emotion I'd never associated with my sister. "You know what else he told me? He thinks once we have kids, I'm going to quit my job. I'm only twenty-four. I don't even know if I want children. And I sure as heck am not devoting my life to them." She shivered. "Can you imagine becoming Mom?"

It was another bullet point on my list of Reasons Why Phee Should Not Marry Joel Allen.

Phee paused and looked at me expectantly. Old Perci was a listener, a sympathizer. I was the one who hummed and yes'ed and of course'd my way through conversations. I'd always pushed my instincts to the side, second-guessed myself, deferred to my mother, who surely knew best. What would she say if I spoke up?

New Perci would speak up.

Phee refolded her napkin and set it on the table. "Anyway, thanks for listening."

"Maybe he's not the right person for you," I blurted.

"What?"

"You're a different person when you're around him."

"What do you mean?"

I took a fortifying breath. "You let him answer questions for you, you wear different clothes. Heck, you barely eat when he's around. You're different, and not in a good way. That whole 'you make me a better person?' It's the opposite when you're with him. Look, I know I'm not the kind of sister you come to for advice. My life is a mess, right? You were always the one who knew exactly what you wanted, but when you're with Joel, it's like you've lost your way. You're not you and that's sad, because you're amazing."

She said nothing for a long time, her eyes unfocused. So long, I was sure I'd said the exact wrong thing and was already composing an apology in my head.

"You're a good sister, Perci," she said, her smile small and sad.

Then she changed the subject, and I let her.

TWENTY-FIVE

"Always choose kindness.
And two-ply toilet paper."

—*MIMI*

"Sal, which one?" I held up two bottles of nail polish—one a conservative pale pink (very Old Perci), the other electric blue (hello, New Perci).

Sal stared at me with unblinking eyes of love, his fin waving serenely.

"You're right, blue it is." I settled back and painted the first two toes and then admired how the bold color shone against my skin. "I like it."

I needed some pampering after this week. It was only Wednesday, but it was also spring break for the area schools. Miss Marge's had been overrun with school-aged kids off for the holiday and all of us were working double time to keep up with them. Survival week, Miss Marge called it.

"It's these holiday weeks and the summer that keep us afloat the rest of the year," Miss Marge explained.

I'd been helping with the bookkeeping for a few weeks now and she was right. The daycare stayed afloat, but barely. Miss Marge refused to raise her rates.

"Parents need to have good childcare," she'd said when I asked her about it.

Finishing the last toe, I flopped back on the couch and snuggled into my favorite cardigan. A sharp knock sent me hobbling to the door. Through the peephole, Nate came into view. Judging by the tic in his jaw and the agitated way he rubbed the top of his head, he was not happy.

I'm not going to lie—it was a good look on him.

"Just a minute." Pressing my back to the door, I forced myself to take deep breaths to slow my stampeding heart. It had been a few weeks since The Kiss and I'd become expert-level good at avoiding him. The thought of looking him in the eye made me break out in a sweat.

"I think you should just go knock on his door and get it over with like an adult," Mathias had advised. "It was just a kiss."

"Just a kiss, huh?" I'd stared him down. "Fine. I'll do that just as soon as you go knock on Phee's door and get it over with like an adult."

He'd glared at me. "I hate it when you throw my words back at me."

From the other side of the door, Nate said now, "Sorry to bug you."

With one last desperate lurch of my heart, I channeled New Perci, Mimi, and anybody else who'd like to throw her hat in the ring, and opened the door. He looked even angrier without the door between us. My voice squeaked when I spoke. "I know you probably have some questions for me about... about the... the thing. The thing that happened with the thing. I know that was awkward, and I put you in a weird position."

He held up a hand. "It was a—"

"I never expected you to even know about it. Which, I know, doesn't make it any better. In fact, it makes it sound worse. Sometimes I don't think before I say things and my mother knows how to get under my skin."

"I just—"

"I know she loves me, but sometimes it's really hard being her daughter. Anyway, thank you for playing along. You really sold it. I mean, that kiss was... awesome."

Yep, that's what I said.

He huffed a laugh and his eyes, more brown than green today, dropped to my mouth. The memory of that kiss slammed into me. "Do I look like someone who would do anything they didn't want to do?"

A little warm shiver raced down my spine and pooled in my stomach. "No."

"Don't worry about it. But I do have a problem. It's Lilah. She locked me out and I don't have my phone or keys. Can I use your phone to call the manager?"

He hadn't wanted to talk about the kiss at all. Which meant I'd just made a fool of myself. Again. I ignored the feeling of wanting to crawl in a hole and spend my life living with naked mole rats. "Of course. Sure. No problem."

I pulled up the building manager's number on my phone and held it out.

Phone to his ear, his gaze traveled the room before landing on me. I was acutely aware of my zebra-striped pajamas (thank you, Mimi), zero make-up, and messy nest of hair, while he radiated the cool carelessness of James-freaking-Dean in jeans and a white t-shirt.

Did I even have a bra on?

"Yeah, I'll hold." Nate wandered into the kitchen and paused in front of the refrigerator. I casually followed him to see what had caught his attention.

That stupid list of resolutions was still hanging right there for the world to see. Just the thought of him seeing those—the dating one or the one about being more confident. *Oh. My. God.* The weight loss one. He could not read that list. I reached around him and yanked the paper down. His eyes sliced in my direction, a question there.

"That was nothing." I shoved the list into my cardigan pocket. "If you want, I can go talk to Lilah."

He nodded and turned away when someone answered the call.

I padded down the hall and knocked. "Lilah? It's Perci."

After a long moment, a soft voice answered. "Hi."

"Is everything okay? Do you need help or anything?"

A beat. "Where's Daddy?"

"He's in my apartment calling the manager for a key."

Another beat. "Is he mad at me?"

"I don't think he's thrilled."

Something thudded against the door. It sounded suspiciously like a small foot.

"But I bet if you let him in, he'll get over it. I'm sure he's just worried about you." Crouching, I lowered my voice. "Why don't you tell me what's wrong and maybe I can help?" My question was met with silence. I slid to the ground in front of the door. "Okay, you don't have to tell me. Guess what? I saw another cardinal."

"You did?"

"Yep. It was on my back porch when I got home from work. Gave me a funny little look and flew off."

"Does it make you feel happy? When you see it?" Lilah asked.

"Hmm. I've never thought about it. I guess it's kind of comforting."

"Yeah, comforting." Even though I couldn't see her, I imagined her nodding with certainty.

"You want to tell me why you locked your dad out?"

She sighed with feeling. "The babysitter can't come tonight, and Daddy says I have to go with him to school 'cause he has a big test and he has to take it, but it's boring to go there with him."

"Your dad has to take a test? For what?"

"He's working on his Bachelorette degree."

I stifled a laugh. "I see."

"Daddy says school is important, which is why he needs to go. He says he moved to Texas to make a better life for us, and he can't get any distractions."

This only brought more questions to mind. *Not your business, Perci.*

From the corner of my eye, I saw Nate move down the hallway. "You could stay with me tonight. If your dad's okay with it."

"What am I okay with?" Nate stood above me, a fierce wrinkle in his brow.

I rose. "Lilah could stay with me while you take your test. If you don't mind. You wouldn't have to take her with you, and I feel like I owe you for, you know, the thing."

"Could I stay with Miss Perci? Please?" Lilah asked through the door.

A rush of air blew past Nate's lips. "Fine."

Slowly, the door opened and revealed Lilah, dark hair damp, dressed in pink and green pajamas along with her trusty rain boots. She glared at her father. "I don't like how you sounded."

Nate ducked down, meeting her eyes. "I don't like how you locked me out of the apartment, so I'd say we're even."

The two battled each other silently, and it was then I saw a strong resemblance—less in how their faces were formed and more in how they used their faces to form identical mutinous expressions.

With a growl (that may have made my toes curl a little), Nate ducked inside and returned with a backpack slung over his shoulder. "Are you sure you're okay with this? I wouldn't ask, but I have a midterm tonight and I can't miss it."

"It's okay. I don't mind."

He pressed his lips together and rubbed a finger over one of his eyebrows. Finally, decision made, he pulled the door closed and the two of us trailed behind him as he marched down the hallway to my apartment. He stopped and wheeled around to face us.

"Lilah, be good. Listen to Perci. Don't touch anything unless you ask first. Don't ask a million questions. Do not tell her about the mating rituals of storks or whatever, and don't force her to watch any of those nature shows."

Lilah rolled her eyes. "Daddy, please."

With a huff, he turned to me. "Thank you for this. I appreciate it." He handed me his phone and asked me to program my number in. "I'll text you with mine."

"Is there anything else I need to know? Has she eaten dinner?"

"Yeah. A small snack is fine. Nothing to drink after 7:30."

"Is she a gremlin?"

He bit back a smile. "Oh, and... just a second." Dumping his backpack, he jogged down the hallway and ducked back into his apartment. When he returned, he held up a small pouch. "No peanuts. She's allergic. If something happens, do you know how to use an EpiPen?"

I nodded. "All of Miss Marge's employees have been trained."

"Good." Nate hesitated, giving us one last long look.

"We'll be fine," I said with a smile. "I swear."

He heaved his backpack on his shoulder. "This is a huge help. Thank you."

"It's not a big deal. Neighbors help each other out, right?"

With a small smile, he turned and was down the hall by the time I heard Lilah call from inside my apartment.

"Oh, is that a betta fish? Did you know bettas are very smart? You can train them to do tricks and they even recognize faces. Did you know that?"

Smiling, I followed her inside.

TWENTY-SIX

"A friend in need is a friend indeed.
  Especially when it comes with a free meal."

—MIMI

"Mom, I'm pretty sure he has plans," I said. For the fourth time.

I'd spent the morning helping Bria fill out job applications, then done some grocery shopping and baked cookies to take to work the next day. But the siren call of sunshine had been too strong to sit in my air-conditioned apartment.

Now I was enjoying the weather in the small garden area in front of my apartment building. Or I had been until I'd accidentally answered my phone before looking at the caller ID. Rookie mistake.

"What plans could he possibly have on Easter? He has no family here. It's a holiday, so he can't be working," my mother said impatiently. "I think it would be nice to get to know him more. Unless, of course, you're no longer dating."

Yet another opportunity to come clean. Maybe she'd even

forgive me, considering the holiday. I mean, probably not. "I just
don't—"

"Perci!" My head snapped up. Lilah skipped toward me,
Nate a few feet behind. She waved a newspaper in my face.
"Guess what? Duke Crosby is coming on a tour."

"Hold on, Mom." I pressed the phone to my chest. "Duke
Crosby is the bird show guy, right?"

She nodded, her pigtails bouncing. "I want to go meet him
so bad, and Daddy says we could go."

"I said we'd have to see if we can get tickets," Nate said with
a shake of his head.

I pointed at the phone and whispered. "It's my mom.
Sorry."

He nodded and put a hand on Lilah's back. "Let's stop bothering her."

As they walked off, I put the phone back to my ear.

"Did I just hear Lilah and Nate?" Mom asked.

Did she have superhuman hearing too? "Yes, but they're
already gone. So sorry."

"Persephone, I need a head count for lunch, and he was
right there. I don't see what's so difficult about asking him."

"And I already told you, I'm pretty sure they have plans for
Easter."

"I don't understand why a man you're dating wouldn't want
to spend time with your family."

I snorted. "Maybe we can have lunch soon or—" I stopped
when a hand appeared in front of me. My eyes jerked up and
widened when they connected with Nate's. How much of that
had he heard?

"Let me talk to her," Nate said.

I frowned and mouthed, *No, it's fine.*

He did not take the hint. In fact, he sat next to me and
gently pulled the phone from my hand.

"Mrs. Mayfield, how are you?" he said. Into the phone. To my mother. What was happening here?

With a gasp, I tried to take the phone back, which was useless because he was bigger and faster. To deter me, he stood and grinned down at me.

"I don't have any plans for Easter," he said. Then after a beat, "That sounds like fun. Lilah and I would love to come. Can we bring anything?" Another beat. "We'll see you then."

He held the phone out to me. I took it, all the while staring at him like he was an alien. After all, who on earth would volunteer for this torture?

"How hard was that?" Mom said in my ear. "Really, Persephone, sometimes you make things so much harder than they need—"

"Bye, Mom," I said, hanging up while she was still talking. I gawked at Nate. "What did you just do?"

Nate shrugged, still smiling. "We didn't have plans, and I thought I could help you out at the same time. I have to go. Lilah's waiting in the lobby. Let me know the details."

I watched him as he walked away. Yup, an alien. An alien that looked really good in a t-shirt, but still an alien.

"The plan is to eat and get out as soon as possible," I said, leading Nate and Lilah to the front door of my parents' house. A giant springtime wreath covered half of it. In fact, the whole front porch looked like an Easter basket had exploded over it.

"It will be fine." Nate patted my back reassuringly.

I was not reassured. "You don't know these people."

Mom opened the door before we even rang the doorbell.

"Thank you for having us." Nate handed her a bouquet of flowers he may have purchased at the grocery store. It was like giving Martha Stewart store-bought dinner rolls.

"Oh, aren't these lovely," she said politely. It was then she noticed Lilah who, as usual, had been allowed to choose her own outfit. "Well, don't you look... festive."

The rabbit ears wobbled as Lilah took a bow. She was dressed head to toe in a rabbit costume, bushy tail and whiskers included. I'd tried to encourage a dress, but she would have none of it and I'd finally given up trying to convince her otherwise. Someone should be comfortable at this lunch. It sure wasn't going to be me.

"Is lunch ready?" I asked.

"Persephone, really. You just got here." We followed as she led us to the living room where everyone was gathered. Phee waved and Joel Allen gave us a finger gun salute. "Why don't we all relax and visit in here."

Relax. Visit. Sure. Great plan.

"Lilah, I think the Easter bunny left you a little present here." Mom took her hand and led her over to a small colorful basket on a table.

As I began to follow, Nate caught my arm and tugged me back. I turned to face him, struck again by how nice he looked in the pale yellow dress shirt and tie he was wearing. No t-shirt and jeans today. "Smile. It's going to be fine."

I attempted a smile. "I can't believe I put you in this position again. I'm so sorry."

"You didn't do anything. I volunteered, remember?" Absently, he brushed a piece of my hair that had fallen across my cheek.

The touch was small, light, but I felt it everywhere just the same. God, he was really, really good at this fake boyfriend stuff. What would he be like as a real boyfriend? I probably wouldn't be able to withstand it.

"Right. It will be fine."

With a smile, he caught my hand and pulled us further into the room. Toward my family and probably my doom.

. . .

Mimi sat next to Nate at lunch and proceeded to monopolize his time and most of the table's conversation. The few times Mom tried to break in, Mimi steered the discussion right back to safe waters. Honestly, that woman deserved a Nobel Prize for her work in Outsmarting My Mother at Every Turn.

Finally, when Mimi had to refill her wine glass, Mom pounced.

"I have a little announcement, since you're all here. I've decided to go back to work part-time and work with your father. I've found that I have extra time on my hands. What with Phee being busy and Persephone pursuing other ventures..." Mom's smile was a little thin.

What did that mean? *Pursuing other ventures?*

"Nate, Persephone says you work in real estate development? We should get together and talk more about that. I'll be looking for property to invest in."

Nate shot me a confused look. I'm not sure what my face said, probably abject misery, but he smiled and played along. "That sounds great."

"Daddy, what does real state development mean?" Lilah asked, looking up from the book she was reading now that she'd finished eating. My mother had barely contained her comment when Nate had allowed it at the table. "I thought you worked at—"

Nate cut her off. "Lilah, what are you reading about?"

She held up a book about animals. "Did you know a blue whale's tongue weighs as much as a whole elephant?"

"That's fascinating," Daddy said with a chuckle. "Tell me more."

Mom had other plans.

"Girls, I was thinking we need to plan another dress shopping day. I know the perfect dress is out there." She turned to me. "And we need to talk about bridesmaid dresses. Do you think if we got a dress two sizes smaller, you could fit into it in a year? If you really, really tried?"

"Mom!" Phee said, at the same time Mimi shouted, "Bobbie Jo!"

I choked on a bite of ham and grabbed for my water glass but managed to knock my napkin, a knife, and a dinner roll off the table instead. I pushed my chair back and bent over. The biscuit had rolled under the table farther than I could reach. Which is how I found myself sitting under the dinner table during Easter lunch with my family and fake boyfriend.

I covered my face with my hands. This could not be my life.

"Hey, you okay?" It was Nate. Sitting right next to me. Under the table. Anytime the floor wanted to swallow me whole, that would be great. "I usually have to have a lot more alcohol in my system before I end up under a table."

I laughed despite the strong desire to burst into tears.

Mimi and Mom were now arguing about Mom's name change.

"What a mess." I sniffled.

"Come here." Nate wrapped an arm around my shoulders and pulled me to his side.

I sagged against him and took a steadying breath. Warmth radiated through his shirt. "You need to stop being so nice about this." Seriously, my heart couldn't take it.

Now Phee and Joel Allen were arguing about wedding venues.

"I don't mind. Really." He gave my shoulders another squeeze. "So, what's the plan here? Do we grab Lilah and sneak out? I could distract them by throwing brussels sprouts across the room."

I pulled my head away and smiled. Our faces were inches apart and even though the light was dim, I could see the spray of tiny lines at the corners of his eyes and how his eyelashes were thick and straight. How had I ever thought he was un-handsome?

Dad was now trying to calm Mom down.

"Thank you," I whispered.

For just a split second, I swore his eyes dropped to my mouth. "No problem."

Mimi's head appeared under the table. "You two gonna get back up here anytime soon?"

We got back in our seats just in time for Lilah to say, "Did you know kangaroos can't fart?"

TWENTY-SEVEN

"The truth hurts, but it'll heal.

On the other hand, lies tend to cut to the white meat and leave a scar for life."

—*MIMI*

Wednesday evenings soon became my favorite night of the week. Nate had class and needed someone to watch Lilah. I had a wide-open social calendar and, besides, I liked Lilah. We had fun together, baking, watching television, painting our nails, or discussing the many illustrious qualities of whatever bird-of-the-week had caught her eye.

One evening in May, Nate knocked on my door just after dinner to drop Lilah off. Except Lilah wasn't with him.

I leaned out the door and peeked down the hallway. "Where is she?"

"Being hard-headed." Stretching a hand on the wall beside the door, he glared toward his apartment. "Move it, Lilah."

"Not going well?" I asked.

"You know, my mom used to tell me she hoped I had a kid

just like me when I grew up." The door slammed and Lilah stomped down the hallway, arms crossed.

"Oh? You liked birds too?"

The corners of his eyes crinkled. "Not quite. Let's say I was... What's the word? Stubborn?"

"I bet you were just focused."

"No, ornery."

"Determined?"

Nate grinned. "Obstinate. Willful. Mule-like. Cantankerous. Unreasonable. Trouble with a capital T."

Nose in the air, Lilah brushed past us without so much as a hello.

He snapped his fingers. "Oh, I remember. Pigheaded."

"You're rude," Lilah said from the living room.

"I really hate that my mother was right." He put his hands on my shoulders and I ignored the shock that buzzed through me. "You are an angel for watching her. I could kiss you."

"Yes, please. I wouldn't mind at all."

I realized my mistake in an instant. I hadn't thought that; *I'd said it*. Out. Loud. My face went nuclear, and I was pretty sure I was one step away from disintegrating into a pile of burnt ashes and embarrassment. "No, that's not what I meant to say. I meant, I wouldn't mind at all if Lilah came over every day. That's what I meant."

He grinned slowly. His eyes warmed with humor and something else, something that made my stomach flip. It made me wonder what would happen if I leaned in just a little. What would he do? Would he kiss me again?

"Pu-lease," Lilah yelled.

With a wink, he dropped his hands and shuffled around me. What had just happened? *Absolutely nothing. Get it together, Perci.* I fanned my face and took a steadying breath, before following him into the living room.

Lilah was sitting on my couch, feet propped on the coffee

table. Already showered and in her pajamas, her hair resembled a tangled nest constructed by drunk birds in the dark.

She scowled. "Don't you have to go to class?"

Nate dumped her backpack on the dining table. "Lilah."

Lilah put a hand to her hair. "I hate when you brush it."

"If you won't let me brush it, we're cutting it."

Tears glistened at the corners of Lilah's eyes. "You can't cut it. Mommy said my hair was pretty."

With a grunt, Nate dropped his head and ran a hand over the back of his neck, but not before I caught a flash of pain. Was he thinking about Lilah's mother? And here I was, fantasizing about kissing him. Not that I'd ever ask him, but I couldn't help wondering about Lilah's mother. Had she and Nate been married? Was he grieving the loss of the love of his life? Did he think of her often and wonder how his life would be different if she were still here? Despite his heartache, he seemed to be adjusting well to life as a single dad. But maybe he was sad or lonely, even scared about the future?

It's none of your business, Perci!

After a moment—I suspect he counted to ten—he raised his eyes and said, "Look, you need to brush your hair. And you can't talk to me like that. Maybe I need to reconsider you being in that talent show."

That caught her attention. Mine, too. I had heard nothing about a talent show. Lilah scrambled to her feet and held her hands out, palms up. "I'm sorry, okay? I'll brush my hair, I promise."

After leaping over the coffee table, she grabbed her backpack and rummaged around before pulling out a wide-toothed comb. "See?" She stuck it in her hair and yanked. The comb didn't budge.

She winced; I winced.

"How about I comb Lilah's hair?" I said.

Nate tugged his phone out of his pocket, glanced at it.

"Fine. I have to go. But"—he pointed a finger at Lilah—"we aren't done with this. Your attitude..."

"I'll be good, I promise. Please, I really want to be in the talent show. You already signed the forms."

"Just remember that I can un-sign them. Got it?"

Lilah nodded meekly, her eyes large and liquid-filled. "I got it."

"Be good." He pulled her close and planted a kiss on her forehead, his voice gruff. "Love you."

"Love you too."

Nate hitched up his backpack and turned to me. He hesitated, the corner of his mouth tipping up. "Thanks, again."

"No problem."

In the living room, Lilah was pawing through my nail polish stash. She bounced on the balls of her feet and held up a vibrant purple.

"No nails until we get through your hair." I found a bottle of leave-in conditioner and sat on the couch. She settled on the floor between my feet.

"So, a talent show?" I asked, spritzing on conditioner.

Lilah nodded. "Uh-huh. For the end of the year. The day before school gets out, in front of the whole school."

"What are you going to do?" I winced as the comb encountered a particularly nasty knot.

"Guess."

"Spontaneous napping?"

"No," she said with a giggle.

"You're teaching an earthworm circus tricks?"

A gap-toothed smile was my answer.

"I have no idea."

"Bird calls."

"I'm sorry. What?"

"Bird calls." Hopping to her feet, she cupped her hands

around her mouth and let out a nasal, loud honk. "That's the snow goose. Pretty good, right? I've been practicing."

My mouth hung open in either disbelief or horror—it was hard to differentiate between the two. Before I could form words, Lilah let out another call, this one in three parts.

"That's a whippoorwill. Do you hear it?" She repeated the sound. "It says its name—whip-poor-will."

She could not do this in front of the entire school. The other kids would tear her apart. How had Nate said yes to this? Didn't he know how mean kids could be? How mean adults could be? I couldn't even imagine my mother's reaction if I'd tried to do anything like this when I had been a kid.

There'd been one time when Mom had insisted I take dance lessons. I'd been six years old and even then, I'd known tutus and high kicks were not my thing. Thirty seconds into the first recital, it had all gone horribly wrong. I'd tripped and fallen flat on my face. While I lay there, too afraid to cry, Miss Alicia, the dance instructor, stood backstage and whisper-yelled to the other girls to keep dancing. I blinked up at the hot stage lights, fighting tears, while eight other girls in leotards and too much make-up twirled and leaped around my body to a jazzy pop song.

Afterward, all I wanted to do was cry on my mother's shoulder, or receive a pat on the back, something to let me know she didn't believe I was a complete failure. Instead, she sighed and took my hand. When we got in the car, I kicked off the black dance shoes and picked at the hole I now had in my tights.

"I'm sorry, Mommy," I whispered.

She started the car without replying. When we were almost home, she finally spoke, her voice low. "There's always next time. Next time will be better."

I never went to another dance class. But it was replaced with soccer, music classes, gymnastics, any number of things I never took to. One humiliating experience after another, one failure after another.

The difference between Lilah and me was I understood other people were laughing at me; she didn't. I couldn't let her do this.

"Lilah, do you think this is a good idea?"

Her face scrunched in concentration. "You don't think the whippoorwill call is good enough? I thought about doing a peacock and a great horned owl and a cardinal."

I held out a hand to her. "Come here."

She sat next to me on the couch. Her warm little body curled next to my side and my heart climbed into my throat.

"I think you sounded great. I love that you know all about birds, but I'm not sure other people will like your bird sounds—"

"Calls. Bird calls."

"—calls, sorry, the way your dad and I do."

She pushed back from my side. "So?"

"So? If you do this in front of the entire school, they might make fun of you."

Her shoulder lifted and fell. "Okay."

"Okay?"

"I don't care if they say things. Daddy says I should always be me."

"Kids can be very mean."

Her little hand patted my knee as if to comfort me. "I can handle it."

With that, she climbed off the couch, settled again on the floor at my feet, and handed me the comb. She practiced her bird calls the entire time I worked the tangles out of her hair.

TWENTY-EIGHT

"You can lead a horse to water,
or you can drag it inch by inch.
Either way, it's gonna get thirsty sometime."

—MIMI

Bria had been avoiding me. I'd called, I'd texted, I'd made Mathias go with me to the fast-food place she worked at, but she was always too busy to talk. She was as slippery as a snake coated in baby oil, as Mimi would say. It hadn't escaped my notice, and I was worried.

When I brought my concerns to Stella, she'd explained that Bria had taken a third job. "Her grandmother asked her to send more money to help with her brothers."

"She can't work three jobs. That's ridiculous. When is she supposed to sleep or eat or study?"

Stella smiled sadly. "This is the way it is, Perci. Some women get overwhelmed and get back in trouble. Other women like Bria, they work themselves to death trying to make up for their failures. It's a lot of pressure they put on themselves."

So, I decided if I couldn't go to Bria, I'd have to bring her to me. I had to resort to trickery, but it was for her own good, which was why I was sitting in Stella's tiny office on a Tuesday night. But I had such exciting news for her, I wanted to tell her in person.

"She said she was coming, right?" I asked.

Stella didn't lift her face from the paperwork she was filling out. "Yes. For the twelfth time. She's coming."

"Okay. Good." I pulled out my phone and puttered around on it, checked the time, crossed my legs, and tucked the phone back in my purse.

Stella lifted her head and flipped the braided rope of her hair behind her shoulder. She set her pen down and leaned back in her chair. "Just don't give her any unrealistic expectations. Let her know the facts and let her decide what she wants to do."

"Right, of course. But this is a huge opportunity, and I don't want it to slip through her fingers."

Stella rubbed a hand on her forehead like she had a headache coming on. "Just be honest. No false expectations."

A knock sounded. I hopped up and opened the door. "Hey, stranger."

"Yo." Bria stuffed her hands in the pocket of her hoodie, which she wore despite the heat of the late spring day.

I wrapped my arms around her for a hug. She held out for a handful of seconds before patting me twice on the back. "I've missed you."

"Come have a seat," Stella said.

Bria plopped into a chair and slouched down, looking from the director to me. She was make-up-less, and her face looked strange without her drawn-on eyebrows. "What's going on?"

"I hope you don't mind. I asked Stella to get you to come," I said, sitting in the chair beside her. "I've been trying to get ahold of you."

Bria sucked her teeth, the sound strangely loud. "Sorry. I've been busy."

"Yeah, I heard. Is everything okay?" I touched her hand. "I've been worried."

She shrugged and stared at her feet. "It's all right. I'm just tired."

"I have good news." I paused and pulled out a packet from my purse. "I might have found a job for you, a good one."

"Yeah?"

I held out the papers, and she took them slowly. "It's with an oil company and they have benefits and a tuition reimbursement program for when you start taking classes. I called and talked to the person in charge. I told her about you, and she seemed excited to meet you. What do you think?"

Bria thumbed through the application. "She knows about me, you know, having been locked up?"

"She said it wasn't something that would lessen your chances." I nibbled on my thumbnail for a long moment. "I, ah, I already set up your interview."

"What?" She dropped the papers on her lap; one slipped off and drifted to the ground. "I don't even know if I want to apply."

"She said the slots were filling fast, and I wanted to make sure you got one. It's at the beginning of September. You have ages to prepare and—"

"I don't know anything about oil or working at some fancy company."

"They'll train you."

She crossed her arms. "Man, look. I'm tired of applying for these jobs and getting turned down. Besides, I can't afford to take time off for some interview that's not gonna work out, anyway."

I leaned forward. "I think if we polished up your interview skills, and you tried your hardest—"

"I've been trying my hardest and it ain't ever good enough. What makes you think this is going to turn out right for me?"

Her words made my throat tighten. I understood that feeling. Hadn't I felt the same way more times than I could count? Hadn't I fought it my whole life? A fierce fire started in my gut, a determination that Bria was going to overcome this. She would succeed.

"Bria, look at me." The silence stretched, but I waited her out. Her eyes met mine. She swallowed and pressed her lips together. "You can do this. Right, Stella?" I glanced at the other woman, who'd been suspiciously quiet.

She nodded. "If Bria wants to do this, it sounds like a good opportunity."

"I'll help you. Mathias will help you. We'll get you ready for that interview and you'll blow them away."

Bria blinked and looked away, her voice thick when she spoke. "I guess I can give it a—"

She hadn't even finished the sentence before I threw my arms around her. "Oh, yes, this is going to be awesome. Just you wait and see."

Bria hugged me back and, in a tentative whisper, replied, "I hope so. I really hope so."

TWENTY-NINE

"If you're looking for a hero,
you've already lost your way."

—*MIMI*

Lilah cleared her throat and repeated the squawk she'd been perfecting for the last thirty minutes. "Was that better?"

"Sure," I said and set a tiny chair atop a tiny table. Lilah and I were the last two people at Miss Marge's this evening. While she practiced, I cleaned up the room.

Lilah frowned. "Are you even listening to me?"

"Of course I am. How could I not?" I'd have to be deaf or in another country to not hear her. Despite my attempts to turn Lilah on to some other talent—singing, dancing, stand-up comedy, miming, baton-twirling, anything else, she would not be swayed.

The last few weeks, she'd subjected me to an encyclopedia of chirps, tweets, squawks, screams, grunts, and chortles. The kid was both relentless and cheerful in her mission to share her passion. But I couldn't help that bit of panic wedged in my heart, the worry she'd be laughed off the stage, the image of her little face crumbled in tears.

"Did you finish my costume? Can I try it on this weekend?"

"That's the plan." A couple of weeks ago, Lilah had hit me up with big, pleading eyes to make her talent show costume. Since I couldn't seem to say no to her, I'd found myself hunched over my old sewing machine, attaching hundreds of feathers onto a custom-made owl costume.

"I can't wait," Lilah said.

I could. Every time I thought of Lilah performing in front of what was sure to be a mob of critics, my heart broke a little. A clap of thunder pulled my eyes to the window where an angry rain pounded. That had to be a sign, right?

If Nate was concerned about the impending fiasco of the talent show, he hadn't shown it. Once or twice I'd almost brought up my concerns to him but caught myself. He hadn't asked my opinion, and I didn't want to overstep.

Lilah let loose a loud, high-pitched whistle that made me cringe. "What about that one? Did that sound like a nightingale?"

Then again, maybe I didn't have much of a choice.

The knock on my door a week later caught me in the middle of belting out show tunes for Sal's listening pleasure. I scrambled to turn down the music and raced to the door, patting at the fine sheen of sweat on my forehead.

It was Nate. Of course.

"Oh, hey," I said, wishing I didn't have on my new pajamas, the ones with the Men of Marvel pictured shirtless across the front. "What's up?"

Eyes twinkling, Nate flashed a half-smile. "Sounded like a party in here."

"No, just me and the fish living it up at nine o'clock on a

Friday night." I winced. "I mean, I was cleaning house and then I was going to take a shower and wash my hair and—"

Grinning, he rocked back on his heels. "No explanation needed."

I blew out a breath. "Did you need something?"

"I was wondering if I could borrow"—he pulled his phone out and squinted down at the screen—"a cup of sugar?"

"Sure." I hurried into the kitchen, measured out some into a baggie, and handed it over. "I put a little extra in. Just in case."

After he thanked me, I closed the door and turned the music back up, not as loud as before. Five minutes later, another knock interrupted my touching performance of Bette Midler's classic "Wind Beneath My Wings." I think Sal even teared up a little.

"Yes?" I said when I opened the door to Nate again.

"Sorry." He glanced at his phone and frowned. "Do you have an egg? I have two, but I need three."

"Yup." I handed over the egg and watched him walk down the hallway toward his door.

"Oh, hey, wait." He jogged back to me. "Do you have any baking soda? Did you know there's baking powder and then there's baking soda? I thought they were both the same thing." He shrugged. "Who knew?"

Me. I knew that. I bit back a smile at his confusion. For once, it was nice to see he was the uncertain one. "Are you making something, or just stocking your pantry?"

"I went to this family night at Lilah's school, and the next thing I knew one of those PTA moms was talking real fast and asking if she could sign me up to help with the bake sale. Thought I'd be setting up tables or something." He rubbed the back of his neck. "But it turns out I'm supposed to make three dozen cupcakes for tomorrow."

"I could help you. I mean, I'm sure I have all the ingredients."

His shoulders relaxed. "Are you serious? I have no idea what I'm doing here."

After checking on Lilah, he brought over the business end of a baby monitor so he could hear her if she woke. He handed over his phone. "This is the recipe I'm using."

"You can't use some random recipe you find on the internet. What are you? A heathen?" I pulled out the notebook I kept of Mimi's recipes. "We'll use a Perkins family recipe. I know I have one in here."

As I thumbed through the book, he leaned over my shoulder, his breath shifting the hairs at the back of my neck. My entire body warmed. I flipped faster. "Here it is. Let's preheat the oven to 350 and I'll get you an apron. We got some bakin' to do."

The next thirty minutes we measured and sifted and stirred, and something strange happened. My nervousness melted away.

"Not much of a baker?" I asked. We were sitting side-by-side on stools at the island, waiting for the first batch of cupcakes to bake.

He snorted and adjusted the apron he'd borrowed from my stash. It was one I kept for Mimi which read, *I'M STILL HOT. IT JUST COMES IN FLASHES NOW*. "Nah. I'm sure Lilah has told you we eat a lot of mac and cheese and hot dogs. Oh, and spaghetti. I can make a mean sauce."

"Impressive. I've never made homemade spaghetti sauce."

"My mom made me learn when I was in high school. She said a good man isn't worth a thing if he can't make a good sauce. Besides, the ladies like a man who can cook."

I laughed. "But you can only make the one thing?"

"Trust me, I only need the one thing." He winked. "I'll make it for you one of these days. You'll see."

My stomach flipped over. Was he flirting with me? Also, had the air conditioning quit working? "I'll take you up on that."

"It's a deal," he said and held out a hand.

My fingers slid against his until our palms touched and his hand swallowed mine. I could feel the dry, warm skin, and I shivered. Our eyes met and held. The tiny creases at the corners of his eyes, that little white scar on his eyebrow, the sharpness of his jaw fascinated me. Warmth traveled up my arm and down my spine, settling low in my stomach. Why did everything about him captivate me? I wondered if he could hear the rapid beating of my heart. I wondered if his heart felt the same way. Without realizing, I leaned toward him and maybe I imagined it, but he tugged on my hand.

And then the oven timer went off.

I jumped, pulled my hand back. "Oh, the cupcakes. I should get them. Out. I should get them out."

Without waiting for a reply, I rushed to the oven, took out the cupcakes, and put the next batch in. I busied myself putting away ingredients and wiping down counters while my heart returned to normal.

"Would you like something to drink? Water?" I asked.

"Thank you, please."

I got him a cup and handed it over, careful not to touch his fingers. He frowned down at his water. A rustle came through the baby monitor and then it quieted again. Lilah, probably turned over in her sleep, likely in the middle of a dream about the life cycle of pigeons. The silence stretched until I couldn't take it. So, of course, I said the exact wrong thing and ruined the warm, gushy, comfortable feeling.

"I'm worried about Lilah. Do you think this talent show is a good idea? Don't you think the other kids are going to make fun of her?"

His head tilted to the side. "Why would they make fun of her?"

Was he kidding? "Because she's going to make a fool of herself in front of the entire school."

"She's not going to make a fool of herself."

"Are you purposely trying to not understand? They're definitely going to make fun of her. Do you know what it feels like to have an entire room of people laugh at you? You've probably never experienced that level of embarrassment. You don't understand how soul-crushing that can be."

He scoffed, the lines of his face hardening. "You have no idea what I've experienced."

"You're right. I don't. I just thought, I don't know, as a friend, I could say something."

With a shake of his head, he pushed his glass to the side. "Look, I appreciate your concern and don't take this the wrong way, but I need you to butt out. It's my decision."

"Got it."

"Good."

For a moment, it had felt like there had been a... something, a connection, that Nate might, just maybe, be interested in me. But this was a good reminder. If his wife were still around, he wouldn't need *my* help. I just happened to be conveniently located right next door. He was here to make cupcakes, not declarations of love.

I glanced at him and his Jaw of Steel. *Nope, don't get any ideas. He's not interested.* My heart pitter-pattered a little dance, anyway. Frowning, I turned to stare at the oven timer, willing the next fourteen minutes to speed by.

THIRTY

"If it sounds too good to be true,
    you probably haven't read the fine print yet."

—*MIMI*

Next night, I got home, ate a peanut butter and jelly sandwich, and sprawled on the couch in front of the television, staring at the two envelopes I'd received in the mail. Both were for Nate, one an offer from a credit card company, the other from a Caroline Russo.

This was the fourth letter I'd accidentally received from her. I'd been tempted more than once to ask Lilah who she was. A search of Facebook only proved there were a lot of women named Caroline Russo in the world. Maybe she was a sister or a cousin or his mother?

I glanced at the time—a little before ten. That wasn't so late. Surely, he'd still be awake. Should I take them over? Maybe feel out the situation. Was he still angry with me for bringing up the talent show? What about that weird moment when our hands had touched? Had he felt something too? Why had I opened my big mouth?

I sat up and turned to Sal. He stared back at me with all the love in his tiny fish body. "Do I take them over?"

A big dark eye stared back at me.

"Good idea. I'll take some blueberry muffins to be neighborly."

Nate opened his door a minute later. I shoved the plate in his hands. "I thought you and Lilah would like some muffins for breakfast. I hope you like blueberry. They're kind of the pizza of berries, and everybody likes pizza."

He took the plate from me. "Thanks."

I stared at him; he stared at me. His eyes were dark green tonight, almost the same shade as his t-shirt. Finally, we both spoke at the same time.

"I should get back—"

"Do you want to come in and I'll give your plate back?"

I nodded. "Um, sure."

Nate's apartment was a mirror image of mine—kitchen in front, long exposed brick wall, small dining area, and living room. But where I'd painted and decorated with abandon, this apartment was bare bones.

Couch—brown. Recliner—beige. Giant television. Nothing hung on the walls—no art or family photos. The only pops of color appeared to originate from Lilah. Bright yellow high-tops in the middle of the living room floor. Her bird backpack on the counter. A small bookcase overflowing with her books. Crayon drawings covering the fridge door.

The only photograph also hung on the fridge, a five-by-seven of a child with giant eyes—certainly Lilah—sitting on the lap of a young woman. In the photo, Lilah's little hand was pressed against the woman's cheek as though she was turning her head. The woman was pretty with dark eyes, despite the smudges under them and the gray-striped scarf wrapped around her head.

This must be Lilah's mother.

"Here's the plate." Nate set it on the island and pushed it toward me. He motioned to the muffins he'd placed in a plastic container. "These look good."

"Hope you like them." I gripped the plate until my knuckles turned white. "I'm sorry if things were weird last night. I didn't mean to upset you."

"I'm sorry if I got defensive."

"No, I get it. I guess it reminded me of stuff from my child-hood that never quite worked out. Plus, if you haven't noticed, I have a way of saying just the wrong thing."

"I like that I never know exactly what you're going to say." His eyes met mine, warm and unguarded, for a few seconds.

"Okay," I whispered.

He grinned, shifting the mood. "Besides, I can be a jerk sometimes. I can give references if you don't believe me."

"I'll keep that in mind." I pulled the two envelopes out of my back pocket and slid them across the counter to him. "These came in the mail today."

Nate picked them up and frowned at the letter from Caro-line. Without opening it, he ripped it in half and tossed it in the garbage can next to the island.

Don't say anything. It's none of your business. Do. Not. Say. Anything. Then my mouth opened. "Why'd you do that?"

"Do what?"

"Throw that letter away. Who's Caroline Russo?" I winced and shuffled back toward the door. "I'm sorry. I did it again. That was nosy. It's none of my business."

"She's my mom."

"Oh."

Ducking his head, he snapped a lid on the container of

muffins. I stood there watching him. Again: awkward, thy name is Perci.

"I'll just head out now." Waving the plate in the air, I scurried toward escape. I only made it halfway before he spoke.

"My sister died last year. Last week was the anniversary."

Slowly, I turned and walked back to the kitchen. "I'm sorry."

He pulled the photo from the fridge and stared at it for a long moment, before passing it over to me. "This is her, Mara. Mara was three years younger, but we were close."

My hand shook as I picked up the photo. Up close, I could see the sharp angle of her nose and chin, like her brother. "She was beautiful."

"She's Lilah's mother. I'm her uncle."

My eyes cut to his face as I pulled out a stool at the island and eased onto it. "But she calls you Daddy."

"I'm the only dad she's ever known. She heard her friends calling their dads 'Daddy' and when she started using it, I didn't have the heart to correct her."

He smiled faintly as his fingertips skimmed the photo. "We grew up in a rough area and it was hard to stay out of trouble. This scar?" His fingertip traced his eyebrow. "Bar fight when I was sixteen. I never passed up the opportunity to fight."

"How did you get into a bar at sixteen?"

He arched that same eyebrow, a wicked spark in his eye. "I was good at being bad. Mom had her hands full with me."

"What about your dad?"

"He left when I was eight. Haven't seen him since." He held up the photo. "Now, Mara was a good girl, always reading and studying. She wanted to be a teacher."

"What happened?"

"Me. Or rather, the people I hung out with." He turned to hang the picture back up, his shoulders rigid. "We were guys with no real plans for the future. I started community college after high school, but that didn't last long. Too many things to do that led to nothing good. My best friend took a liking to Mara. They dated, she got pregnant, and then he got busted for drugs."

I stacked my arms on the counter and rested my chin on them. "Wow."

"He's never met Lilah, and that's just fine. We did all right, Mara and Ma and me. I straightened up and got a good job. Mara started taking classes." He shrugged. "Then, about three years ago, Mara was diagnosed with breast cancer. The doctors all said it was rare for someone so young."

"Oh, Nate. I'm so sorry."

"Toward the end, she knew." His shoulders hunched forward, and he rested his forehead on the fridge door. "She knew she wasn't going to make it. So, she got a will real cheap off the internet and asked me to take care of Lilah. She died three weeks later."

A flood of icy-hot sorrow burned in my throat. These were the moments when words seemed inadequate.

With a humorless laugh, he gestured toward the trashcan. "My mother didn't think I had the ability to raise a kid. Some days, I'm not sure she's wrong."

"You seem to be doing okay," I said. "Is that the reason you moved here?"

"Partly. I needed to get away from home. That neighborhood was no place to raise a kid. I guess I ran away. But yeah, I wanted to prove to myself and to my mom I could do this."

"Maybe she's ready to apologize?"

His frown was fierce and immediate. "Maybe I'm not ready to hear it. The thing is, I want a better life for Lilah. For me, too. I'm in school. I have work. I can't afford any distractions."

"Distractions?"

With a firm nod of his head, he continued. "I need to keep my focus. When I was a kid, I let myself get distracted. I can't do that again. I have Lilah now. She comes before anything else."

"That makes sense. Keep your eyes on the prize, and all that." But a tiny part of my heart shriveled right there on the spot. *I* was clearly not a distraction. He wouldn't have any problems being distracted by me. I was the opposite of a distraction, an un-distraction. That was fine. Totally fine.

Relief tinged his smile. "Exactly."

"I think that's admirable, and I think your sister would be proud of you."

His eyes drifted back to Mara's picture. "I hope so."

"Well, I should get back. I'm glad we talked." I made my way to the door and hesitated. "Is having friends too much of a distraction? Everyone needs friends."

I waited for him to reply, my heart beating too hard in my chest. When he didn't, I pulled open the door.

As I stepped into the hallway, the quiet sound of his voice reached me. "Yeah, a friend would be nice."

THIRTY-ONE

"Beauty's only skin deep.
  So, make sure you pay attention to the stuff
  on the inside you can't moisturize."

                                                        —*MIMI*

"Are you sure this looks okay on me? I tend to stay away from animal prints." My face scrunched as I stared at my reflection in the department store mirror.

It was a Saturday afternoon and I'd promised Mimi I'd take her to the mall for a little retail therapy.

"Of course it does. It looks very nice with your skin tone," Mimi said with a firm nod. Long feather earrings grazed across her shoulders with the movement.

I could imagine Mathias vehemently disagreeing with that claim.

I pulled a black tea-length dress with cap sleeves and tent-like volume from the nearest rack. "What about something like this?"

Mimi scowled. "No black. Honey, you aren't in mourning. You're young and beautiful, so dress like it."

I snorted. Maybe I was in mourning. Over a body that never quite looked the way I wanted it to. Round, chubby, fluffy. Whatever the euphemism, they all meant fat.

My grandmother stomped over to me. "What was that sound about? You *are* young and beautiful." Wrapping her fingers around my wrist, she half dragged me back to the mirror and turned me so I was facing my image. "Now, tell me what you see."

"Me?"

"That's all?"

I craned my neck to meet her eyes over my shoulder. "Is this a trick question?"

"No trick." Fingers on my chin moved my head back to face the mirror. "Let me tell you what I see. I see a young woman who's hiding behind her clothes, who doesn't realize beauty isn't what's on the outside. I see kind eyes and a sweet smile. I see someone who loves other people. I see someone who worries about other people more than she worries about herself. I see someone I am proud to call my granddaughter."

Chest tightening, tears pricked the backs of my eyes.

"Being beautiful doesn't mean you're perfect." She moved in front of me and placed the tips of her fingers, painted a deep crimson, over my heart. "Beautiful is in here."

I waved a hand down my body. "I'm not sure what to do with all of this. I'm not like you."

"Oh, honey, you are, though." Her smile was quiet, thoughtful. A hand closed around my arm. "I'm not what most people would call beautiful. I'm too short and round and loud, and I know that. The thing is, I don't care because I'm happy with who I am. If you don't like yourself, if you can't see the good parts, no one else will either."

I bit my lip. My eyes drifted back to the mirror, and I examined myself—the weight I carried in my hips and my thighs and my boobs and all the other parts in between, the make-up-less face, the lazy ponytail. "It's hard to see the good things," I said, a hitch in my voice.

"I know." She pulled me in for a hug. "You aren't ever gonna be a beauty queen like Phee, but that doesn't make you less than her. I hate that you think that. Sometimes I want to take your mama out in the backyard and find a good switch to use on her."

I laughed, imagining that scene.

"She doesn't mean to wear you down. But sweet baby Jesus, once she gets something in her head, there's no changing her mind." Cupping my shoulders, she pulled back. "Sometimes you gotta fake it till you make it. You gotta walk tall when you feel small. Lift your chin and you can face anything."

"Fake it till you make it, huh?" I lifted my shoulders back and raised my head.

Mimi moved to the side and grinned at me in the mirror. "That's right. And remember, it's the parts on the inside of you that count the most."

Pink spots of color highlighted my cheeks, and my eyes shone back at me. No, I was still the same person. It wasn't a magic confidence pill Mimi had given me, but something felt... changed.

"And honey?"

"Yes?"

With a wink, she smacked my butt. "Don't forget to shake what your grandmama gave you either. Now, let's go buy this dress."

THIRTY-TWO

"Men are visual.
Dress accordingly."

—MIMI

On a Friday, Mathias and I had a dinner date to catch up. He'd been busy with work, and I missed him.

After work, I rushed through a shower to wash away the fine dusting of glitter I'd acquired at the daycare. Wrapped in a towel, I stood before the bathroom mirror. A thin layer of steam covered the entire surface. I used my hand to swipe an oval there. Something about the lighting in bathrooms brought out imperfections, made my skin splotchy, and displayed the tiny lines around my eyes with more clarity.

Turning away, I dropped my towel, stepped on the scale, and held my breath. Over the past few months, I'd seen the number on the scale slip downward with no intention on my part—more a consequence of walking to work, wrangling preschoolers, fewer fast-food trips.

Glancing up, I caught the image of my body in the mirror

and frowned. If I'd lost weight, I couldn't see it. Turning to the side, I sucked in my breath and pressed my hands on my stomach and then released it all at once.

Flab.

Flabby.

The flabbiest.

Mimi would be angry at me for thinking those things. I could hear her voice now, reminding me to be kind to myself, just as she had when we'd gone dress shopping.

"Fake it until you make it," I muttered. "Okay, then." I leaned over the counter and inspected my face. "I have nice eyes. My hair isn't too bad. People seem to like my smile. I like my smile." I pressed a hand to my chest. "And I like the stuff in here."

So, maybe I sounded like a commercial for a cheesy self-help video. But I couldn't deny the kernel of warmth unfurling inside me. That feeling spread through my body and something strange happened: I believed what I was saying. My hands tingled with the need to prove this feeling was true.

Before I could second-guess myself, I marched to my closet and pulled out the red zebra-striped dress.

I ran my fingers over the cool, stretchy material and cringed a bit at the pattern. After dressing quickly in my underthings, I put it on, anyway. It hugged my body to my knees. Channeling Mimi, I slid my feet into black wedges with three-inch heels and wobbled back to the bathroom to apply make-up. When I finished, I was sure I hadn't worn this much eye make-up since senior prom. Biting my lip, I felt my confidence waver.

"Stand tall when you feel small." I adjusted my posture, straightened my shoulders, pushed my chest out. I had to admit, I looked pretty damn good. Not at all like I usually did, but maybe that wasn't a bad thing.

Giggling, I spun in a circle. My foot connected with the bathroom scale, and I frowned. Stupid scale. How many mornings had it made me wince or panic or cry, sometimes all three at once? I kicked it. It bounced on the tile floor with a clatter. Snatching it off the floor, I strode into the kitchen, pulled a garbage bag from under the sink, and shoved the scale in it.

That felt good. So good, in fact, I didn't stop there.

I yanked the inspirational weight loss calendar Mom had given me from the wall and stuffed it in with the scale. Next, I hustled to my bedroom. From my top dresser drawer, I pulled out every Spanx, body shaper, and tummy control apparatus my mother had ever purchased for me and tossed them, too.

The tips of my fingers tingled, and I felt a little drunk with excitement. I looked for another victim. The cookbooks! The lowfat, low-carb one, the high-protein one, the eat-like-a-cave-woman one, the gluten-free, dairy-free, soy-free, nut-free one. I gathered them all and dumped them in the garbage bag.

The cabinet by the stove held an entire shelf of supplements—pills that encouraged weight loss, suppressed appetite, and claimed to take inches off my waist. The bottle of essential oils that stimulated weight loss was there too. Above them, the vat of whey protein mix for those meal replacement shakes I'd tried for a half a week, the bars, the sugar substitutes, and the digital food scale—I chucked them all.

Grinning, I tucked my fists at my waist, enjoying the wave of freedom washing over me.

New Perci was a badass.

Next, I raced over to the bookcase by the TV where an entire row of exercise videos—Pilates, Zumba, yoga, kick-boxing, core and abs (I really hated that one), dance it off—taunted me. I tossed them, too.

A fine sheen of sweat coated my forehead. Apparently chucking all the stuff I bought to lose weight was an intense workout. Ironic.

I half dragged, half carried the two garbage bags into the hallway, to the elevator, down to the first floor, and through the service door. It took a few tries, but I hefted them into the dumpster. From the corner of my eye, I swore I saw a flash of red swoop by. Grinning, I marched back into the building.

When I got in the lobby, I slipped my shoes off. I might have to rethink wearing heels that night. But what I didn't do was pay attention to where I was walking. Three steps later, I bumped into Nate. Literally—my head on his shoulder. Nice shoulder, very solid.

Flustered, I scrambled back and tucked my shoes behind my back. "Sorry. Didn't see you there."

Then I *curtsied*.

Nate grinned. "Hey."

A small band of kittens chased a ball of yarn in my stomach at the sound of his voice.

Lift your chin and you can face anything, Mimi whispered in my head.

Right. Yes. Play it cool.

I smoothed a hand over my hip and edged around him. The elevator dinged, and he pressed a hand to keep the door open and indicated for me to enter.

We both faced the doors as they closed, me barefoot and clutching my shoes, Nate, all smiley eyes and slashing mouth. I was jumpier than a virgin at a prison rodeo. (Mimi stole that one from an episode of *The Golden Girls*.) It made eye contact hard, like college-statistics-hard.

Nate leaned against the elevator wall. "You going somewhere?"

"I'm meeting Mathias for dinner."

"That's your best friend, right?"

"Yes."

"And he's in love with your sister?"

"Correct."

"But she's engaged to the news guy with the hair plugs and the fake tan?"

I laughed. Mathias and Nate would get along well. "I'm impressed."

"Thanks. Watching soap operas with my grandma when I was little is paying off." He grinned. "So, how do you think it will all turn out?"

The elevator jerked to a stop, and the doors opened. We both stepped through, my shoulder brushing his arm, and started down the hallway.

"At this point, it's not looking good for Team Mathias. And that means I'm going to be related to Joel Allen." Abruptly I stopped and turned to face him. "Do you know what he called me? A mouse. I am not a mouse. Would a mouse wear this dress?"

He surveyed me from top to bottom, stalling on my legs. "Nope."

"That's right. No. Of course not. Because I'm not a mouse."

"Definitely not a mouse," he murmured and flashed another smile.

"That's why I like you. I mean, as a neighbor, you know. Not like, like..." I winced.

Go into your apartment. Pack all your belongings and move. Tonight. Maybe become a nun. In one of those orders that doesn't speak. Never, ever speak again.

I dropped a shoe and slid it on. Balanced on that foot, I tossed the other shoe too hard, and it skittered across the hallway. I limped toward it the same time Nate moved.

"I got it," he said.

Strange, wonderful things happened in my belly at the sight of his hand holding my shoe. Instead of handing it back, he crouched and brushed his fingers over the top of my bare foot.

I sucked in a gasp as that small touch sent tingles in all directions. "You don't have to do that."

But even as the words fell from my mouth, my foot lifted of its own accord. His touch was gentle as he slid my foot in, secured the strap around my heel, and stood. It all took a handful of seconds, and yet, my entire body felt sluggish and warm, like my insides were made of honey. I sagged against the wall and resisted the urge to fan my face.

The extra few inches from the heels put my eyes right at his neckline and they lingered on the olive-colored slice of skin there. I bet it was warm to the touch and smelled like his soap. I bet the soap on his skin smelled amazing, probably one of my favorite smells in the entire world, and I'd never even had the pleasure of...

"Have fun."

I dragged my gaze to his face. The smile from his eyes traveled to his mouth. Gosh, it was hot in this hallway. "What?"

He hung his head, and I swore his shoulders shook. But when he looked at me again, he was straight-faced. "Have fun. With Mathias."

"Oh, right. Him."

With a quick grin, he started down the hallway to his apartment in sure, even steps, clearly unaffected by this encounter.

Unlike me.

"See you later," I said to his back.

At his door, Nate hesitated, his keys jangling in his hand. "You look nice, by the way."

I pushed my shoulders back and channeled Mimi. I strutted —oh, yes, I did—down the hallway, watching Nate watch me. I was freaking New Perci.

His smile widened; I put an extra swing in my hips. By some miracle, I made it down the hallway perfectly. No hesitation, no falling, no twisting an ankle, no bumping a table with my hip and knocking over an urn that held the ashes of my boyfriend's grandmother and thereby ruining any chance of making a good first impression on his parents. That last thing had only happened once. So far.

"Thanks," I said, my voice a little deeper than usual.

He opened his door; I opened mine.

"No need to thank me for the truth," he said and winked.

I stumbled and pitched forward. With an unladylike "Oomph," I fell against the doorframe. Ignoring the pain in my shoulder, I righted myself and prayed Nate had not witnessed that. But when I peeked around the door and down the hallway, there he was, looking cool and calm and so dang untouchable, a knowing little hitch at the corner of his mouth.

Plastering on a smile, I waved. "I'm fine. Everything's fine. I'm good."

"See you later, Perci," he said.

"You too, neighbor. Good seeing ya. We should do this more often. You know, talking in the hallway, and stuff. You have a good one, buddy."

This time, I was sure I heard him laugh as I hurried inside my apartment.

THIRTY-THREE

"Money can't buy you happiness,
  but it can help you look for it on a nicer street."

—MIMI

The day of Lilah's school talent show bloomed clear and sunny. I took off half a day of work, stopped for a small bouquet of daisies, and drove to the school.

Neat rows of children sat on the floor in the front of half of the gym, adults crowded in back on plastic chairs. Nate waved from the seat he'd saved me. He'd come straight from work. I knew from experience he'd smell of sweat and dirt and a hint of that fruity, clean smell I couldn't seem to name. My heart skipped a beat, which is what it did most often these days when I caught a glimpse of him.

Being *friends* with Nate was an experience. He joked with me more, seemed less tense, smiled more. Twice, we ordered a pizza and ate it together with Lilah. He borrowed milk one night. It was all very neighborly and friendly and not at all distracting. At least for him.

For example, I was in no way distracted when he answered his door shirtless one evening. My eyes managed to remain firmly planted on his face the entire time.

Nope. I was completely friend-like.

So what if I might have had a dream about him one time, or four? And maybe one of them involved a steamy kiss and a declaration of love in the middle of a rainstorm while he was wearing a hard hat and a tool belt. But it wasn't like I stared at him a little too long when he dropped off Lilah that Wednesday night. I played it all totally cool.

Because we were friends. Friends don't have kissing dreams about their friends.

I fiddled with the cellophane wrapper on the flowers as I sat down. I offered Nate a stick of gum. I nibbled on my thumbnail.

"She'll be fine," Nate said and patted my knee.

The lights dimmed and the assistant principal acting as emcee announced the first act—a troupe of little girls dancing to an 80s song, complete with leg warmers and scrunchies. Next, a magician wowed the audience with his tricks, followed by two tiny singers with big voices, and then another dance routine.

Lilah was next. She waddled onto the stage in her owl costume, feathers blowing in the breeze from the AC.

"Adorable," I heard someone whisper behind me. I straightened in pride.

"Today," she said, her voice tiny. The entire audience leaned forward to hear better. Nate held up his phone to film. "I'll be performing sounds of our friends, the birds." She waved one of her wings with a flourish.

Someone chuckled.

"First, a peacock." A screeching noise erupted from Lilah. I winced.

"Oh, brother," a voice muttered somewhere to my left. A spattering of giggles came from the front.

Next to me, Nate frowned. "I told her not to start with the peacock."

"And the great horned owl," she said, and followed it up with a few hoots.

The next three minutes felt like the longest of my life. At first the audience played along—aside from a murmur here or a laugh there, they didn't seem to mind the performance. But around bird call number seven (the pine warbler), it was clear patience was running out.

"Another one?" one of the parents near me muttered when Lilah announced number eight (the American crow). "Let's get this over with."

Number nine (the tufted titmouse) elicited more than a few laughs and one of the kids yelled, "She said tit!"

"How many is she doing again?" I whispered.

"One more," Nate said. "She's doing great."

But every laugh and groan from the children sounded louder than the one before, and poor Lilah looked so tiny and helpless on that big stage by herself.

"The last one," she said and waited for a handful of kids to stop cheering, "is my favorite bird, the cardinal." She pursed her lips just so and whistled out a high-pitched melody.

A few kids squawked back, another quacked, and more honked. Half of them laughed and ignored the cue to applause when she bowed. For the first time, Lilah's smile melted a little. Then she took a deep breath and began to toss out air-kisses with abandon.

"Thank you, thank you," she half sang, half shouted, grin bright with confidence. Just like a professional who dealt with hecklers all the time.

Still, I hated the idea she could hear those laughs and jeers. I had to do something. My purse and the flowers tumbled to the floor as I jumped to my feet. Clapping as loudly as I could, I said, "Great job, Lilah. Great job."

But the murmur of the audience drowned me out, and the fact that we were way in the back meant Lilah couldn't see me. I flung my arms in the air and when that still didn't work, I grabbed Nate's shoulder and climbed onto my chair. "Lilah!"

Laughing at me, Nate rose and let out one of those mouth–finger combination whistles that could be heard from three blocks away. "That's my girl!"

Lilah grinned and waved both wings before bouncing off backstage.

After the show, Nate and I met Lilah in the crowded hallway.

Nate lifted her in the air, feathers and all, and squeezed her. "You did a great job!"

"Do you think everyone liked me?" She nibbled at her lip.

"What's important is that you weren't mean or unkind or hurtful. And besides, the people who matter"—he waved a finger between him and me—"like you a lot."

His words brought a smile to Lilah's face. "I gotta be me, right?"

"Right."

Nate was a good father, and I was glad Lilah had someone like him to tell her she was okay being exactly who she was. I wished, just once, I'd heard that message from my parents. They may have said the words, but everything my mother did proved the opposite. A wave of sadness rolled through me. I shook it off and held up the flowers. "For you, my dear."

"Thank you," Lilah said and buried her nose in the daisies.

Nate set Lilah down, and she grabbed his hand and mine as we walked toward the exit. Halfway there, a thin boy with bright blue eyes, Harry Potter-esque glasses, and a bow tie stepped into our path.

"Hello," he said, his face serious. "I wanted to tell you I enjoyed your bird calls. I especially liked the blue jay."

"Thanks," Lilah said, equally serious.

"Perhaps I'll see you around school tomorrow."

Lilah smiled. "Okay."

The boy nodded at Nate, turned on his heel, and marched down the hallway in the opposite direction.

"Who was that?" Nate asked as we walked out of the building.

"That's Caleb. The kids say he's kind of weird," Lilah said.

"Is he?" I asked.

Lilah shrugged. "I like him. He's my friend." She skipped ahead to the car, flapping her owl wings with abandon.

There was something sweet about the whole thing. Lilah's bird obsession and quirky clothing made her stand out from the crowd, and kids like Caleb could see that and liked her for who she was.

I'd spent my whole life trying to fix all the things I thought were wrong with me—my body, my ambitions, my failures—but what if I was doing this all wrong? What if I just needed to be happy with who I was and never mind what my mother or anyone else thought? What if slightly awkward, slightly chubby Perci with her loud fashion sense and emotional support fish was fine being exactly who she was? What if it took being New Perci to see that Old Perci was pretty okay being exactly who she already was?

As we reached our cars parked next to each other, my gaze drifted to Nate and my heart wobbled. And maybe, just maybe, there was someone out there who would like me for being me.

Perhaps he was thinking of me too, or he likely felt the creepy weight of my stare, because he turned to me then. The corner of his mouth tipped in a half-smile. "I think we need dessert. You want to come?"

Lilah jumped up and down. "Yes! Yes! Please come with us, Perci! Can I still wear my owl costume?"

"Sure," Nate said. He opened her door, and she climbed in.

He tipped his head toward me. "You coming? We can come back and get your car when we're done."

"Okay." Like I could say no to dessert. Or Nate. Or Nate offering me dessert. He opened the passenger door. His fingers skimmed the small of my back, warming my skin through my shirt, and guided me into the seat.

He closed the door and was rounding the car when Lilah gasped and pointed out the side window. "Look, do you see it?"

I whipped my head around in time to see a cardinal swooping from tree to tree, carrying a brown feather in its mouth that resembled the very ones I'd made Lilah's costume with.

"I see it," I said as Nate slid into his seat.

"What?" he asked.

"It was Mommy, letting me know she was around," Lilah said.

Nate scowled and started the car, his hands tight on the steering wheel. "We've talked about this, sweetheart. Cardinals live in Texas year-round, that's all."

"Okay, Daddy," Lilah said in the most accommodating voice a kid has ever used.

I flipped down the visor and found Lilah's eyes in the mirror. I winked; she covered her mouth to stifle her giggle.

Nate side-eyed us. "What was that?"

"What was what?" I asked.

"Nothing," Lilah said at the same time.

"Fine, don't tell me." But his smile was indulgent and the whole bird business seemed forgotten by the time we pulled up to the ice cream shop and tumbled out of the car.

And yes, even though it was dangerous and stupid, I pretended we were a little family the whole time.

·   ·   ·

Later that night, long after I'd parted ways with Nate and Lilah, I was too restless to sleep. Instead, I scrubbed my face and pasted on a mud mask. While I waited the fifteen minutes before washing it off, I called Mathias, who was trapped in North Dakota.

"The most exciting thing we've done is drive two hours to take photos the client's mother insisted on."

"What was two hours away?"

"A twenty-six-foot-tall buffalo statue."

"Well, you wouldn't see that in Texas."

"And thank God for that," he said with feeling.

I was laughing when I heard the knock on the door. It was past ten, so I made Mathias stay on the phone in case it was a serial killer.

"It's Nate," I whispered into the phone.

"Kind of late for a visit from our friendly neighborhood fake boyfriend. Whatever could he want? A cup of milk?"

"Goodbye, Mathias."

"Or maybe he wants to use your—" I hung up before he could finish.

I opened the door. "Hi."

Nate straightened and his eyes widened. "Ah, hi. If this isn't a good time, I can come back."

"It's fine. Is everything okay?"

He shook his head. "Yeah, everything's fine. I just wanted to thank you for today—the talent show. I'm glad you were there. It was nice."

"I'm glad I was there too." I leaned my hip against the door jamb and looked at him expectantly.

He stared down at me, brow crinkled. He did not speak.

I cleared my throat and asked again, "Are you sure everything's okay?"

"I was hoping you'd have dinner with me next weekend."

I blinked. "Dinner?"

"Yes. That meal we eat in the evening. I have a sitter next Saturday."

My mouth twisted to the side. Dinner? Without Lilah? But with Nate? Alone? Just the two of us? Like a date?

Danger! Danger! Do not go down that path.

I shook my head to clear those thoughts and reminded myself that Nate had told me himself he wasn't looking for anything that distracted him from Lilah and his plan. A friendly dinner wasn't a distraction. It was just dinner. Talking, but with food.

"Okay."

"Great." With a smile, he took a step back. "I'll see you later then."

The whole conversation whirled in my head as I watched him walk back to his door.

With a snap of his fingers, he turned. "Oh, and maybe for dinner, think about losing the face mask thing."

I gasped; he grinned and disappeared into his apartment.

THIRTY-FOUR

"Perfection is boring.
Be imperfect. All my favorite people are."

"Jeans or a skirt?" I asked Mathias as I stared into my closet. "What says this-might-be-a-date-but-I'm-not-sure-and-don't-want-to-look-like-I'm-trying-too-hard?"

"Go with jeans."

"Right. Jeans."

"Do you have any shirts without kittens on them?"

"Ha. Ha. Yes." I tucked the phone between my ear and shoulder and pawed through my closet. I did have a lot of kitten t-shirts, now that I paid attention. "Here's one. It's blue with little yellow flowers on it. How's that?"

"Probably tragic, but it will do."

"Your faith in me is overwhelming." I laid the shirt on my bed, next to my nicest pair of dark-wash jeans. Then I threw myself on my back next to them and stared at the ceiling. "What am I doing?"

"You're having fun. I have a lot of fun. Having fun is... fun."

I gnawed on my thumbnail. "I want it to be fun, but my feelings are sort of wrapped up here. What if his aren't?"

"Just go with it for now. You overthink everything. Be you and let him be him and see what happens."

"I don't overthink everything. Do I?"

Mathias laughed. "No comment. Now, you kids have fun on your... whatever it is you're doing. Relax. Maybe he won't even notice what you're wearing."

I took extra care when I got ready, slathering on lotion and letting my hair air-dry (with the help of hair product and a diffuser on my blow-dryer) to soft waves. Standing in front of the mirror, I examined myself and I liked what I saw. I felt that more and more these days. Happy with me, the extra pounds didn't bother me as much as they used to. Come to think of it, I hadn't much thought about calories or weighing myself in weeks. I ate when I was hungry, and I ate what I wanted.

Nate knocked on my door at 6:30, freshly showered, his expression uncertain, almost nervous. He held out a bouquet of wildflowers.

"They're beautiful." I took the bouquet and cradled it in my arms like it was precious. The kittens were back, tumbling in my stomach. "I'll go put them in some water."

Nate waited in the hallway, and we walked to his truck in silence. On the drive, Mathias's words replayed in my head. *Just go with it.* Good advice and I wanted to try, if I wasn't such a ball of nerves and potentially embarrassing phrases.

We arrived at a tiny bistro about fifteen minutes later. Nate held the door open for me, and I was greeted by a man around my father's age with a full black beard and shiny bald head. He escorted us to a table by the window. Strands of twinkle lights draped from the ceiling. The walls shone a warm soft yellow in the flicker of the tabletop candles.

"This place is amazing," I said as I examined the artwork decorating the walls. They ranged from framed hand-drawn pictures to oversized oil paintings. Nothing matched. I loved it. "How did you find it?"

"I asked a few people at work." His eyes drifted around the room. "It reminds me of you, actually."

Our gazes met. A smile hovered around the corners of his mouth; my cheeks heated. "I'll take that as a compliment."

The server brought water and a breadbasket. The kitten party in my stomach almost made it impossible for me to eat. Almost.

While I slathered on rosemary-garlic butter, I stole glances at my companion. This was another side of Nate—not cool construction dude or cool responsible father or cool college student. Tonight, he was just... cool hot guy. His shoulders filled out his navy coat jacket. A plaid button-down peeked from underneath. He was undeniably handsome now—the kind of handsome that grows on you. I swallowed and looked away.

Nate cleared his throat. "So, Persephone, huh? Where'd that name come from?"

I scowled. "Please forget you know that."

"Too late. What does it mean?"

"It means my mother was in charge of picking my name." I sighed. "Persephone was the Greek goddess of springtime and flowers. She married a charming guy named Hades, aka Lord of the Underworld. They struck a deal—she'd spend six months of the year in Hades and six months topside every year."

"So, the original prenup, then?"

"I guess you could say that."

"Goddess of springtime and flowers. That fits you."

"That's very nice of you to say."

"I'm not saying it to be nice." He paused. The dim light

spilled across his face, reveling in the sharp crags and edges. "Do you know what I like about you?"

"Honestly? No."

The corner of his mouth ticked up. "You always seem to make me smile."

"I don't think that's on purpose most of the time."

"I know. But you still make me smile. Haven't felt much like that since Mara died."

"I'm glad I can help," I said, my voice low. "I'm glad we're friends."

He frowned and leaned back in his chair. "Friends. Right."

But it was hard not to imagine what else we could be.

We spent the next hour enjoying a good meal and better conversation. We talked about things we liked to do as kids— reading for me, skipping school for him. We discussed our favorite movies and music and foods. We joked, we laughed, we enjoyed each other's company, and it was good. Great. Fantastic.

Just like familiar friends of old.

After dinner, the slow descent of the sun had cooled the air enough for Nate to suggest a walk around the neighborhood.

"Thanks for bringing me here and for paying. You didn't have to," I said.

He frowned. "I asked you out to dinner so yes, I did."

"I mean, as friends, I don't expect you..." My eyes lit on a storefront a half a block down and across the street. With a gasp, I jerked to a stop and grabbed Nate's arm. "I know that place! When I was a kid, my dad took me. It's a nickel arcade. I can't believe it's still open."

"Wanna go?"

"Yes! If you don't mind? But my Skee-Ball game is strong. A

lot stronger than my bowling game. I don't want to embarrass you."

He grinned. "Them are fighting words."

"Let's do it. But don't come crying to me when I win."

"We'll see who's crying."

After that, things felt easier, less tense, and less date-like. After all, who goes to a nickel arcade on a date? That realization both disappointed and relaxed me.

We spent another hour and a half playing pinball and Ms. Pac-Man and Skee-Ball—I was, indeed, the victor. We pooled our tickets together and had just enough to become the proud owners of a miniature stuffed armadillo, which Nate insisted I keep. We walked back to the car, laughing and a little sweaty from the warm arcade and warmer night. At the car, he held my door open and guided me in with a touch on the small of my back.

"Such a gentleman."

With a hand flourish, he bowed. "I do my best."

Without food or games to distract us, silence fell on the ride home and continued all the way to my apartment door. Nate shoved his hands in his pockets. "Can we do this again soon? Maybe next weekend?"

I nodded. "I live twenty feet away from you. All you have to do is knock."

Rocking back on his feet, he looked almost confused. "Okay, sure. Ah, goodnight."

"Night." With a little wave, I stepped inside my apartment, closed the door, and pressed my back against it. I'd followed Mathias's directive. I'd gone with it tonight, and we'd had fun tonight. Fun. Like friends. Friends who just have fun together.

A sharp knock sounded on the door. I pulled it open to find Nate.

"Oh, hey, did you—"

Nate cut me off. "This was a date. You know that, right?"

My brow furrowed in confusion. "What?"

"I asked you to dinner." He held up a finger. "I got a sitter for Lilah." Another finger.

"But..."

"I took you to a restaurant with candles on the table. I asked you out for a second date." Two more fingers.

I stared at him, slack-jawed. "But no. Never once did you use the word 'date.' I think I would remember that."

"You know, I used to be pretty good at this. I almost feel offended," he said, more to himself than to me. "It was a date."

"No."

"Yes."

I crossed my arms. "I thought you didn't want any distractions?"

"Well, maybe I needed the right kind of distraction."

"Okay, fine, if this was a date, you didn't even kiss me at the end of it. Isn't that how dates are supposed to end?"

I wanted to take back the words immediately, but they were out there now. Right there in the two feet of space that separated us, which suddenly seemed terribly wide and yet terrifyingly narrow.

Nate straightened. "I can take care of that now."

"W-what?"

"A kiss."

"I—"

But that was all I got out before he was in my space. He wrapped an arm around my waist and tugged gently. With a squeak, I fell against his chest. I barely had half a second to process this before his other hand cupped my cheek and his mouth was on mine. My hands fluttered, unsure where they should go, or perhaps what they should touch first, before they curled into the fabric of his shirt.

His fingers slid from my cheek to tangle in my hair. My body melted until it was impossible to tell where he stopped, and I started. He deepened the kiss, nudging my mouth open. A bolt of something hot and wild shot through me. My toes curled, my knees shook, my mind jumbled into flashes of bright pinks, fiery reds, blinding white.

Unlike the last time, this kiss wasn't for an audience. It was just for us and that left no wiggle room for confusion.

Holy crap. I'd just gone on a date with Nate Russo.

THIRTY-FIVE

*"A Southern mama is no different than any other mama.
She's just more polite when she lays on the guilt."*

—MIMI

On my list of Most Unexpected, Wonderful Surprises in Life, dating Nate was numbers one through a hundred.

We had gone on a second date. After which, there'd been hand-holding and long kisses while sitting on my couch. At least, until the sitter called and reminded Nate that she had to be home by eleven. The third and fourth dates only got better, and by the fifth, I was all in—the dreamy-eyed, floating-on-a-cloud kind of smitten that annoyed other people. I didn't care.

He was so sweet. Flowers just because, a note found hanging on my door in the morning to wish me a good day, a text message just to say he was thinking about me. And the touching. He couldn't pass me without brushing his fingers along my cheek or smoothing my hair or kissing the top of my head. Every time he did it, my heart flipped, and my cheeks warmed, and I wanted to throw open a window and shout, "Nate Russo is my boyfriend."

I didn't. But I was tempted to.

Maybe it was because we lived next door to each other, but we slipped into each other's lives easily, like it was meant to be. We ate most of our meals crowded around his table or mine, Lilah chattering on about some new animal fact she'd learned. We spent hot summer afternoons at the park with Lilah or swimming at the community center.

We'd go to the movies on a Saturday night when Nate could get a sitter and make out in the back row like teenagers. (My mother would have been scandalized.) We even grocery-shopped together. I pushed the cart while Lilah's pleas for candy and Pop-Tarts went largely ignored, and Nate tossed in ingredients for lasagna. With his famous homemade sauce. And oh, yes, it was real good.

Although it might have been the hot guy cooking it for me that made it better. Or that he was *my* hot guy.

Together we decided to not let Lilah know, at least for now. It was Nate's idea, but I agreed. It was all so new, and we didn't know where it was headed. Neither of us wanted Lilah to be a casualty if it didn't work out. Plus, I'm not going to lie, the sneaking around added an extra layer of excitement.

Sometimes I wanted to pinch myself, to make sure I wasn't living in some fantasy world. And although things seemed to be going well, a small part of me waited for the other shoe to drop. I couldn't stop the nagging feeling it would all be over as quickly as it had started. I told him that one night after Lilah had gone to bed and we were snuggled together on the couch to watch a movie. Although, I was watching him more than the movie.

I sighed. He was just so... perfect.

He glanced down at me. "What's the matter?"

"Nothing. Everything is perfect."

The corner of his mouth hinted upward. "Oh, yeah?"

"Yeah. I mean, *you're* perfect." I dropped my eyes and picked at a ball of fuzz on the blanket we were under. "Sometimes I wonder if you're going to figure out that I'm not."

He frowned. "Not what?"

"Not perfect. I just keep waiting for you to get that and then you're outta here. I make mistakes, I screw things up. Plus, there's your classes and Lilah. What if I'm making things harder for you? What if I am a distraction?"

He kissed me, a soft press of his lips, but it did the job of quieting me and led to a much deeper kiss that had me a little starry-eyed and a lot disappointed when he finished.

"Everything is fine," he said, stroking my cheek with the pad of his thumb. "I'm not perfect and I don't think you are. We're not-perfect together."

"Hmm," I said, still recovering from the kiss. "Okay."

"Just okay?"

"I mean, another kiss might convince me..."

He grinned and did just that.

"You are almost unbearable," Stella said one Saturday morning. "Like, disgustingly happy all the time. It's giving me a headache."

I grinned. "Thank you very much."

She rolled her eyes and stomped into her office but left the door open. I followed her and sat in the wobbly chair across from her.

"Stop smiling," she grumbled without looking up from her clipboard. "And sit down."

Between Nate, my job at the daycare, and even my plans for the anniversary party, it felt like my life was falling into place at last; like I'd spent most of my life trying to be an edge piece in a puzzle and I'd realized I was an inside piece the whole time.

I was the girl *after*. The one who starts out frumpy and

broken and finds everything she ever wanted by growing her hair out, changing her wardrobe, and becoming a new, vibrant person.

Sure, my mom and I didn't talk to each other, it was more *at* each other. And my sister was marrying a jerk, and Bria was MIA again. And I'd lied more than I ever had before in my life during the last few months, but life was good. Right?

I plopped into the lone wobbly chair in Stella's office.

"I gotta talk fast. Bria is here. She just found out about the internship."

"She got it?" I asked, excitement buzzing through me.

"No, she did not. The interview went very badly." She shuffled some papers on her desk. "It went so badly, the guy from the oil company called me after to let me know. She bombed it. Arrived ten minutes late, wore shorts and a tank top, and refused to answer half the questions."

My smile retreated. "What? We practiced. She was ready. Why would she do that?"

"I think you'll have to ask her that yourself." Stella chewed her lip, her dark eyes serious. "Just remember, it takes a lot for a person to change what they've always thought about themselves. She's angry at herself, but that's not who she's going to take the anger out on."

With a sigh, I stood and walked to the rec room. Bria was slumped on an ugly beige couch, a pillow held to her stomach. She flipped through the TV channels mindlessly before pausing on a cooking show.

"Hey," I sat opposite her on the couch. A rock of concern laced with a dollop of guilt settled in my stomach. "How's it going?"

She flipped through more channels and stopped at a wrestling match.

My hands twisted in my lap. "I heard about the interview. You want to talk about it?"

Nothing, but her breathing changed, became rougher.

"Or not. We don't have to."

The television clicked off. We both stared at the black screen.

I touched her arm. "I'm sorry, Bria. I wish I could do something to make it better."

The remote flew across the room and hit the wall, plastic raining down. Bria stood and turned the full force of her anger at me then, her eyes burning.

"You know what? I'm tired of you trying to make things better for me. I'm not a stray you find on the street and clean up and hope that solves all its problems."

Her words made me flinch and that feeling in my stomach turned sour. "I-I'm not trying to solve all your problems."

Bria snorted. "Aren't you? I'm a failure. I'm always gonna be a failure. Ain't nothing gonna change that. I don't need you or your help anymore."

Her words hurt, but it was the look on her face that made my insides twist. "That's not true. It's not."

But what if it was true? What if I'd done to Bria what my mother had been trying to do for me my whole life? What if I'd just seen her as a "problem" I could fix? That made me just like my mother, didn't it? A sharp pain spliced my chest.

She leaned down. "It really is. Once a screw-up, always a screw-up. You know exactly what I mean, don't you? Takes one to know one."

I sucked in a stinging breath at her words and held it until my lungs burned. Bria stomped out of the room, slamming the door behind her. But I didn't hear it. All I heard were her words over and over, like a mantra, *Once a screw-up, always a screw-up.*

THIRTY-SIX

"Wishin' and hopin' is not the same as doin'."

—*MIMI*

"Do you think Duke Crosby will sign my limited-edition *Duke Crosby Encyclopedia of Birds?*" Lilah asked, practically vibrating with excitement.

"Yes, for the hundredth time, yes," Nate said as we made our way through the hordes of fellow Duke Crosby devotees.

And there were a lot of them, apparently. The tickets had gone faster than Nate expected, and Lilah had been crushed. When Phee had found out, she'd worked a little magic. She'd talked her way into doing a piece about the event. Sometimes it paid to have a sister who worked for a news station.

"There's Phee," I said, pointing to my sister standing in front of a news van. Despite the stifling heat, she was dressed in a navy knee-length dress and heels, her hair pulled up in some complicated twist that probably involved a lot of bobby pins and hairspray. Oversized sunglasses covered half her face.

Lilah dropped Nate's hand and took off, screaming Phee's name.

"I think she's excited," I said.

"That would be an understatement. She's been up and dressed since five o'clock this morning." He tugged my hand, so I stopped and faced him. He smiled. "Thank you for this. It means a lot to Lilah. And me."

That smile was worth promising Phee two extra dress shopping trips with Mom for the tickets. "It was my pleasure."

His smiled turned wicked. Now *that* smile would make me do a whole lot of other things. He glanced toward Lilah and, satisfied she wasn't looking, he kissed me right there. Long enough, my knees turned to noodles and I had to clutch his shirt, even after we parted.

"You should thank me more often," I said. Behind him, I caught sight of Lilah dragging Phee by the hand toward us. "Here they come. Look casual."

"My, my," Phee smirked. "I was worried you two got lost."

"They didn't get lost," Lilah said matter-of-factly. "They were kissing."

"No, we weren't," Nate said.

"Of course not," I said at the same time.

Phee laughed. "Is that so?"

"They kiss all the time. They think I don't see but they aren't very good at sneaking, so I just pretend I don't know."

Nate rubbed the back of his neck. "Can we just keep pretending? Please?"

"Sure." She shrugged, then turned to Phee. "Did you see Duke yet? Does he have all his birds? Can I meet him now? Please? Please? I'll be so good, I swear."

Phee gave one of Lilah's pigtails a tug. "Slow down. I have met him. In fact, see this tent over there? He's in there right now and he knows I have a special friend who wants to meet him."

"Now?" Lilah squealed. "Can I go now?"

"Let's go." Phee led us into a large tent. It was set up circle-style, with seats around the edge and a center performance area.

Lilah froze. "It's him. It's really him. He's beautiful. Daddy, isn't he beautiful?"

At the center of the tent stood an older man with a notice-able paunch and an oversized handlebar mustache. He was dressed head to toe in khaki. A brightly colored bird perched on his arm.

Nate cleared his throat, probably to hide a laugh. "Do you mean the bird or Duke?"

"Both," Lilah said, her eyes wide with excitement. She grabbed Nate's arm and pulled him toward the object of her affection. "Let's go."

"I thought I could steal Perci away for a little," Phee said.

"Daddy, hurry up!"

Nate waved us off. "Take your time. Something tells me we're going to be occupied for a while."

Phee linked arms with me and directed us to a semi-circle of food trucks not too far away from the tent. We both ordered something to drink and a fried pickle to share. (This was Texas. Most any food could be found in fried form.)

"How are you not melting?" I asked, pulling my tank top away from my sticky skin. We'd found a seat at a table under a slightly wilted umbrella that provided very little relief.

"I am. You just can't see it under all the make-up. Occupa-tional perk, I guess." She pushed her sunglasses on top of her head.

I took one look at her and my sister-sense went wild. "What's wrong?"

She froze and took a deep breath. "Nothing's wrong. Every-thing's fine."

And then she burst into tears.

"Oh, Phee." I patted her hand and handed her napkins.

When she'd calmed down some, I asked, "Do you want to talk about it?"

She shook her head but started talking anyway. "Everything is just so... weird."

I waited a beat and when she didn't go on, I prodded her. "With what?"

"With everything. Joel. The wedding. My job." She sniffled and whispered, "Mathias."

"Did something happen?"

With a nod, she settled her head on my shoulder. "On my birthday. Mathias showed up at my apartment and wanted to talk. We haven't talked much since..."

"...he kissed you?"

"You know about that?"

"Phee, he's my best friend. He tells me stuff."

She looked away. "Yeah, since the kiss. He said he had something to tell me."

"And?"

Her fingers tangled in her lap. "He said he's in love with me."

"He did what?" I half yelled. "He didn't tell me about this."

She sniffled. "It surprised me too."

"What did you say?"

"Nothing at first. Then he said some things. I said some things and then he left. I've tried to text, but he won't respond." Eyes filling with tears, she sat up and swiped at her cheeks.

"Phee, I'm so sorry."

"You know when we first met, back when he was just regular Mathias before all the clothes and hair, and we were kind of seeing each other? It wasn't serious. But it could have been." A small smile broke through the sadness and just as quickly, disappeared. "Then one night, Mom figured it out and she sat me down and told me that Mathias was a nice boy but that I needed a man who could take care of me, help me reach my goals."

My jaw dropped. "She didn't."

"She did. And Perci, I wanted those things too. At least back then. You can't blame it all on her."

I totally could.

"So, I shut him down. Even though he didn't know the real reason." With a steadying breath, she turned to face me. "Do you think he hates me?"

I shook my head. "But I think he wishes he could." I covered her hand with mine and squeezed. "Have you thought that you might feel the same way about him?"

"I-I'm engaged to be married."

The misery in her voice made my own heart break a little. "I know it would be hard to call off the wedding, but an engagement doesn't mean you're married yet. You have choices."

She shook her head. "I can't do that to Joel. Or to Mom. She'd lose her mind."

"Mom isn't the one who's getting married. She would get over it." Probably. Maybe.

She dabbed at her eyes with a napkin and plastered on her pageant smile, even if it wobbled a bit. "Joel and I are getting married. In fact, he asked me to move in with him at the end of the month and I said yes."

The next Monday, Miss Marge greeted me with a shout from her office as soon as I arrived at work. Even though it was before 7 a.m., a fine sheen of sweat graced my forehead from my walk in the hotter-than-Hades September weather. Fall was a myth in Texas.

Work was going well. Miss Marge had finally allowed me to digitize the sign-in/sign-out sheets, and I'd helped her set up direct deposit for payroll. Which she'd even grudgingly admitted was easier. She'd offered me the position of head preschool teacher. The pay was the same, but with more responsibility.

I, of course, had said yes.

I peeked into Marge's office. "Morning."

Glasses perched on her nose, she flicked her eyes from the computer screen—yes, my evil plan had succeeded—to me. "Perci. Good, just who I needed to talk to. Come, have a seat."

I sidled into the office. "What's up?"

She pulled off her glasses, her face serious. "I wanted to give you plenty of notice. The daycare will be closing in October."

"What do you mean, closing?" I dropped into the chair across from her.

"The property was purchased, and my lease is up. The new owner hiked up the rent. I've been trying to see if I could make it work and I just can't."

"But what about the kids? What about you?" *What about me?*

"Clients will get notified tomorrow. I wanted to let all the employees know today." She rubbed her eyes with the palms of her hands. "I've been here for over twenty-five years. I'm old and tired. It's time for me to go spend time with my grandbabies. I guess I'll sell the house and move to Austin to be closer to them."

I slumped in my seat. "I love it here. This job has been so good for me."

"And you've been good for this place." She leaned forward, her face serious. "You're good with the kids, with the parents, with all the business stuff. My son still can't believe you got me to start using computers."

"I'll miss you," I whispered, and got myself out of that office before I started crying.

. . .

The rest of the day dragged. No amount of hugs from the tiny monsters or declarations of love from three-year-olds pulled me from my funk. I'd spent the last several months falling in love with this place. More than that, I'd found a job I loved, and I'd become a version of myself that I loved while doing it. Sure, it wasn't the most lucrative in terms of money, and it wasn't a job my mom "approved" of, but it made me happy, excited to wake up each morning. And now? It would be gone, and I would be back to square one. I wanted to throw up at the thought of looking for a new job. Eventually, I'd have to tell my family that I'd lost another job, failed at another thing.

As other employees received Miss Marge's news, the mood grew somber. By the time 3 p.m. rolled around, I slunk out the door with a heavy heart. The sun beat down without mercy. Slipping on my sunglasses, I turned onto the sidewalk and stopped. My feet rooted themselves right there and refused to move.

There was a sign—one of those inexpensive FOR RENT signs on metal prongs—pushed into the patch of grass next to the sidewalk. I was sure it hadn't been there this morning.

I blinked, wanting to shake my head in the exaggerated way a confused cartoon character would. This wasn't right. It couldn't be real. But no amount of silent prayers changed it.

My chest tightened, face growing hot with disbelief and then with flat-out, white-hot anger as I read the sign in its entirety.

FOR RENT. FOR INFORMATION, CONTACT MAYFIELD HOME MORTGAGE

THIRTY-SEVEN

"I may be poor but it don't cost nothing to pay attention."

I spent the rest of the week equal parts in awe of my mother's ability to ruin lives in a single action. Even Lilah and Nate couldn't lighten my mood. Every time I had a moment to let my mind wander, it went right back to the sign in front of Miss Marge's, or to Phee crying in front of a food truck.

Mathias fielded my ranting texts and phone calls, even at midnight. He was a good friend, and I couldn't help but wonder what would have happened with him and Phee if our mother hadn't interfered.

The thought of seeing Mom made me feel sick to my stomach. But the anniversary party loomed ahead and although I prayed for an excuse—the flu, a broken leg, leprosy—to get me out of it, it didn't happen. Instead, I spent the week double-checking the vendors, confirming tables and food.

Then there was that stupid slide show I hadn't even started.

By the weekend, when I made it over to Mimi's apartment

to search through her old photographs, I was a mess of emotions, teetering on some imaginary ledge. It would take nothing more than a tiny breeze for me to fall, and I wasn't sure what would happen if I did.

Mimi was making potato salad and humming along with Patsy Cline when I arrived. She took one look at me and frowned. "What's wrong with you? You look like a vegetarian bear at a barbecue."

That was a new one. "I'm fine."

She hummed but didn't push further. "All right, then. I took out all the photos I could find and made a big stack on the kitchen table."

"Thanks."

"Got a little teary-eyed looking at them. Your mama was cute as a bug when she was little." Mimi danced over to the fridge in her three-inch heels and pulled out a pitcher. "Tea?"

I nodded and wandered over to the table, where several albums and a couple of shoeboxes rested. Flicking through a few photos in one box, I came across one of me holding Phee when she wasn't more than two years old. I smiled, remembering how I'd carted her around like she was my very own living doll back then.

Mimi handed me a glass, and I caught a whiff of cigarette smoke on her clothes. "You promised you'd quit smoking."

"I'm only smoking a little now."

"That's like being a little pregnant."

"Don't you worry about old Mimi. I'm indestructible."

"So was the *Titanic*. And Rome. And Crystal Pepsi. You can't be the Crystal Pepsi of grandmothers. I need you."

"Honey, I'm not going anywhere." She sat and flipped through an album before stopping on a photo of herself and my mother. Mom was about five or six in the picture, her dark hair pulled up in pigtails, a smile full of missing teeth set in a round face. "Look at those cheeks. You looked just like her at that age."

She pointed at the photo I was holding. I laid the pictures beside each other and squinted at them. The resemblance was undeniable—dark hair, dark eyes, same rounded cheeks and wide grins. Somehow, this annoyed me. I wasn't sure I wanted to have anything in common with my mother. I closed the album and rooted around in the box of photos.

We spent the next twenty minutes lost in memories. Sometimes, Mimi would stop and show me a photo—almost always of her and Mom—a dreamy, faraway look in her eyes.

"It was always the two of us for so long—me and my girl against the world."

"Did you ever think about getting married again?"

My grandmother flipped another page in her album. "Oh, sure. I dated a little and when your mama was about ten, I was hot and heavy with a gentleman caller. But he and Bobbie Jo got along 'bout as well as a cat at a dog show. Lots of barking and hissing between the two of them. Never could figure out how to make them tolerate each other. After that, I dipped my toe into the dating pool now and then, but I was too tired to put a lot of effort into a long-term relationship."

"That's kind of sad."

"Goodness, I worked three jobs to make sure my girl had what she needed. She was the most important thing I ever did with my entire life." Her gaze met mine, a sadness there that made me uncomfortable. "Still is. Mamas do an awful lot for their babies, even when it's not appreciated."

I squirmed, not wanting to feel an ounce of sympathy and understanding for my mother. I opened another album. A grainy Polaroid of my parents stared back at me. In it, my mother—dressed in jeans, a college sweatshirt, and rocking some major feathered hair—sat on Dad's lap, an arm slung around his shoulders.

Mimi leaned closer. "Yep, that's about when they met at college. She was always so serious about going to school and making something of herself. Had a good head on her shoulders. Very driven. Your sister gets that from her. But then she met your daddy and plans changed."

She pulled the album toward herself and flipped through the pages, pointing out pictures, commenting on them, and allowing me to photograph them for the slide show. My parents looked so happy, carefree. Mom wasn't quite so thin or quite so perfect, and she looked so much more relaxed.

"And here are the wedding photos." She tapped on the album.

I flipped through the pictures of my parents at the courthouse, in a smallish room, a judge presiding over the blessed event. Mimi was there in a truly awful garment of purple sequins, while my mother wore a simple white shift dress and an enormous smile. Dad was in jeans, his hand clutching Mom's.

"They look different. Young, happy," I said, wishing I could have known these versions of my parents.

"They were."

I flipped the page to a photo of their first married kiss, my mom and grandma hugging, everyone posing with the judge. It seemed like such a small event, so ordinary for my mother to be a part of. The next page was of Mimi signing what I assumed was the marriage license as a witness. Next to that was a photo of that license up close. I read as much of it as I could—my parents' names, the place, the witnesses' names, and the date.

That's where I paused, squinted, leaned over the book and reread the date. "This is weird."

"What's that?"

"The year is wrong on their marriage license." I took the photo out of the album and showed it to Mimi. "They were married thirty years ago, not twenty-nine."

Mimi grabbed the photo. She studied it, making a clicking sound as she did so.

"Mimi?"

She didn't reply.

"If this is right... I'll turn twenty-nine this coming February. That would mean..."

"That's right, honey." Mimi set the photo down with a sigh. "It seems your mama never quite told you the story of why they rushed down the aisle. She was pregnant with you."

I pushed the photo of the marriage license away from me like it was on fire. "Why would she never tell me that?"

Mimi shrugged. "I can't say I understand everything about your mother, but I think she didn't want anyone to know she was pregnant." Her finger traced a wedding day photo of Mimi and Mom together. "History repeated itself, I guess. I got married because I got pregnant and so did she. Maybe she thought if you girls didn't know, you wouldn't make the same mistake."

And there it was. This explained so much about my relationship with my mother, why I was never good enough or smart enough or pretty enough for her. I hadn't been part of her plan. In fact, I was the reason she'd had to get married instead of finishing school. My chest tightened, ached with this realization.

To my mother, I wasn't just a failure, I was a mistake.

THIRTY-EIGHT

"The real measure of a man is not when he does something right,

it's how he reacts when he screws something up."

—MIMI

Pericles the Demon Dog bore his bottomless death eyes into the back of my head as I stacked fancy clear plastic plates in my parents' kitchen. It was the day of the anniversary party and I'd been here all morning making preparations.

"Stop looking at me." I glared at him. "I'm not afraid of you."

The dog regarded me for a long moment before letting out one sharp, ominous yip. I startled, pressing a hand to my heart.

"Nope, not scared of you at all."

"Are you talking to the dog again?" Phee asked, hovering by the doorway.

"Is there a dog in here? I'd hardly noticed." *Take that, Scary Perry.*

I ripped open a box of plastic forks with more force than

necessary. They scattered across the island, bouncing to the floor. With a groan, I bent to pick them up.

I'd been a jumble of nervous energy since the moment I'd woken up. A giant ball of tension lay smack in the middle of my stomach, like an omen of bad things to come.

Phee crouched beside me. "You okay?"

"Me? I'm fine. Just lots to do."

My sister nodded, frowning as she stood. Dressed in white capris and a bright pink ruffled tank top, her hair and make-up done with a steady, knowledgeable hand, she reminded me of a carnation. She looked lovely. I hated it.

"We'll get it all done."

"You know what I could use? A drink." I pulled a bottle of wine from the fridge and grabbed a couple of plastic cups.

"It's not even noon yet."

"It's not every day you throw your parents an anniversary party." I held out a half-full glass to her and took a sip of mine. "Time to start celebrating," I said, and even I could hear how miserable I sounded.

An hour and two glasses of premium, screw-top white wine later, a pleasant numbness had replaced some of my tension. Phee was arguing with the rental delivery man, Mom was out getting her hair and nails done, Daddy was tucked in his office.

After one more swig of wine, I marched down the hallway to his office and knocked.

"Come on in."

I relocated a stack of files on one of his chairs and sat. "Daddy, I have a question."

Head still bent over his papers, he motioned with his hand. "Of course."

"Do you own the building of the daycare where I work?"

He paused. "That would be some coincidence, huh? Where's it located?"

I told him the address and waited while he dug around to

find the information, gnawing at my thumbnail. The room felt hot and stuffy. Sweat gathered on my brow. The idea to ask this question had been brewing all week, but the desire had only intensified in the last few days—right around the time Mimi had dropped that wedding bombshell on me.

"Well, I'll be." He tapped a finger to his computer screen. "Looks like we bought that about two months ago. I think this was one your mother found."

A strange choking sound worked its way from my throat. There was the confirmation. I knew it but hearing it out loud made it even worse. This was a new low, even for her. Her actions had now affected more people than just me. Miss Marge had to close her business. All those families had to scramble to find a new daycare.

"So, it was Mom."

"Must have been. You know how she's been working here part-time? She's really enjoying the property management side of things."

"Great," I muttered as my stomach churned with wine and anger. Not a good combination.

Dad leaned back in his chair, folding his hands over his stomach. "Now, what's this all about?"

"No reason."

Daddy stared, looking for all the world like he could read my mind. His mouth opened at the same time the doorbell rang.

"I should get that. I bet it's the caterer. Thanks for looking." I hustled out of his office, wobbling more from anger than wine. In hindsight, that turned out to be a very bad combination.

I opened the back gate for the delivery men and tromped back to the kitchen to get some lunch before completing the 1,400 things on the to-do list. The room was empty. The quiet allowed me time to fixate on the many ways my mother was ruining my life.

How should I deal with it? With her? How would I make it through every single day of my life without exploding?

I made sherbet punch, stirring it with too much vigor. The frothy pink sloshed over the side and onto the counter. Pausing, I took another swig of my wine.

Should I tell someone about this fake-iversary? Was that necessary?

Then again, was it *necessary* for my mother to ruin the job I loved? Or to try to control everything about my life? None of those things was okay. My mother couldn't seem to help herself, bulldozing into my life whenever she saw fit.

I scowled into the punch bowl and took another sip of wine.

New Perci was in charge of her life. New Perci didn't second-guess herself, and New Perci didn't let her mother walk—

"Persephone, there you are," my mother said. Hair straightened, face freshly spackled with make-up, she slid into the kitchen with a smile. "Where's Pericles? I haven't seen my little baby in hours."

"Outside with Phee."

"Oh, good. I need to put his outfit on him. Did you know they make tuxedos for dogs?" She surveyed the kitchen. "Is there anything I can do?"

Stop ruining my life? I snorted and gulped the rest of my wine, gripping the glass until my fingers hurt. "Nope, we have it under control."

"Are you sure? I'm ready to serve."

Oh, right. Serve your own evil plans! I laughed out loud. My mother shot me a curious look, and I slapped a hand over my mouth.

"I'm fine. We're fine. Everything is fine."

"Will you be wearing this"—she waved a hand in my direction—"outfit to the party?"

I yanked on my neon-yellow tank top and almost lost my

balance. *Hmm. Probably should lay off the wine.* "No, Mother. I brought a change of clothes."

"Good." She came closer and pressed a kiss to my cheek. Her Mom Scent surrounded me and for one stolen moment, I wanted to curve into her, to let her hug me tight until this weird pressure in my chest disappeared. Didn't matter how old a person was, mothers meant comfort. "I want everything to look perfect."

And then I remembered the part about her ruining my life. And me ruining hers.

I straightened. "It will."

Mom pressed a hand to her stomach. "Then, I'll go make myself scarce. See you at five, dear."

She disappeared into the hallway and my eyes followed her. That was the last time I saw Mom before the party started. The calm before the storm, or something like that.

THIRTY-NINE

"Never trust a man if his teeth are too white,
or he's got two first names,
or he says, 'Trust me.'"

—*MIMI*

I'd brought two dresses with me—one a sensible, black dress in deference to my mother. But I decided not to wear it. Instead, I changed into a pale green boho dress and white sandals, pulled my hair up at the sides, and stuck in dangling gold earrings.

It made me a little sad Nate wasn't here, but he hadn't been able to find a sitter for Lilah. Mathias had decided not to come for... reasons (namely, Phee). I'd even toyed with the idea of inviting Bria, who I knew would laugh outright at attending, but at least I'd have an ally. Except since our last conversation, my calls and texts to her went unanswered, her silence clearly communicating we were not allies, not even a little, at the moment. I was on my own.

Mom greeted guests, giving out hugs and air-kisses and making sure to point out the anniversary necklace my father had purchased for her. "It has thirty diamonds, one for every year we've been married."

I grimaced each time she said it and it was getting harder and harder to not stand on the nearest chair and shout, *Lies! You've not been married thirty years!*

An hour into the party, and my parents' home was cozily packed with one hundred of their closest friends. The group spilled into the backyard and settled around the many small tables strategically placed throughout. Even the weather had cooperated today, with highs only in the eighties and a tolerable amount of humidity.

In the front room of the house, the flat-screen television was playing the slide show on a loop. I searched my mother's face in the photographs for any indication she'd resented me as a baby. Had I disappointed her even then?

The fourth glass of wine slid right past the lump in my throat.

But I held myself together, thank you very much. I smiled and nodded. I directed guests to the bathroom like a boss. I help the servers in the kitchen. I shooed Phee out of the way to go mingle. I was an efficient, organized machine, damn it.

Outside, I surveyed the festivities to look for any weaknesses, but all the guests seemed happy.

"Perci!" Mimi shouted across the yard where she'd settled in at a table next to the open bar. "Get over here."

Mom's head shot up at the sound, a pasted-on smile frozen on her face. Her eyes met mine and told me in one look to take care of the old lady and do it now.

I trotted over to Mimi. "What's up?"

"Come sit down and have a drink." Mimi waved a hand at one of the servers. "Bring my girl an old-fashioned."

"I shouldn't have any more to drink," I said, sliding into a chair across from her.

"Nonsense! You can never have too much alcohol or chocolate."

"I'm pretty sure you can."

She shrugged. "Just have a little and stay with me. I doubt your mother will come over here anyway. You're safe."

Good point. I nodded and sipped at the drink. The sugar and heat of the bourbon warmed me from the inside and went straight to my already fuzzy head. I set the glass to the side.

Mimi patted my arm. "You've done a great job. The food is delicious."

"Yep. It's all going along swimmingly." Swimmingly was a good word, and it reminded me of Sal, and that reminded me I'd much rather be home, curled up with a good book or maybe making out with Nate in a closet while Lilah watched a movie. I hiccupped and giggled too loudly.

"You have had a bit to drink, haven't you?" Mimi frowned.

My head felt heavy and light all at the same time. How was that possible? New Perci shrugged. Who cares?

"Let's get you some water." She pushed the plate toward me. "Try the artichoke dip while I get it. Good stuff."

Pressing a finger to my lips, I studied the plate before choosing a baby carrot and dipping it in hummus.

Mimi placed a cup of water at my elbow. "There you go. Now, drink up."

But I didn't drink it. I hunted down the artichoke dip and a cracker. This was much better than dumb vegetables, and I was hungry. A gnawing sort of hunger that seemed bottomless. I shoved another cracker in my mouth. "This is delicious."

Mimi scooted the glass closer. "Now, slow down and drink that water too."

I ignored her. Dip fell off a cracker on its way to my mouth and landed half on my cleavage, half on my dress.

"Well, shoot." My voice sounded loud to my own ears. I used my fingers to scrape off the dip and shove it in my mouth.

It was good dip, no need to waste it. In the process, my elbow banged into the cup of water, and it took a dive off the table and landed in my lap.

I sucked in a breath when the ice water made contact and shot to my feet with a loud—and very impolite—curse word.

"Oh, lawd," Mimi muttered. She stood and started dabbing at me with little white-and-gold napkins I'd had made for the party. They read: CRAIG AND ROBERTA MAYFIELD, THIRTY YEARS OF WEDDED BLISS. Underneath that was their wedding date.

Lies.

My whole life was surrounded by lies. My parents had lied about their wedding date. My mother lied about how she felt about me. My sister was lying about Joel Allen. I couldn't be blamed for all my lies lately, could I? I was following in the family tradition. Liars beget liars, or something.

"Here comes your mother," Mimi said. "Let me handle her."

I was tired of lying, though. It took a lot of energy.

"What is going on over here?" Mom hissed. "Everyone is looking at you."

When I glanced around, dozens of eyes were fixed on me.

"Are you drunk?" Mom asked, wrapping a hand around my arm.

"Maybe? I don't know." I frowned. "I have to tell you something."

"Lower your voice."

I straightened and scowled. "No. You can't tell me what to do anymore. New Perci is her own person."

"Let's go in the house and talk."

"Nah-uh. I'm going to say it now." I flung an arm out. "I pretended Nate was my boyfriend because I didn't want you to think I was pathetic Old Perci who couldn't get herself a date. But guess what? We're dating now. Oh, yes, we are. A-and he's a construction worker. Ha! Oh, I lied when I said I had my job even though I have it now, but I didn't have it then, and now it's closing, and I won't have any job." I turned to the crowd of gawkers. "And Brent and I didn't go our separate ways like my mom wants me to say. He broke up with me on the radio because I'm boring."

I paused, leaned against the table. "I guess I ended up being pathetic, anyway. Who lies about a job and a boyfriend, huh? Me. Mimimimi!" I sang that last bit while turning in a circle. I jerked to a stop when I spotted a certain onlooker. "Who's boring now, Brent? By the way, your ties are super ugly. All of them."

Several people chuckled.

"You aren't making any sense at all," Mom hissed.

"Is the truth hard to understand?" A little dizzy, I sank into my chair. "Now. I told you the truth. It's your turn."

Phee pushed her way through the growing crowd. "Perci, lower your voice, please."

Pasting on a smile, Mom waved a hand at the guests. "I'm sorry for our little scene."

No one moved a muscle, including Joel Allen, who stood front and center with a smirk on his stupid, fake face. After he married my sister, we'd be related, and I would have to make up excuses to avoid him. How many kidneys did I have? Four? That would get me through a couple of holiday dinners if I donated them at just the right time, but then... I jolted upright in my chair. In the name of honesty, I should tell Phee this.

So, I did.

"Phee, Joel Allen is stupid and fake. You shouldn't marry him. If you marry him, I'm going to give away all four of my kidneys just so I don't have to see him at Christmas. Do you want that on your conscience?"

Phee crouched beside me, eyes wide and panicked. "Please. Go inside."

I did not go inside.

"And," I continued, poking a finger at Phee's stupid pink shirt, "you are not even in love with him."

My mother glared at me with the vitriol of a thousand angry cats. "Persephone Amelia Mayfield, stop this at once. Your sister does not need—"

"My sister is a liar. It runs in the family, I guess." I picked up a sausage wrap and spoke around the bite I took. "Did you know she really hates you butting into her life all the time? Oh, and she's in love with Mathias even though you don't want her to be."

"Perci!" A stricken look washed over Phee, draining the color from her face. Her eyes darted between Mom and me. But I noticed she didn't search out Joel Allen and she didn't correct me.

"Is this true, Phoebe?" My mother asked, or, rather, demanded.

"Go ahead. Tell her, Phee." I gestured at my sister, but she only shook her head. "Fine. I will. Mom, butt out of her life. She's not a little pageant girl for you to mold. She's got her own plans and you have to let her live them. You should understand what it's like when something screws up your plans, right?" A hiccup popped out of my mouth, and I giggled.

"What is that supposed to mean?" Mom demanded.

Before I could answer, my father pushed his way through the crowd and put an arm on my mother's shoulders. He smiled widely at the onlookers in the crowd. "Ladies, isn't it time for the cake?"

A murmur rolled through the crowd, but no one moved. In fact, I'd say they all leaned in a bit closer.

Mom tipped her chin up. "No, I want to hear what Persephone meant by that."

I selected a stuffed shrimp from the plate on the table. "I saw your marriage certificate at Mimi's house. Did you know you've only been married twenty-nine years, not thirty? Mimi told me you were pregnant with me. That's why you had to get married, right? Because I was a mistake. What a screw-up I've been."

Something like horror flashed in my mother's eyes, but it was my father who spoke. "Cupcake, that's not true. You were never a mistake."

"Oh, really? Why are we pretending this is your thirtieth anniversary then?" I stood up, slid my shoes off and began to pace in the little patch of grass in front of me. "Why does Mom constantly complain about my weight and my clothes? She tried to talk Brent into proposing." I plunked down in the chair. "That daycare building she bought? She hiked up the rent so much, now it's closing."

Dad took a step back and turned to Mom. "Is that true?"

Panic edged Mom's voice when she spoke to my father. "What was I supposed to do, Craig? You don't know the whole story. You know as well as I do that daycare job of hers was ridiculous, but you let me be the bad guy. That's how it works. That's how it's always worked."

My father stared at his wife of thirty—no, twenty-nine, years, face flushed. He opened his mouth and a choking growl emerged before he slammed it shut. With a shake of his head, he turned on his heels and stalked away. Mom's eyes followed him, but she didn't go after him.

"Well, this is turning out to be quite a party," Mimi said.

Mom's eyes gleamed as she swung around to face her mother. "This is your fault. You have ruined everything."

"Now, Bobbie Jo."

My mother growled and turned on me. "How could you do this here? Now? Are you trying to embarrass me?"

My heart clunked against my chest and then began to beat double-time. "Like all the times I embarrassed you? Oh, it's Perci? She can't get anything right. Here, I can do it better."

I swiped at my cheeks and my fingers came away wet. That made me angrier. I didn't want to cry. I wanted pure, unadulterated rage to pour out of me. Then I wanted my mother to hug me and tell me everything would be okay.

Mom's fists balled at her sides. "That's not true. Of course I'm not embarrassed by you."

Mimi snorted.

"Shut up, Mama!" Mom's eyes narrowed on Mimi. "You always do this, turn her against me. She's my daughter, not yours."

"Oh, is that what I'm doing?"

"Yes! It's always been about you, even when I was a child. You had to dress like that." She pointed a finger at Mimi's dark green leopard-print caftan. "You had to be loud. You could never just fit in with the rest of the moms."

"I wasn't like the rest of the moms." Mimi held up her hands, the skin paper-thin and covered in wrinkled lines. "You might remember, I had to work. It was these two hands that worked every day to make sure you had food on your plate and clothes on your back."

"How could I possibly forget? Everyone knew I was Mona Raye Perkins' daughter, and they pitied me. 'Look how hard she works, and just for hand-me-downs and thrift store bargains. Had that baby so young and no man to help her.' And you never let me forget we couldn't afford this or that." Mom's hands twisted at her waist, her normally placid expression laced with frustration, anger, hurt. "Is it my fault I want better for my daughters?"

"I didn't realize life was so difficult for you," Mimi said, and for the first time I could remember, an edge of bitterness crept into her voice. "It didn't go exactly how I planned either."

"Well, you never could afford the double-wide trailer of your dreams," Mom bit out.

Pain flashed in Mimi's eyes. Jaw ticking, she climbed to her feet, a full drink cup in her hand. In slow motion, Mimi's hand tipped and spilled all its contents—on my mother.

With a hiss, Mom froze and stared at the dark stain overtaking the front of her dress. The crowd gasped. Phee scrambled to get out of the line of fire. My jaw dropped.

Mom's eyes shot to Mimi, her face grim. "I cannot believe you did that."

"I apologize," Mimi said in a very non-apologetic voice. She picked up a tiny ham-and-cheese quiche from the table, held it up like she was about to take a bite, and paused. "You know, Bobbie Jo, for a girl who came from a trailer park, you sure act like royalty. You weren't raised this way."

And then, instead of eating that quiche, she threw it. At my mother's face. "Whoops."

Mom blinked; red slashes burned her cheeks. With blurring speed, she reached over and grabbed a cracker topped with artichoke dip from the plate of Mr. Sinclair, who lived three houses down, and lobbed it at Mimi.

The crowd released a collective, "Oooo."

Mimi swiped at her cheek. She selected a cream puff from the plate and took aim. It landed in the middle of Mom's cleavage, where it clung for a moment, before taking the dive into her dress. A deep, rolling laugh burst out of Mimi.

"That is it, Mama!"

"Bring it on, baby girl."

With a screech, Mom turned and snagged a cup of punch from a startled guest's hand and hurled the contents at Mimi.

I swiped at the drops of red liquid that sprinkled on my arm. Old Perci would dive for the nearest safe place and wait for the war to die down. But this was New Perci.

I grabbed a meatball and flicked it. It left a trail of gravy as it slid down Mom's hair to the floor. "That meatball has forty-five calories, and I didn't eat it. Aren't you proud?"

"Persephone, please."

It's hard to take someone who has a cream puff in her bra seriously, though. With a grin, I followed up the meatball with a cheese-and-cracker combo.

Then all hell broke loose.

"This is for ruining my job," I shouted, and tossed a berry-beef bite at my mother. "One hundred calories."

"This is for setting me up on dates." A bacon-wrapped fig. "One hundred and thirty calories."

"For every chance you take to remind me of how much I weigh." Brussels sprouts and ricotta toast. "Three hundred and forty calories. Ouch. That would have gone straight to my hips."

Phee dove in front of us, but despite her good intentions, it only got her covered in cream cheese and shrimp.

"Hey, knock it off," she yelled when a hunk of dip smacked her in the face.

Mimi lobbed food without mercy—at my mother, at Phee, even at me. When she ran out of appetizers from the table, a glass of wine magically appeared in her hand. She sipped at it while looking on with amusement.

And my mom? Never once did she defend herself against me. She stood there and took everything thrown at her—the food, the words, the anger. If I hadn't been high on the rage, I might have noticed the slump of her shoulders and the tears shining in her eyes.

The crowd watched with rapt attention. I glimpsed a phone recording, flashes of a photo, or twelve, being taken. This would be all over the internet in the next couple of hours. My mother would be devastated and even that didn't make me stop.

For a half-second, I wondered if New Perci was who I wanted to be. She was kind of a bitch.

Who knows how long we would have gone on like that for? As it was, it felt like hours. But all the damage had been done in under five minutes.

"Stop this right now." It was Phee, yelling as she stood on a chair, berry sauce dripping from her hair. "Just stop."

Silence washed over the yard. My heaving breath drowned out any other sound except one—a sob.

Mimi frowned. "Bobbie Jo?"

But Mom stood stock-still, tears running down her face, mingling with bits of food. Her eyes darted around the yard, at the faces of her family and friends.

"I-I'm sorry," she blurted, and then she ran away.

Fifteen minutes later, Phee had gone to look for Dad, Mimi had gone to look for Mom, and the guests, having seen the show, had mostly departed. Within minutes, whatever alcohol-induced fog that had filled my brain before shifted and my world became bright, stark, and very, very real.

The backyard looked like it had barely survived a war. Bits of food covered the rental tables and chairs and the linens in the line of fire. I took a step and something soft squelched between my toes.

My mother had been devastated. Not angry or hurt—devastated. What daughter did that to her mother? I sank to the ground, my feet in front of me like a three-year-old who needed someone to tie her shoes.

The tears overwhelmed me, blurring my vision, and that's probably why I never even noticed Pericles until he was right beside me. Delicately, he nudged my arm with his tongue. At first, I thought somehow the Demon Dog had figured out I was at the end of my rope. With a sniffle, I patted his head. "Thanks. That's nice of you. Does this mean I have to stop calling you Scary Perry?"

The dog paused and tilted his head as though he were listening. And then he went back to licking barbecue sauce off my arm.

"Hey."

I blinked, clearing my vision, and looked up. It was Nate. Of course it was. "You're here."

He crouched in front of me and used the pad of his thumb to wipe away a clump of soft cheese from my cheek. "I found a last-minute sitter for Lilah and thought I'd surprise you. So, surprise."

"Oh, great," I moaned. "How much did you hear?"

His eyes were infinitely kind. It almost hurt my chest, how kind they were. "Somewhere around 'New Perci is her own person.'"

A sob escaped me. "I-I think New Perci might be a bitch."

He didn't correct me or tell me I was wrong. Nor did he tell me how to fix all the problems I'd just created. Instead, he stood and put his hand out. "Let's get you up and I'll help you clean up some of this."

"Okay," I whispered, and took his hand.

FORTY

"The loudest one gets heard;
the quietest one gets revenge."

—*MIMI*

Next day, the hangover was enough to swear off wine for the rest of my natural life. But that wasn't the worst of it. Regret was my constant companion. Every time I shut my eyes, I pictured my mother, drenched in appetizers. I couldn't shake the look on her face just before she ran away, how broken and defeated she'd looked.

Mathias called in the morning to tell me he'd seen the photos already.

"What was I thinking?" I said. "She must hate me, and I don't blame her. I think I hate me."

Like the good friend he was, he wisely brought me tacos and let me cry.

The next few days were met with silence from everyone in my family until Daddy asked to meet me for coffee at the office. Unease took up space in my stomach as I opened the door to

Mayfield. Miss Ruby peered at me over the top of her glasses. "Well, well. Are you gonna throw a donut at me?"

I scowled.

She leaned back in her chair and folded her arms across her chest. "Your father's been sleeping in his office all week."

"Really?"

"Really. He's like a lost little puppy." The phone rang, and she ignored it. "And, let me tell you, if he asks me if his shirt matches his tie one more time, I'm going to whack him with a newspaper and put him in the yard."

"Is he that bad?"

"Worse."

"I've made such a mess of everything," I said, feeling a little lost myself.

"I've known your parents for a long time and the two of them need each other. I suspect they'll figure that out sooner than later."

The ringing stopped and then started again in the next breath. This time Miss Ruby snatched up the receiver and said, "We're closed," and slammed it down without ever taking her eyes off me.

"Plus, sometimes a fight can be the best thing for a relationship. Gets the truth out in the open."

That had happened, although why the truth always had to feel so hard to hear was beyond me. "I guess."

She returned to her computer screen, where she began the familiar hunt-peck-hunt-peck. As I shuffled down the hallway toward Dad's office, I heard her say, "Though most people like to fight in private and usually not with meatballs."

Dad's office was even more crowded and messy than usual. Somehow, he'd managed to clear off the loveseat in the room and the remnants of his nights on it included a throw blanket and toss pillow. If that wasn't proof enough of his sleeping arrangements, his appearance was. A few days' worth of salt-

and-pepper growth covered his normally clean-shaven jaw. His dress shirt was so wrinkled, it looked like he'd slept in it and hoped the tie would cover up the damage. It didn't.

I braved circumventing his desk to give him a kiss on the cheek. "Hi."

"Cupcake, thank you for coming." He waved a hand toward the other side of his desk. "I got you coffee."

"Oh, um, thanks." I settled into a chair across from him and wrapped my hands around the cup. Although I had no idea why he'd brought me here, I did have something of my own to say. I'd spent hours over the last few days revisiting that scene in my parents' backyard. For once, I hadn't filtered my words or bit my tongue. For once, I'd spoken *to my mother*. But I'd gone about it the wrong way. I'd done it in public, and I'd done it with appetizer grenades. I had to accept the results that came with that and admit when I'd screwed up.

"I'm sorry about the anniversary party. I shouldn't have said what I said, how I said it." My voice broke.

"I'll say one thing, it's an event that's not likely to be forgotten anytime soon. And you aren't the only one who needs to apologize. Your mother and I had a discussion afterward and" —he took a deep breath and continued—"I'm sorry that I've been sitting back and letting your mother take care of everything. I haven't been a part of our family the way I should. I'm just on the outside looking in."

"Daddy, that's not..." Shaking my head, I stopped before I said the easy thing. I didn't want to hurt his feelings, but if I was going to speak my mind, I needed to do it even when it was hard. "I know how important work is to you, but sometimes, it feels like it's the only thing that matters to you."

"That's my fault," he said, his voice gruff. "If it's not too late, I'd like to change that."

"It's never too late, Daddy." At least, I hoped it wasn't. I gestured toward the couch. "Are you sleeping here?"

He nodded. "For now. I think it's best. Your mother and I have a lot to work on, and I'm worried we'll go right back to our old ways if we don't make a change. I made an appointment with a marriage counselor. We're going tonight."

"*You* made the appointment?"

"I did. I think she's mad about that too, but she's going to go and we're going to spend some time on us, our marriage. We only knew each other for five months before we got married. It was a wedding and baby five months after that. We never had that time for just each other. And I spent all my time working, while she spent all her time with you girls, and now that you're both gone, I think your mother has been struggling for a while. I've been too much of an idiot to see it until now."

"Is Mom okay? She won't take my calls. I'm worried about her." And I needed to apologize to her, too. I needed to apologize every day for the next thirty years. At least.

"She's hurt, Cupcake, and she's embarrassed. It's like poking at a porcupine. She's tough on the outside and nothing but mush on the inside. She loves you and Phee very much, but she knows she's made mistakes. Just give her time. Give us all time."

But it felt like the more time passed, the less likely it was to mend our relationship. I'd screwed up in a way my mother couldn't fix. I'd said things I couldn't unsay. It felt like I'd broken our relationship beyond repair. Could my mother forgive me for this? Could I even forgive myself?

Maybe forgiveness was the wrong word. I didn't just want her to forgive me, I wanted things to change. I wanted my mom to accept me for exactly how I was. Until now, every single action and word and outfit and meal had been noted, inspected, and judged. If our relationship was broken, I wanted to rebuild it, but differently, better.

Still, I was pretty sure I held the top spot on the list of Worst Daughters in the World. In case I needed a reminder, I just had to log onto YouTube and view the five videos uploaded hours after the party.

My sister, considering her job, had taken the brunt of the public response, which spanned the spectrum of amused to disgusted. On air, she'd taken it with gracious humor, but in private, I'd heard very little from her since. I'd called and texted, apologizing as much as I could, but she'd remained quiet just the same.

My allies could be numbered on one hand: Nate, Lilah, Mathias, and Mimi.

And soon, I would lose two of those.

FORTY-ONE

"When it rains, it pours.
Best hope your umbrella opens in time."

—MIMI

The second Friday in October marked the final day of Miss Marge's Preschool and Daycare. By then, most parents had made new arrangements for the kids. Lilah's last day had been the week before, and only a handful remained until the bitter end. On my final walkthrough, my heart grew heavy at the empty classrooms and bare walls.

Miss Marge hugged me before I left and shoved a baggie of cookies at me. "Take these. They're left over from the party, and they'll just go bad."

"Remember to keep me updated on Facebook."

Somehow, I'd convinced her of the merits of social media, set her up on Facebook and given her a crash course in how to upload photos so we could stay in touch. Especially now she was moving three hours away. "I will."

My gaze drifted out the window to the spot by the sidewalk

where the preschool sign had been. Only a small bare patch of
dirt remained, surrounded by green grass and that FOR RENT
sign. I'd never told Miss Marge the Mayfield Home Mortgage
that held her lease was the same Mayfield of my last name.
Maybe she'd put two and two together at some point but, if she
had, she hadn't held it against me.

"Thanks for giving me a job." I sniffled and blinked to hold
the tears at bay. "I know I wasn't exactly prepared."

"Hush, now. Sometimes you go with your gut. My gut told
me you were a good person." She patted my arm and gave me a
watery smile. "And it was right. Besides, you're good at this. You
have a heart for the kids."

I wandered home, soaking in the last time I'd make this trek
from Miss Marge's. There was something satisfying about using
my own two legs to get me where I needed to go every day, and
now I wouldn't have a reason to do it. A few shop owners waved
as I walked by, and I tried to smile in return. Even a glimpse of
red feathers in a tree I passed under did nothing to lift my
mood.

My phone vibrated in my pocket. I slipped it out and smiled
at the text message there.

> **Nate**: *I hope you had a good last day. There's a surprise
> outside your door.*

My heart lightened. Nate did that to me. A bouquet of
tulips waited on the welcome mat in front of my apartment. A
little tag attached to it read: *They reminded me of you. Dinner,
tonight?*

Clutching the flowers to my chest like the besotted dope I
was, I opened my door and danced over to Sal. He gazed at my
gift with one interested black eye.

"Yes, Sal, I'm pretty sure I love this guy."

. . .

Lilah bounded into my apartment a little after six, Nate trailing behind her.

"Perci! Perci! Guess what?" She held up a baggie containing a tiny chip of white. "I lost another tooth."

"Don't forget to put it under your pillow."

She rolled her eyes and stuffed the bag in her pocket. "Of course. Else the tooth fairy can't find it and I won't get"—she side-eyed Nate—"the newest book in the *Wonders of the World* series."

"When I was a kid, we got a dollar," Nate said.

Lilah stuck out a hip and put her fist on it. "That was in the old-time days."

I snorted and Lilah skipped over to show Sal her tooth.

Nate pulled me into a hug. I closed my eyes and burrowed my face into the soft spot by his neck. "Hi."

"Hi," I breathed against him. "Thank you for the flowers. They're my favorite."

"I thought wildflowers were your favorite."

I tipped my head back. "They're my favorite because they're from you."

I think Sal even rolled his eyes at all the cheesiness, and I didn't care.

He gave me one of his slow smiles. His fingers tangled with mine and he pulled me toward the hallway. Without taking his eyes off me, he said, "Lilah, Perci's going to show me something. Just wait right here."

We turned the corner and stopped. My back bumped against the wall as he took a shuffling step forward. "What am I showing—"

He cut me off with a kiss. Humming, I melted against him. One of his hands threaded in my hair, the other settled on my hip.

"Perci?" Lilah said, from close by but not visible.

With a huff, Nate rested his forehead to mine. I pressed my fingers to his lips and giggled. "Yes?"

"Those cookies look good. Can I have one?"

Nate moved to my neck, leaving tiny little kisses along the path. "Sure," I said. "Yes, that's fine." He hit the spot right where my neck and shoulder met. Lovely, lovely. Toes curling. "Oh, my."

He laughed against my skin and whispered, "Right there, huh?"

I hummed in agreement, and he did it again.

"This is a good cookie," Lilah said from somewhere in the living room. "I've never had a cookie that tastes like this before."

Nate's arm wrapping around my waist distracted me before I could answer. He pulled me in for another long kiss.

"Daddy, my lips feel spicy," Lilah said from the other room.

Nate straightened. "What do you mean, spicy?"

"They feel funny."

Concern flashed in his eyes. He rounded the corner, and I hurried after him. Lilah stood in the middle of the kitchen, a half-eaten cookie resting on the counter in front of her. Nate reached her and tilted her face. Drool trailed to her chin from the corner of her mouth.

I couldn't speak, as the full weight of what was happening hit me.

Lilah coughed and her breathing changed to shallow inhalations. Fear crept into her eyes as she took labored breaths. "I-I can't..."

Nate's eyes darted around the room and landed on the cookie. He turned to me, a wild look in his eye. "The cookie. What's in the cookie?"

My heart was racing. "They're from work... I'm not sure."

He lunged across the island, snatched a cookie, and sniffed it. "Shit. Shit. Shit."

"I don't feel so good," Lilah said. The wheezing echoed in

the room, louder and more terrifying with each pull of air. And then she puked.

I rushed across the kitchen, grabbing paper towels, panic bubbling inside. "I didn't know they had peanut butter in them... I had no idea..."

Nate ignored me, racing toward the front door. "Big breaths, honey. I'll get your medicine. It'll be okay."

My heart dropped. *Would it be okay?*

The door slammed into the wall when he pulled it open. Lilah slid to her knees and puked again. I bent over and shoved a bowl under her face, rubbed her back.

I let her have those cookies without even thinking about what might be in them. What had I done?

"I'm scared," Lilah said. Her voice sounded strange—thick and garbled—through noticeably swollen lips.

I was scared too. Terrified. My hand shook as I brushed back hair from her face.

Lilah closed her eyes.

"Your dad will be here with your medicine, and it will be okay," I said, trying to sound soothing. I'd never felt so helpless or hopeless as that moment, watching her struggle to breathe while my own lungs constricted with panic. I couldn't live with myself if something happened to Lilah.

Nate stormed into the room and slid to the floor beside Lilah, clutching a thick tube in his fist. He yanked off the top cap and placed a hand on Lilah's knee closest to him. "Hold on, Lilah."

He stabbed the end into her thigh, hard, and counted to three before pulling it out and tossing it on the ground. With his palm, he rubbed her thigh where he'd injected the medicine. It took only a handful of seconds before Lilah's breathing came easier, but it felt like forever. Relief coursed through me. She would be okay now. She would be. I dropped my head and took some deep breaths of my own.

Nate pressed his forehead to Lilah's. Tension layered his back and shoulders, evident in the harsh set of his jaw, the ruler-straightness of his back. I put my hand there, and he jerked. Alarm zinged through me. But I knew he had to be sick with worry. It meant nothing. But when I didn't move, he slid from under it and stood with Lilah in his arms.

"We need to get to the hospital," he said.

I rose slowly, my heart beating heavy in my chest. A feeling of foreboding settled in my bones. Something was wrong. It wasn't that Nate moved in sharp movements, or that he shrugged off my touch, or that his voice held a shaky quality.

No, the wariness sliding through me had everything to do with something else: he couldn't quite meet my eye when he said it.

The emergency room at the children's hospital had Lilah in a bed faster than Nate could say, "allergic reaction" and "epinephrine." An hour later, she was breathing well and looked much better. She'd have to stay several hours under observation, but otherwise, tragedy had been avoided.

Nate hovered around her, sitting, then standing to adjust her pillow, helping her flip through the channels on the television, and staring at her with a mixture of love and relief that almost brought tears to my eyes.

I'd been responsible for this—for letting her eat that cookie. The ball in my stomach tightened each time I thought about what could have happened.

Later, after Lilah drifted to sleep, I rose from the chair I'd been sitting in for the better part of two hours and stretched.

Lilah shifted and then curled on her side. Dark lashes resting on her cheeks, she propped a fist under her chin. Her mouth curved into a small smile from whatever dream played in her head. Tears pricked behind my eyes for the second time this evening.

How close had we been to losing Lilah? My hands tingled just remembering her labored breathing, and the terrified glint in her eyes as she'd struggled. But she was okay now. She was okay. I brushed aside a tear that had escaped, unable to quell the rush of gratitude.

"Can I talk to you in the hallway?" Nate asked.

This time his eyes met mine. He looked as though he'd aged twenty years in a few hours. I bit my lip and nodded.

He followed me and closed the door with a quiet click before turning my way. A hand ran over the top of his head and stopped to rest on the back of his neck. His face was drawn tight with tension. But his eyes were busy looking anywhere but at me.

I held my breath and waited for him to speak, waited for what I knew was coming, the moment Nate Russo was going to break my heart. I knew he wouldn't mean to. He wasn't cruel, but I'd just put his daughter in grave danger. She could have died. And I was responsible. I'd break up with me.

We both spoke at the same time.

"I'm so sorry," I said. "I should have checked the cookies."

And he said, "I don't think we should see each other anymore."

A small gasp escaped as my heart deflated. I tried, and failed, to come up with any kind of response.

He squeezed the back of his neck. "My job right now is to keep Lilah safe. It's my number one priority."

I nodded, forced myself to look him in the eye. "I know tonight was scary."

He straightened and set his shoulders. "I've already lost my sister. I can't lose Lilah. I can't lose another person I love. You're a distraction I cannot afford."

The words felt like a punch to my gut, so much so, I took a

step back to steady myself. My fingers twisted at my waist as I fought back tears and forced myself to get the next words out.

"I understand. I know I screwed up," I whispered, then took a deep breath and raised my voice. "I-is there anything I can do to help, or...?"

A small choking laugh escaped him, but his voice was gentle. "No, there's nothing."

A part of me had known this wouldn't work out. After all, I screwed up everything one way or another, but a small piece of my heart had stupidly held onto a hope that Nate was different, I was different, and we could be different together.

"I'm sorry," I whispered. "About tonight and Lilah and everything. I know you must be angry."

Fingertips on my chin, he turned my head. His murky eyes shone with something unreadable to my brain but recognizable to my heart, something soft and precious, and I was losing my chance at ever seeing it again.

"I am not angry with you. I'm angry with myself. I let myself lose focus."

Words clogged my throat. I nodded.

"I'm sorry, Perci." He sounded a little helpless. "I need time and maybe you need some, too." He pressed his lips to my forehead and any hope I had of this working itself out shattered along with what was left of my heart.

I took a shuffling step back, away from him, away from the person who'd made me feel happy and whole and loved for maybe the first time in my life. The person whose smile and laugh and kisses I longed for. The person who was breaking my heart.

I blinked away the sting of threatening tears. "Um, I should go then. Tell Lilah goodbye for me and that... that I love her and I'm glad she's okay."

As I hurried away, I wondered if Nate understood Lilah wasn't the only Russo I loved.

FORTY-TWO

"Stick that bottom lip out any further and I'll sit on it."

I holed up in my apartment for two weeks. Sat on my couch until the imprint of my butt was permanent. Ate frosting straight out of the canister. Showering was optional. By optional, I mean I only showered once, after I fell asleep with half a carton of ice cream resting on my chest and woke to a melted mess. I didn't have a job, I didn't have a boyfriend, I didn't even have a mom or a sister who would talk to me.

On the third day, that stupid cardinal landed on my patio. With its tilted head and penetrating eyes, it seemed to scold me. Me? What had I done?

"Go away, bird. We are not friends." I closed the curtains to the patio and didn't open them again.

I cried—body-wracking sobs—while I pressed my face into a pillow in case Nate happened to walk by and hear me. And then there were the much sadder, silent tears that streamed down my cheeks as I watched *The Notebook*. Three times in a row. Okay, fine, four times.

Mathias tried his best to tempt me to leave my apartment.

Mathias: *Get dressed and I'll buy you a milkshake.*

Me: *Don't try to bribe me with ice cream.*

Mathias: *Now I know you really are in a dark place. That usually works.*

Me: *You're hilarious.*

Mathias: *You know I love you, right?*

Me: *I know.*

Mathias: *You're going to survive this.*

I wished I had his optimism. Even Sal shot me gentle, admonishing looks. Or they could have been looks of pity. It was hard to tell.

When the third week rolled around, I forced myself off the couch. I called every daycare and preschool in the area, but no one was hiring. I broke down and put in an application at a couple of accounting firms.

After two solid weeks of calling and interviewing and not getting the job and eating ice cream because I didn't get the job, I found myself staring at the name I'd pulled up on my phone, a lingering sense of loss heavy in my heart.

Maybe this was how it was all meant to work out. Who was I to think I could change myself? I'd always be the Mayfield Failure. Attempting to become New Perci hadn't changed that. In fact, she might have made everything worse.

My finger shook as I hit *call* and waited.

When he answered, the words forced themselves out of my throat. "Hi, Daddy. I wanted to see if I could get my old job back."

The next Monday, I pulled out one of my old boxy black suits. It surprised me how big it was, even without the Spanx. I straightened my hair and stopped by the donut shop on the way. Twenty minutes later, I pushed open the door to Mayfield Home Mortgage.

Miss Ruby frowned. "What are you doing here?"

"I'm back," I said with little enthusiasm.

"Why'd you do a fool thing like that?"

"Maybe this is where I'm meant to be."

Her eyes narrowed, but she didn't reply, just stared at me, her mouth puckered like she'd sucked on a lemon.

Marianna shrieked when she laid eyes on me. "You're back. I can't believe it. And none too soon. The replacement they hired left last week after I made her cry. It was not my fault, I swear."

She chattered away as I rearranged my desk supplies, logged into my computer, and checked my schedule for the day. Marianna paused when her phone rang. When she finished, she said, "So, listen, my mom's in town and I have an appointment. Do you think you could take my client?"

Like muscle memory, I didn't even have to think of my answer before I said it. "Sure. No problem."

The next few weeks, I slipped right back into my old life. I put away my bright clothes and dangly earrings and pulled out my trusty, sensible shoes and suits. Everything was fine. I was fine.

Sure, I cried myself to sleep most nights, but everything was okay. I had a job. I had a purpose to my day. It was awful. No less than I deserved.

I avoided Nate and Lilah as much as I could. I knew their schedule like my own, so it wasn't hard. The one time we managed to run into each other, he politely held the door to the lobby open for me. It was fine; it didn't feel like a knife twisting in my heart or anything.

I would have gone on like this, maybe forever, if two things hadn't happened.

The first was Mimi.

On the Saturday morning before Thanksgiving, she pounded on my door. "Come on. I know you're in there."

I shuffled to the door and opened it. She strutted by me in a trail of sequins and... "Are you wearing feathers?"

"It's new. You like it?"

I gawked at the combination of black feathers and gold sequins. "'Like' is a strong word."

"I'm not taking fashion advice from you." She pointed a finger at me, scowling at my sweatpants and oversized t-shirt. "In fact, look at this place."

She flipped the overhead light on, marched across the room and threw open the curtain to the patio door. Brightness flooded the room. I squinted against it. When my eyes adjusted, I took in the empty bag of chips, the pile of used Kleenex, the indent from my body on the couch.

"You've been wallowing," Mimi said.

"I have not."

"Oh, honey." She cleared a spot on the couch. "Come sit with me."

I plopped next to her. She slung an arm around me and pulled my head to her shoulder. "I'm sorry."

"For what?"

Mimi sighed. "For being a pot-stirrer when I could have been a peacemaker."

I pulled my head up to look at her. "You don't have to apologize for being you."

Mimi continued, "This might be hard to believe, but I've made an awful lot of mistakes in my life, and I've felt like a failure more than once myself. Truth be told, I'm not feeling so good after that party."

"Mom won't return any of my calls and it's almost Thanksgiving." I sniffled. "I guess I'm not invited to dinner. She must hate me."

"She doesn't hate you." She patted my knee. "I'll take care of her. You won't be alone on Thanksgiving, I'll guarantee you that. But it's time for you to take care of you. Is this how you want the rest of your life to go? You, in your pajamas, eating ice cream in the dark? Alone?"

"It's not all that bad. I have Sal."

"Honey, I think even he would agree, you need actual people too. Going back to the way things were is not the answer. You weren't happy then, and you aren't happy now. But for a while, you were, and you can be happy again. Just because bad things happen, it doesn't mean you're on the wrong path, it just means you can't give up. You understand?"

"I understand," I said. Although I wasn't sure I did.

"It's like this: failing isn't bad. Failing means you tried. Sure, you won't fail now because you aren't even trying. You can stay in your safe little cocoon, at a job you don't care about, keeping yourself all bottled up. But that's not living."

Her words poked at me, making me feel uncomfortable with the truth in them. I rubbed my stinging nose. "It's not that easy."

"The good things in life usually aren't." With one more pat on my knee, she stood. "I've got to get back home and get gussied up. I'm going to dinner with a gentleman friend."

"Like, a date?"

Mimi winked. "Yep, exactly like a date. Now, don't make me come over here again."

. . .

The second thing happened after Mimi left.

I closed the curtains and crawled back onto my spot on the couch. Mimi's words played on repeat in my brain, no matter how hard I tried to shut them out. I turned on the television. I tossed and turned to find a comfortable position. I ordered Chinese food delivered for lunch. I listened to every depressing song I could find on my playlist. But nothing seemed to drown out my grandmother's voice.

"Maybe Mimi is wrong this time, huh?" I said, staring at Sal.

Sal fluttered away. Even he took her side.

"Whatever." I stuffed my hands into my cardigan pockets and thought about getting pizza for dinner. But I got distracted by the crumpled piece of paper I withdrew.

Opening it, I snorted at the words written on the page in Mathias's bold, block handwriting: PERCI'S NEW YEAR'S ANTI-RESOLUTIONS.

Mathias and I had been sitting on this very couch last New Year's Eve when we'd written this list. "You can't possibly fail at these resolutions," he'd said.

1. I will not try to lose weight.

I hadn't tried to lose weight, but those walks to and from work had done the job, anyway. And I'd stopped obsessing about food. It wasn't taking up head space, and that freed me up to relax, be okay with me and this body. It would never be perfect, but it was a good body, strong and healthy.

2. I will not try to be more confident.

Somewhere along the way, I'd stopped worrying so much about what other people—namely, my mother—thought. I'd stopped worrying about keeping quiet and not creating a problem. I'd managed to become more confident that what I thought mattered and now, I wasn't so afraid to speak up. Although I'd also learned that if I was confident enough to speak my mind, I also had to be confident enough to deal with the consequences —good or bad. For example, the giant mess I'd made with my mother.

3. I will not put more effort into my job.

I sat up slowly. I hadn't put more effort into my Mayfield job, but once I'd started working at Miss Marge's, I hadn't minded staying late. Somehow, I'd managed to help Miss Marge with the new computer programs and spreadsheet. And the kids, I'd loved them. Not too many reasons I was willing to get puked on, except those kids. Even though it was now over, at least I'd had a job I loved for a few months.

4. I will not date.

Major fail. Not only had I dated, but I'd also gone ahead and fallen in love. And then I'd screwed that up too.

5. I will not be a better daughter and sister.

I crushed the note to my chest. This might have been the only resolution I'd kept.

My mother wasn't even speaking to me at present. Phee was ignoring me. True, I'd made mistakes, big ones. But my mother had, too. Had I been wrong to finally take charge of my life? To share what I was feeling? The results seemed to have been spectacular in their failure.

But as Mimi said, failing meant at least I'd tried. Failing meant I'd cared enough to change the situation. It hadn't been pretty. There had been fighting and uncomfortable conversations, but this year had changed me.

New Perci wasn't so new. She was Old Perci who wasn't afraid to fail. I was still a little awkward and said the wrong thing at the wrong time. I still wasn't sure of myself, in the same way a baby bird didn't understand what wings were. But like that baby bird, I'd jumped out of the nest, anyway. I'd tried. I'd failed. I'd tried again.

I stood and a cascade of cookie crumbs tumbled off me. Brushing them away, I stumbled into my bedroom. I couldn't go back to my old life. I couldn't spend the rest of my life at a job I hated. I couldn't wait for my mother to make the first move. I couldn't let Phee ignore me or Bria freeze me out. I'd find a way to keep Nate as a friend. It wouldn't all work out. I could, and *would*, fail, but it would be okay. Because at least I'd tried. I had to try.

Surveying my closet, I pushed aside the Suits of Neutral Colors and picked out a lime-green t-shirt and leggings and dressed quickly. The time for wallowing was over.

Now it was time to try.

FORTY-THREE

"An apple a day keeps the doctor away.
*   Which is a hell of a lot cheaper than a health insurance*
plan."

—MIMI

The fast-food joint Bria worked at was quiet when I got there an hour later. Bria was on her break, so I ordered a soda and sat in the corner booth.

I fidgeted with my phone while I waited, unsure what her reaction would be when she saw me. Since that last awful conversation, my text messages and voicemails had gone unanswered. Although I checked up on her often through Stella, I wanted to lay eyes on her; I wanted to talk to her; I wanted to tell her I was sorry.

Fifteen minutes later, she walked through the front door. She must have seen me immediately because she didn't hesitate in making a path to me. I gave her a little wave and took a deep breath.

She slid in across from me and crossed her arms. "What are you doing here?"

"Nice hair," I said. It was dyed a silvery-lavender now and clashed with her yellow-and-orange-striped uniform shirt.

An arched eyebrow was my reply. Okay, tough crowd.

I leaned in and risked touching the hand she had on the table. She let me, so that was a good sign. "I've tried to call."

"I got your messages."

"Oh, good. I thought maybe you got a new number or... something."

"I was busy," she said, and studied her fingernails carefully. Like there'd be a quiz on them afterward.

She was not going to make this easy on me, but I hadn't really expected her to. Bria had a life full of people who'd given up on her. Maybe she thought it was easier to be the one who gave up first. That put her in control.

But I was here to let her know I wasn't going anywhere.

"I'm sorry if I ever made you feel you were less than. You were right. I know how that feels." I paused, surprised by a wave of emotion I hadn't expected. "The thing is that I want the best for you, so I guess I started getting pushy. I guess you could say I learned that from the best."

In some weird way, my mom's pushiness and constant interference made more sense to me in that moment than ever before.

Bria studied me with wide dark eyes that I couldn't quite read. I forged on, wanting to get all of this out while I had the chance.

"I don't have all the right answers though, and I never should have made you feel like my way was the best way. But I want you to know that I'm here. I'm not going anywhere. You can ignore me and not answer my calls, but I will still be here when you need me. Always." I swallowed and waited for a reaction, an understanding, a coupon for free French fries, anything. "I'm done now."

The next moment was long. Bria's face gave no hints, not a smile or a crack in the stern set of her jaw, nothing. Maybe that was all I would get. I'd tried. I'd reached out to her. That was all I could do. If I failed, it was okay. Like Mimi said, it didn't mean I was a failure; it meant I cared enough to try.

I slung my purse over my shoulder and grabbed my cup. "I know you need to get back to work, so I'll get going. Call me, maybe. If you want to."

"I took my GED test."

I froze and tried to keep my voice even and calm, but inside, hope bubbled, sprang eternal, whatever you wanted to call it. "Oh, you did?"

She nodded. "Those stupid word problems were a pain in the ass."

I grinned and shuffled back to the table. "So?"

"I passed."

"Of course you did," I said, my grin widening to a smile.

"It was no big deal. I had a little help," she said with a shrug. Then she let me know without words we were okay—she smiled back.

A couple of days later, Mimi called me at the end of the workday. "Did you see the noon news program?"

"Nope."

"Someone posted it on that YouTube. You need to watch it."

"I'm about to head out. Can it wait until later?"

Mimi ignored me. "Go to the YouTube and type in 'newscaster puts fiancé on blast.' Go ahead now. I'll wait."

Heart beginning to pound, I put my cell on speaker and pulled up the video. I gasped when I saw the still was a photo of Phee sitting behind the KKRE news desk. "Uh-oh."

Mimi hummed in response. I pressed play and cranked the volume.

Phee smiled at the camera. "As I sign off today, it is with a heavy heart I let you, the viewers, know this will be my last broadcast with KKRE. Over the last two years, I'm humbled to have been invited into your homes as I shared the traffic and news of the great city of Houston."

"What in the world?" I said.

Mimi chuckled. "Keep watching. It gets real good soon."

The camera panned out to reveal Joel Allen on Phee's left, a tight smile plastered on his face.

My sister continued. "I've learned a great deal and for that, I will forever be grateful to KKRE. But it's time for me to move on." Phee paused, frowned, and leaned forward in her chair as though she were about to tell us all a secret. "I'm supposed to say something now about how I've got some exciting new opportunities on the horizon and while that is true, I'd like you to know the real reason I'm leaving."

The camera bounced for a split second as though it wasn't quite sure where to focus. Phee's voice sped up with urgency. My heart clanged in my chest as I leaned forward in my seat. I had no idea what she was about to say, but it felt big. Real big.

"You all know that until recently, I was engaged to my co-worker, Joel Allen."

The man in question's head whipped around to stare at Phee, an expression of growing horror dawning.

"I've just learned what a weasely, insecure, lying liar he is. I'm grateful I learned this information before I made the grave mistake of marrying him."

"Holy crap," I yelled, and I couldn't keep the grin from spreading across my face.

"Phoebe," he whispered under his breath, through that fake-forced smile I knew all too well.

She laughed mirthlessly. "That would have been the worst mistake of my life."

Joel Allen turned toward the camera. "Go to commercial, off air, do something!"

"Go!" Someone off-screen yelled.

The screen went blue, and a "technical difficulties" sign flashed. Despite the loss of picture, the audio still rolled.

"Did you really need to do all that?" Joel Allen yelled. "You're making a huge deal out of this."

"You told the producers you'd quit if they gave me a promotion. That's a huge deal to me." Phee's voice broke. "Perci warned me. She told me you were a jerk, and so did Mathias and Mimi. They said you were—"

But the audio was cut off before she finished that sentence.

I slumped in my seat, feeling like I'd just climbed fifty-two flights of stairs and finally reached flat ground. Had that really just happened? I had to call Mathias immediately. "Wow."

"It's about time she told that man off," Mimi said, and I swear I could hear her earrings swinging as she nodded her head. "The fastest way to lose weight is to get rid of the monkey on your back, and that Joel was an awful big monkey."

"Have you talked to her?" I asked.

"Not yet. But don't you worry about your sister. She's gonna be just fine, you can quote me on that."

The knock came at ten o'clock that night. I opened the door to three suitcases and Phee in sweatpants.

"I broke up with Joel," she said.

"I saw."

"He's a weaselly, insecure, lying liar."

I leaned against the doorframe. "I heard."

"The thing is, I don't have a place to live anymore and, well…"

"You could always move in with Mom," I said.

"I'm not sure Mom will be speaking to me for the rest of my life. That might make things awkward."

"Good point. I have a spare room."

For the first time, she smiled. "I was hoping you'd say that."

She took two steps inside and threw herself at me. For a stunned moment, I froze and then wrapped my arms around her. "Thank you for being there for me," she said, her voice stilted, and I realized she was crying. "I know I didn't want to listen, but..."

"Don't cry," I said, my heart swelling. She'd come to me, her sister, for comfort and support. "It's going to be okay. You're going to be okay."

She pulled back and gave me a watery smile, which made her look sad and beautiful all at once. "I'm not even crying over Joel or the job. I'm just relieved it's done. I'm okay with whatever happens next. You taught me that."

I blinked, confused. "Me?"

"Yes, you." She sniffled. "You survived the break-up with Brent and quitting your job. You did it, so I can too. It's like you gave me courage."

"Oh, Phee." Now I was the one with a watery smile.

"This year has changed you. You're different, you're living your life now, not what anyone else wants for you."

I had been, anyway, and I would be again. Phee's words only gave me more resolve.

She swiped at her cheeks and straightened. "Now, I'm expecting there to be a lot of ice cream and wine in your kitchen."

"Well, of course. What else would I keep in there? Kale?" I said with a shiver of disgust.

Phee hooked her arm through mine. "Let's go celebrate."

And that's how my sister moved in with me.

FORTY-FOUR

*"You don't have to like your family
but you do have to love them."*

—MIMI

The ring jolted me awake. I stared, wide-eyed, at the name of the caller: Mom. It was 11:37 p.m. on Thanksgiving Eve. It had been over two months since her name had appeared on my phone.

"Mom?"

"Persephone, did I wake you?"

"Is everything okay?" I snapped on the lamp on my nightstand.

My mother took an audible breath and when she spoke, her voice was infinitely gentle. "It's Mimi."

"What about Mimi?"

"The apartment complex manager called. She was complaining of chest pains, so they've taken her to the emergency room by ambulance." Her voice cracked, along with my heart.

"She's okay, right?" I raced to my closet and yanked a t-shirt off a hanger without even looking at it.

"For now. I think it would be a good idea if you and Phoebe came to the hospital. Your father and I will meet you there."

Phee drove and, on the way, I texted Mathias to let him know. Even though it was after midnight, he texted me right back and told me to keep him posted.

We arrived at the hospital twenty-five minutes later. Daddy was pacing the length of the waiting room. He wrapped us in a hug. "Your mom is worried sick. Go sit with her while I get us some coffee, okay?"

I knew after a week and a half of sleeping in his office, Dad had moved back to the house, and they'd continued with marriage counseling. He said things were getting back to normal. Well, a new normal. A better, more honest, open normal.

While I'd been happy to hear they had reconnected, it still hurt that Mom hadn't tried to reach out to me. Not even once. In the end, I'd stopped trying to call her, too. I'd been afraid I'd make things worse.

My mother sat straight-backed, trying her hardest to appear ladylike in her long white nightgown with the tiny blue flowers Phee and I had dubbed the Old Lady Gown. A pair of sweatpants peeked out from the bottom, and fuzzy pink slippers covered her feet.

Without discussing it, Phee and I took a seat on either side of Mom. Each of us took one of her hands and we sat there in silence.

"Have they said anything yet?" Phee asked, after the quiet dragged on.

Mom shook her head. "We've been waiting for someone to come and tell us something."

"I'm so worried," I whispered.

Mom squeezed my hand. "Me too."

Finally, in what felt like three hours but was more like twenty minutes, a woman in scrubs and a friendly smile entered. "Family for Mona Perkins?"

At Mom's nod, the nurse beckoned us to follow her. She led us to a small room at the end of the hallway. There on the bed lay my grandmother, pale and shrunken, eyes closed. An IV fed saline and whatever else into her arm. The steady beeps of the heart monitor were reassuring.

My mother stepped to Mimi and touched the back of her hand. "Mama?"

Mimi's eyelids fluttered open slowly. "Bobbie Jo, I'm glad you're here." Her voice sounded weak, thready.

"I was worried about you." Mom sniffed.

"Thank you for coming."

"Do you need some water?" My mother scanned the room, her eyes a little wild. "Where did that nurse go?"

"Don't go bothering anyone, now. I'm sure I'll be—" *Cough. Cough.* She placed a hand on her chest.

Mom frowned. "Craig, go find that nurse and get some water."

"Of course, of course." Daddy slipped into the hallway.

After pulling a chair close to the bed, Mom arranged herself in it.

"Perci? Phee?" Mimi waved us closer. When she could, she grabbed my hand and squeezed so hard I almost winced. Her eyes met mine with bright, straightforward clarity. She coughed. Again. "Perci, go close that door for your grandmother. Phee, pull up a chair."

I nodded, suspicion forming by the second, and did as she asked. By the time I returned, Mimi had made a small space on the bed and patted it for me to sit.

"I'm so glad you could come to be with me."

"What happened?" Phee asked. "What did the doctor say?"

"Chest pains, you know. Very serious."

Crossing my arms, I stared down at her. She wouldn't. *Would she?*

"I've told you about cutting back on the butter and the bacon," Mom said. "It's not good for your heart."

"Yes, yes, you're right," Mimi replied meekly.

Meekly?

"But since you're all here now and—"

Daddy opened the door. "Water is on its way," he announced.

"Great," Mimi said. "Now go find me an extra blanket, would you?"

Daddy's brow furrowed. "But I—"

"I'm just so cold." She shivered for good measure.

My mother huffed. "Craig, my mother is in the hospital, and she is cold. Go find her a blanket."

"Fine," Daddy grumbled and left the room.

"As I was sayin', since we're all here, this might be a good time to clear the air."

Mom's eyes narrowed. "What do you mean?"

"I mean that sometimes, in the face of tragedy..." Mimi coughed again. She was laying it on thicker than the frosting on her German chocolate cake.

On a list of People on Their Deathbeds, Mimi's name was nowhere in sight.

"What do you mean by that? Have the doctors told you something?" Mom rose. "Where is that nurse? I want some answers."

"Bobbie Jo, sit down." Mimi's voice brooked no argument. "I'm trying to say I want us to talk. Don't you think it's about time? Now, I understand you're angry with me and I'm sorry. There, I said I'm sorry. That wasn't hard. Who's next?"

"Mama, you can't just say the words and think that's it. You started a food fight. You embarrassed me in front of all those people." Mom leaned over the bed, her stance menacing. "There are videos on the internet."

"I can't apologize for the videos. Had nothing to do with that."

"That is not the point!" Mom's voice grew louder with each word. "It's always been like this. You don't care what anyone thinks about what you do or who you hurt in the process."

"And maybe you care a little too much," Mimi shot back.

"What is that supposed to mean?"

Mimi nudged me. "I brought the horse to the trough. You gotta make her drink."

But it was Phee who answered. "I don't want to be a traffic girl. I want to anchor. I want to be taken seriously. And Perci is right, I do have feelings for Mathias, but I stayed away because you told me to. And I would have married Joel, too, because I knew it's what you wanted for me. I would have married him and had two kids and been a PTA mom and I would have been miserable."

The only sound when she finished was the steady beep of Mimi's heart monitor. Mom's spine went solid. She turned to face the wall, and I heard a sniffle. "And Persephone, do you feel the same way?"

I pulled a breath and willed myself to be honest, even though it was hard. "You're embarrassed by me."

"I'm not embarrassed by you." She whipped around to glare at me. "Why would you think such a thing?"

"I'm a failure in your eyes." I spread my arms wide at my sides. "But I'm not a failure, not anymore at least. This is who I am. I'm okay with myself. I really, really am." Now the other part. "I know I make mistakes. Like at the party and the food fight and the things I said. I'm sorry. I really am. I know I'm not perfect. I fail a lot. I make mistakes and I will again, but I'm not letting that hold me back anymore."

It was the worst time to smile, but I couldn't help it because for once, those words held meaning, real meaning, to me. I *was* okay with me.

Her eyes flashed. "So, what am I supposed to do? Just stop caring? Stop worrying you'll end up at my age and realize you have no idea who you are anymore? Just sit back and watch you make mistakes? I've tried to be a good mother," she said with as much dignity as a woman in fuzzy slippers could muster.

"You *are* a good mother," I said. "I hope to be half the mom you are. I never had to worry about anything as a kid. You fixed all my problems. But at some point, I started to feel like you were trying to fix me, too."

"I wasn't trying to fix you. I wanted you to be happy." Her accent thickened with every word, and she suddenly looked exhausted. "When I was a kid, we had nothing, and it was hard. Mama, I know you did the best you could, but I was always that poor girl with the single mother. I wanted my children's lives to be different."

The door opened and Daddy stuck his head in. "Can I come in yet?"

"No," all of us said at once. With a grumble, he shut the door.

"Then I went off to college and did the same thing. Got myself pregnant. So, yes, I wanted to do everything I could to make sure you had better opportunities. I sent you to good schools. I was involved. Always available. And it wasn't enough, was it? I devoted my life to you girls and... and... now you hate me." The tears that had gathered in her eyes began a quiet descent down her cheeks.

My gut clenched like someone had punched me. In that moment, I saw my mother so clearly. It was the fear of judgment that had driven her to change her hair and watch her weight, to strive for perfection, for herself, and for Phee and me. My heart broke a little for her.

"Mom," I whispered and put a hand on her shoulder.

"Now, you aren't quite right. You might have started down the same path as me, but you made better choices," Mimi said. "Craig is a good man. And it hasn't been all bad, has it? You've got a pretty good life—two beautiful daughters, a husband who loves you, a nice house, friends."

Mom's eyes shone under the yellowish hospital lights. "It has been good. I just worry it's not enough."

"It's not enough for who? Or are you worried that you're not enough?" Mimi asked.

"I don't know, Mama, I just don't know."

"You are, honey. You are enough." Mimi smoothed the back of her hand over Mom's cheek. "Now, I'm probably always gonna embarrass you some. That's just how I'm made. You make some decisions I don't agree with, but that's okay. You are you and I am me, but it doesn't mean I love you any less."

"But you have to butt out," Phee said. "I almost married a weaselly, arrogant lying liar because I was worried about your feelings."

"You can't be the one to decide who or what makes us happy. We get to decide that," I said.

"You're right," Mom said, her voice a little shaky.

I sat back on the edge of Mimi's bed. None of us said a word, lost in our thoughts, examining the words we'd spoken until the nurse bustled in with her rolling cart.

"Time to take your vitals, Ms. Perkins. How's that heartburn doing now?"

"Heartburn?" My mother repeated. "Mama!"

FORTY-FIVE

"The bigger the leap, the higher you might soar.
  But if you fall, it's really gonna hurt."

—MIMI

The week after Thanksgiving, I went into work as usual. I sat at my desk. I listened to Marianna complain about the traffic. I turned on my computer and checked my email. I met with clients. I greeted Brent and ate lunch with Daddy and listened to Miss Ruby bellow down the hallway.

But the whole time, I thought about the letter in my desk drawer. I'd written it last week, printed it, and hidden it there. Waiting.

Now it was time.

Letter in hand, I marched down the hallway and past Miss Ruby.

"What are you smiling about?" she demanded.

"Nothing. It's a good day. That's all," I said, pausing at her desk. "One more week until retirement?"

"Seven more business days, young lady, and don't you

forget." She frowned. "Although your father has yet to hire a replacement."

I grinned and headed toward Daddy's office. "Don't you worry. I'm working on it."

The door to his office was propped open with an egg crate stuffed with spiral notebooks. One entire wall of his office had been divulged of its towering fire hazards, and his hoard looked significantly thinned out. He was bent over a stack of paperwork on his desk, which he seemed to be dividing into two piles.

"Hi, Daddy."

"Come in. Your mother has decided it's time I clean out my office. One stack at a time, she said." He grimaced. "Easier said than done. She threatened to take it all out and burn it, and I think she meant it."

"You have to admit, it already looks better in here. I'm definitely less worried about you being buried alive." I moved a box from a chair and sat, crinkling the paper in my hand. "Do you think we could talk for a minute?"

Dad shoved his stacks of paper aside and folded his hands on his desk. "Of course. There's something I'd like to talk to you about too, Cupcake."

"Can I ask you something? Why is Phee a princess and I'm a cupcake? Is it because I'm, you know, fluffy?"

He looked surprised. "You've always been my sweet little cupcake. When you were little, you'd climb on my lap and ask me for a kiss on the cheek. Then you'd ask me what flavor you were. And"—he shrugged, a little smile curving his mouth—"I would say you tasted as sweet as a cupcake, and you'd laugh and laugh. You remember that?"

At his words, a memory of those times flashed in my head. Mom—pregnant with Phee—had been cranky and uncomfortable, and by the evening was often sprawled dead asleep on the recliner—the only place she could find any rest, a bag of potato chips resting on her swollen belly. I was supposed to be in bed, but I'd wait to hear the door open and tiptoe out of my room to find Daddy.

After he covered Mom with a blanket, he'd take me back to my bedroom. I'd curl up on his lap and he'd ask me about my day, and we'd play the game he was talking about. He'd read me a book, tuck me in, and lay beside me until I fell asleep. I didn't remember it happening once Phee came, but for a while there, I'd had his full attention in those stolen moments.

My heart warmed. "I remember that."

"Now what did you want to talk about?"

"You go first."

Nodding, he slid his glasses on and pulled a folder out of a desk drawer. "Your mother and I had a long conversation this weekend. We discussed some changes." He took a deep breath. "I'm cutting down to three-day work weeks so we can spend more time together. Brent can handle stepping up."

"That's huge. I bet Mom is happy."

"She is. And not just about that. Thanksgiving was extra special this year."

I smiled in agreement. Mom had insisted Phee and Mimi and I come to the house after Mimi was discharged from hospital. Then like an army general, or possibly a witch, she'd produced a first-rate Thanksgiving meal complete with real cranberry sauce and homemade pumpkin pie and whipped cream. Even Pericles had seemed a little less demon-like. But I guess once a dog licks condiments off your arm, you might concede to a lifelong truce.

Dad pulled his glasses to the tip of his nose and peered at me over them, his expression serious. I flinched when he snapped open the folder. "You know your mother and I love you very much, and even though we haven't seen eye-to-eye at times, we only want you to be happy." He paused, and I inched to the edge of my chair, my stomach sinking with each second. He hesitated. "So, in the name of all that, you're fired."

"What?" I waved the letter in my hand. "You can't fire me. I'm quitting. This is my letter of resignation."

"Too late. I said it first." He actually smirked.

"But why?"

"Because we realize you'll never be happy working here." He slid the open folder across the desk. "There's something else."

The folder contained a few sheets of paper, the most important one on top. A deed. "What is this?"

"You are now the proud owner of one recently vacated daycare center."

My mouth opened and closed in a reasonable imitation of Sal. "What?"

"Now, you'll still have to get a loan for start-up costs, but with your business degree and experience, I think you'll be able to swing it."

"Daddy, you can't... this is too much." But my mind was screaming, *yes*. Already, a vision of me walking to work every day and greeting each child as they arrived filled my head. I wanted this. Badly.

"Cupcake, I'll be honest. You're going to have to take it. You're fired for good—you can't come back here. Besides, this was all your mother's idea, and you know what she's like when she gets an idea in her head."

Laughing, I swiped at the wetness on my cheeks and said the only thing I could. "Thank you."

We decided I had two more weeks at Mayfield Home Mortgage, which I would spend hiring and training my replacement. But I also had a special project of my own. One last thing I wanted to do as an employee.

"How's it going trying to find someone to replace Miss Ruby?"

He frowned. "Not well."

"I've been doing some looking too, and I think I have the

perfect person for you, if you're willing to give her a chance. Her name is Bria."

A week later, I burst into my apartment with a song and a bouquet of flowers. Even I was tired of how excited I was about my life, but I couldn't contain it. Mimi said I was walking sunshine.

"Phoebe Anne Mayfield, where are you? You haven't answered any of my texts." I shut the door with a tap from my shoe and waltzed down the hallway. "I'm dying to know how it went today."

Phee had spent the first week sleeping in and enjoying a life of no responsibility. Aside from responding to an abundance of text messages which she grinned over and refused to say who they were from, she'd spent time with me watching movies and painting our toes and being sisters.

However, when it was time to pay her credit card bill, Phee had buckled down to find a new job. But it wasn't like you could snap your fingers and find a job in her field. It was likely she'd have to move to where one was available. The last two weeks, she'd called in every favor, spoken to any connections she'd ever made, flown to Orlando for an interview, then Minneapolis, and Seattle. Three days ago, Chuck, her old producer at KKRE, had called and wanted to "talk."

"You've left me hanging all day." I dumped my purse and the flowers on the counter. Shrugging off my coat, I turned and stumbled. There was Phee sitting on my red couch, and next to her was Mathias. Let me rephrase that. He wasn't just next to her, he was *right* next to her, as in, breaking every rule at a middle school dance. His arm wrapped around her shoulders; her hair tousled. Both of them were flushed.

I froze, my mouth hanging open as my eyes flitted back and forth between my sister and my best friend, before focusing on Mathias. Even from here, I could see his glasses were fogged up. But they didn't hide the shiner his left eye was sporting.

"Why do you have a black eye?" I asked.

Mathias's smiled widened. "I got in a fight."

"What?" I shook my head. "Wait. First, what is going on here? I thought the plan was to get over Phee, not get under her." I gestured toward my sister with a hand. Phee's cheeks brightened to red.

Mathias grinned. "We've been... talking."

I gave him a very pointed look. "Is that what the kids are calling it?"

"And stuff. We've been talking and stuff."

I glanced between the two of them. "So, are you a thing now?"

"We're not giving it any titles. Just seeing what happens and not letting anyone get in the middle of it," Phee said.

"Are you going to tell Mom?" I asked.

"Yes. I texted her and then turned off my phone." She paused, looking a little nervous. "I'm not worried about Mom. Are you okay with this?"

I stared at her a long moment, just to watch her squirm before I laughed. "Are you kidding? It's about time." I tackled her with a hug until she was laughing too, and then pulled back to look at her. "How did it go with Chuck?"

Her eyes sparkled. "He offered me a job as weekend anchor."

I squealed. "What did you tell him?"

"I told him that I would think about it. I'm going to make him sweat it out for a few days before I accept it. Don't want to look too eager, you know."

Then I turned to Mathias. I crossed my arms and tried for intimidating. "If you hurt my little sister, I'll kill you."

"Deal." He hung his hand out for me to shake.

Instead, I threw my arms around him and pulled him in for a hug. "Now tell me how you got the black eye."

"I wish you could have been there, Perci," Phee said. "He went with me to pick up the rest of my stuff yesterday and Joel hit him. It was a sucker punch. Mathias didn't even have a chance to prepare himself."

I gasped. "What?"

"Don't worry about it." Mathias held up his right hand, the knuckles red and a little swollen. "You should see the other guy's face."

Maybe I'm a bad person, but the idea of Joel "Jackass" Allen getting punched out by Mathias was the best news I'd heard all day.

We cracked open a bottle of wine to celebrate. And we might have turned on the evening news, just to see Joel Allen try to make his way through the broadcast with a very noticeable black eye.

FORTY-SIX

"The road to happiness has a whole lotta hitchhikers.
Choose wisely before you pick one up."

—*MIMI*

The elevator door was sliding shut as I entered the lobby, my arms laden with bags and boxes and wrapping paper and a bag of cookies, because who could resist Christmas cookies?

"Oh, hold the door," I said.

A hand shot out to stop their progress—a hand I recognized.

Nate and Lilah stood in the elevator. Next to them was a short, round older woman with out-of-control curly hair and green-brown eyes. She was holding Lilah's hand. I shot them a small smile and stepped in, my hand tightening on the strap of my purse as my heart leaped in my chest.

"Hi," I said.

Despite living practically on top of each other, Nate and I had done an excellent job of avoiding one another. Aside from a brief glimpse here or there as he ducked into his apartment, or the time Lilah saw me across the street and yelled my name, we hadn't seen each other on purpose for over two months.

I missed him. Even now, when I should have had enough time to get over him, just the sight of him made my heart clench. I wanted to touch him, to reach over and kiss him hello. But I didn't.

Lilah flung herself at me as the doors closed. "Perci! Perci!"

I missed Lilah too. I wrapped my arms around her and kissed the top of her head. The smell of her shampoo sent a rush of memories through me. It was the same scent as Nate's, and a memory of snuggling with him on his couch washed over me. "Strawberry!"

Lilah pulled back and stared up at me. "Huh?"

"Your shampoo. It's strawberry-scented."

She nodded. "It's my favorite."

I grinned. "Mine too."

"So, this is Perci," the woman said, her voice so New York I almost didn't understand her.

Nate cleared his throat. "Perci, this is my mother, Caroline. Mom, this is Perci, my... neighbor."

"Oh, wow. Mrs. Russo." I juggled my bags to free up a hand and held it out to her.

But Mrs. Russo shoved it aside and wrapped me in a stranglehold of a hug. "Any friend of my son is a friend of mine." She took a step back, but kept my hand in hers as she surveyed me from sneakers to knitted hat.

I fidgeted and wished I'd known I was going to meet Nate's mom today; I would have dressed better. As it was, I was in my scummiest pair of jeans. I'd spent most of the morning at Miss Perci's Preschool and Daycare, cleaning. Then I'd met with a contractor about some updates. It would take a couple months to get everything worked out the way I wanted it. But my business loan had come through fast, and I'd already started sending out mailers around the neighborhood.

"It's nice to meet you," I said. "This is a surprise."

The elevator dinged, and the doors slid open. We spilled out into the hallway.

"A surprise, for sure," Mrs. Russo said. "I didn't expect an invitation, but I'm glad I got one. It's good to see my baby." She reached up and pinched Nate's cheek. Despite the fierce scowl he aimed at her, she laughed.

I fidgeted with the bags in my hands. "I hope you have a great time."

"We will. Now, don't be a stranger. You come over for coffee and chat. I'll be here until after the new year." She took Lilah's hand and hurried to keep up with the girl as she skipped down the hallway.

I turned toward Nate, trying hard to not notice how his sweater stretched perfectly across his shoulders, or how just the sight of him made my insides warm. "So, your mom, huh?"

"Yeah, I finally opened one of her letters. She wore me down and, well, I thought it was time I got myself together."

"I'm happy for you."

He flashed me a small smile. "Anyway, she's cleaned my house from top to bottom, made three pans of lasagna to freeze, and spoiled Lilah rotten. But it's been good having her. I think we understand each other better now, you know?"

"I do."

"You look happy, Perci," he said, his eyes soft.

"I am happy. I really am." Even I could hear the delight in my voice. Because it was true. The daycare would open soon. My mother and I were venturing on building a new, better relationship. Phee and Mathias were... something. The only thing missing was, well, Nate. One day, my heart would get over him and move on. Probably. "And you? Are you happy?"

The crease in his forehead deepened. "Almost."

A lump of emotion worked its way to my throat, and I felt tears prick the backs of my eyes. I was glad he was happy.

That's all I wanted for him, even if it meant I wasn't there to be part of it. But it was hard to be this close to him and know that we would never be a *we* again. He'd made that clear. I glanced away and studied the hallway tile. "Good. Good. That's good."

Nate shoved his hands in his jean pockets. I shifted from one foot to the other. Our eyes darted around the hallway, taking in everything but each other.

"I should get inside. I have presents to wrap and all that." Plastering on a bright smile, I held out my hand to shake his. "It was good to see you, Nate."

It was all very adult of me.

FORTY-SEVEN

"An ending is just the beginning of something new."

—*MIMI*

The Loveland Hotel ballroom had been transformed into a winter wonderland for the occasion of New Year's Eve. Round tables with oversized centerpieces surrounded the dance floor under dramatic lighting that made the entire space magical. One entire wall of the room was floor-to-ceiling windows that looked out on to the city from the fifteenth floor.

I'd never noticed before how beautiful it was. All the other years I'd been forced to come, wearing some awful, uncomfortable dress my mother had picked out, I'd wanted to be anywhere else. But this year was different because I was different. This year, I was excited to celebrate a new year and a new me. I planned to party like I was Mimi's granddaughter.

"Now, when does the dancing start, is what I want to know?" Mimi said, adjusting the floor-length dress she'd bought specially for the occasion. Lest she appear too tame, she'd spent extra time on her updo, using red feathers liberally. The feathers matched her red boa and red high heels.

"Mama, sit down, please. The dancing is later," my mother said, exasperation threading through her words. "I can't take you anywhere."

Mimi patted her cheek as she strolled by. "You know you love me."

Mom rolled her eyes and turned to survey my outfit from top to bottom. "You look lovely."

I knew it was hard for her to say it. Earlier in the week, I'd announced I would be picking out my own dress, thank you very much.

Mom had objected but I'd stood firm. "I get to decide what I wear or I'm not going."

Which wasn't at all true. I was totally going. But she didn't need to know that.

"Oh, fine," my mother said.

See? Progress.

With Mathias and Phee in tow, I'd headed to the vintage store I passed every day on the way to the daycare, and I'd tried on The Dress. Its 1950s vintage charm with the sweetheart neckline in the perfect shade of red suited me perfectly. Like it was made for me. The salesclerk had showed me a pair of black ballet shoes and a snow-white wrap that pulled the entire outfit together.

Yesterday morning, Mom had treated me to a manicure and a cut and style at the salon. She hadn't even argued when I chose Alisa to work her voodoo on my hair, instead of Jacque. Earlier this evening, Phee had helped with my make-up. I am not too proud to admit I kept walking by mirrors whenever I could, just to see myself.

On a list of People Who Looked Smoking Hot Tonight, I was at least in the top five.

The tables held twelve chairs, and ours were occupied by

Mom, Dad, Phee, Mathias, Mimi, and me. Brent was also there, with a date. She had the same taste in dresses Brent had in ties. A match made in fashion hell.

Bria showed up a half-hour later, looking uncomfortable in a knee-length green velvet dress that, I had on good authority, my mother had picked out for her. Part of me wished I could have sent her to the bathroom and let her put on short shorts and a tank top.

She had started her new job as the front receptionist at Mayfield Home Mortgage. Miss Ruby had stayed on a couple extra days to train her, but it was clear by the end of the first day, Bria could bellow for employees all on her own. At the end of the second day, Bria sent me a text, just two words: *Thank you.*

Bria slid in the chair across from me now, her eyes wide and more than a little apprehensive. She held up one of the three forks by her plate. "This is some fancy shit. Why am I here again?"

"Because," Daddy said, smiling at her, "you're part of the Mayfield family now."

"Oh, great." Bria crossed her arms, but I was sure a small smile flirted with the corners of her mouth.

Dinner wasn't served until close to 9:30 p.m., and the dancing started after. I watched as our table slowly paired off and hit the floor. Mimi found an older gentleman resplendent in a bright red tuxedo and claimed him for her own. Even Bria found a partner in a short, thin man who might be scared to death or having the time of his life dancing with her.

A slow song started, and I smiled as Mathias pulled Phee close. Although they weren't "defining their relationship," I'd say their status would be something like: Disgustingly Into Each Other.

Daddy gazed down at Mom like he was entranced—that marriage counseling was definitely working. I pushed away a wave of sadness—and okay, envy—and drifted around the room. The open bar wasn't so crowded, so I got a cocktail and sipped at it. Later, I took myself off to the bathroom.

I was washing my hands when Mimi burst into the bathroom. "Phew. There ya are. We couldn't find you anywhere."

"Sorry. Nature called."

Mimi examined my face and frowned. "You bring more lipstick in that little purse? Reapply, girl. And hurry." When I didn't move fast enough, she grabbed my tiny black clutch and dumped it on the counter.

"Geesh, okay." I snatched up the lipstick and did what I was told.

"Fluff your hair." She turned me to face her and pinched my cheeks.

"Ouch!"

"You looked a little pale. Needed to put some color in your cheeks. Now smile so I can check your teeth."

"Mimi, this—"

"Smile!" she barked.

I smiled.

"Excellent." She threw everything back in my purse. "I'll hold this for you. Fix your wrap. Come on, then." With a tug on my hand, she pulled me through the door and back into the ballroom.

"What in the world has gotten into you?"

Mimi jerked to a stop. "Listen to me, Perci-girl. You remember that life is full of moments, right? Small moments, big moments. Some moments we don't realize are moments until long after they happen."

I nodded and thought of that moment a year before, sitting in the dentist chair while Brent broke up with me on the radio. Not a glorious moment, but one that had started a whole slew of things I could never have imagined.

"Okay then," she said, and we started walking again. "I

believe you're about to have one of those moments. I want you to go with it. Enjoy it. Just be you, honey."

"Right. And how will I know—"

But that was about the time I couldn't form words anymore. Because there, standing in front of all the people I loved, was a sharp-edged, un-handsome man in a tuxedo. He smiled, and I wanted to melt right there.

Mimi shoved me forward. "Go get him, tiger."

I started toward him, and he met me halfway. We stopped with inches between us.

"Hi," I said, my voice breathy. "What are you doing here?"

"It's kind of a funny story," he said, his face serious. "A few weeks ago, I was sitting on my patio, feeling a little down because I have this friend who I hadn't spoken to in a while. You might know her, she's real pretty, always makes me smile, and I was missing her."

I locked my hands behind my back, lest I reach for him. "Go on."

"The strangest thing, this little red bird lands on my banister. It had these funny feathers sticking up at the top of its head. I stared at it, and it stared at me. And the more I tried to shoo it away, the more it just stared at me like it was trying to tell me something."

"Oh, yeah? What do you think it was trying to tell you?"

"I think it might have been trying to tell me that loving someone doesn't mean they'll always leave you or disappoint you. Sometimes they will, because they're human. But most of the time, they'll make your life a lot better."

I hummed. "Sounds like a smart bird."

He smiled at me; I smiled back. We might have stayed like that if someone hadn't walked by and bumped into Nate's shoulder.

"Do you want to dance?" He held out his hand.

"I'd love to."

As luck would have it, the next song was a slow, sappy love song.

Nate put an arm around my waist and took my other hand. We swayed closer to each other as we danced. His face slipped in and out of shadows as we turned, making his eyes flash dark and light and putting the sharp edges of his face in relief. He was beautiful, and he was here and dancing with me.

"Of course I'm dancing with you." He grinned at me, and I blushed when I realized I'd spoken out loud. Again. "And you're the beautiful one." With a little tug, he pulled me closer until I leaned into him. "I miss you. Turns out I'm more distracted when you're not around." He kissed my forehead. "I think about you all the time." Next, his lips brushed the corner of my mouth. I shivered. "I think about your voice and your laugh and this soft spot right here." I giggled when he kissed the spot where my neck meets my collarbone. "I think about you when I'm with Lilah because she never stops talking about you." With a tug, he brought my hand to his mouth. "And I even think about you when I'm sleeping," he said, his voice low and tickling my spine.

"Oh, my."

We turned and I could see my family now, all lined up like a group of crazies waiting for Walmart to open on Black Friday. Mimi gave me a thumbs-up. Mom waved; Daddy rocked back on his heels.

"I've thought about going over to see you a hundred times. But when I saw you that day in the hallway, you looked so happy. I told myself I'd lost my shot. Then Phee knocked on my door."

"She did?"

"Yeah. She talked some sense into me."

I shook my head in disbelief, more than a little overwhelmed. "She didn't say a word."

"Your family can be sneaky when they want to be. For example, your mom talked to my mom."

"What? She did not."

"Oh, she did." Any space once between us was now gone. We'd stopped moving, too. "They get along famously. It's scary. Your mom got my mom into this scheme to get me here."

"I'm going to kill her," I said, without much heat to my voice. Instead of being angry, I found myself grateful for my mother's meddling this time. Maybe it had its good points once in a while. Because who was I kidding? Nate was here, in a tuxedo, dancing with me on New Year's Eve.

"So, are they watching?" he whispered.

"Who?"

"Your family. Are they watching us?"

I glanced over his shoulder and nodded.

"Good."

Then we were kissing. I heard a catcall I was sure was Mimi, but I was too busy wrapping my arms around Nate and kissing him back. We turned, he dipped me. My wrap fell to the floor, but we never broke that kiss.

Not even when my mother said, "Persephone Amelia Mayfield, really? You are in public."

Nope, we laughed, but we didn't stop kissing.

FORTY-EIGHT

PERCI'S NEW YEAR'S ANTI-RESOLUTIONS

1. I will not get engaged to an un-handsome, wildly perfect man I love dearly.
2. I will not open my own daycare and love going to work every day.
3. I will not have a small wedding in a country church while wearing a flower crown.
4. I will not get knocked up on my honeymoon. (But, as Mimi reminds me, at least I was married first.)
5. I most definitely, 100%, will not be happy just being me.

A LETTER FROM SHARON

Dearest Reader,

I cannot say thank you enough for choosing to read *The Do-Over*. If you'd like to keep up to date with all my book news, just sign up at the following link. Never fear, your email address will never be shared, and you can unsubscribe at any time.

www.bookouture.com/sharon-m-peterson

As a debut author, I'm still wrapping my head around the idea that you—yes, you, dear reader—chose my book out of so many other choices. I know time is precious; thank you for using it to get to know Perci and Nate and the rest of the gang.

I'd love to hear what you think. Reviews are a great way to share that, and they make such a difference helping new readers to discover one of my books for the first time. If you ever have questions, want to chat, or need a random picture of a baby animal to brighten your day, please feel free to find me online.

You can find me on my Facebook page, tweeting nonsense on Twitter, adding too many books to my TBR list on Goodreads, making awkward videos on TikTok, or my website.

As Mimi would say, "There's nothing fuller than a grateful heart. Or my stomach after taco night."

My heart is very full, Sharon

KEEP IN TOUCH WITH SHARON

sharonmpeterson.com

facebook.com/SharonMPetersonAuthor

twitter.com/stone4031

tiktok.com/@stone4031

goodreads.com/68003715-sharon-m-peterson

ACKNOWLEDGMENTS

I know most of you will skip over this part, even though it is arguably the most important. See, this book wasn't just written by me. It took the support, talent, and love of so many people to put it in your hands.

Many, many thanks to my agent, Nalini Akolekar, who has been a constant support and worked tirelessly to get my books into the world. I'm forever grateful that you believed in me, sometimes when I did not believe in myself. Thanks also to the rest of the gang at Spencerhill Associates.

To my editor, Billi-Dee Jones, thank you for seeing something in my stories that touched you. My little book baby has grown fat and happy under your care. To the whole team at Bookouture, you've created such an amazing environment for authors to bloom. Thank you for all you do.

To Courtney Lott, who has been cheering me on since the very first word of my first book, read countless drafts, and given encouragement when I wanted to give up. I could never, ever have finished writing my first chapter without you. You are a blessing, my friend.

To Maria Gonzalez-Gorosito who, along with a group of moms, who barely knew me, surprised me with a new laptop when mine broke. It remains one of the most remarkable gifts I've ever been given. This book would never have been written without your gift. It wasn't just a laptop you gave me; you gave me the courage to write.

To the ladies of the Ink Tank. Your constant support and

the safe place you've provided for me to vent/scream/cry/lament/laugh/celebrate is such an important part of my writing life. You are all amazing. Special thanks to Alison Hammer for your feedback, insight, and friendship.

To Tracey Christensen. I'm sure glad you answered a plea for a critique partner from a random stranger on the internet. Your wisdom and friendship have truly been a gift from God. I'm so very glad I know you, my friend.

Thank you to the members of the Women's Fiction Writers Association and the League of Romance Writers for giving writers support and opportunities to grow.

To my mom and Aunt CC, thank you for being my cheerleaders and believing that I could make a dream like this a reality. Love you bunches.

To my sister Gabbie, who will never get to hold one of my books in her hands. I miss you always; love you forever. And I fully expect you to sell a copy of this book to every single angel in Heaven.

To Daniel, Benjamin, Gideon, and Katherine. I am incredibly blessed to be your mother. Thank you for putting up with a mom who makes you repeat everything you say at least twice because my mind was somewhere else the first time you said it. You are my heart always.

To Carl. You've put up with my exhaustion, my tears, my anger, my disappointment, my excitement, my crazy ideas, my ramblings about made-up people in made-up worlds, and way too many pizza dinners. You've never wavered in your support of me. Ever. I love you.

To the many, many others I can't even begin to list here, but you know who you are. Your endless support, encouragement, and prayers have kept and continue to keep me going daily. Thank you for always believing in me.